FACT

The U...
SECRET

Behind the Story

In 1912, the collector Wilfred Voynich discovered a selection of ancient books hidden in a chest in Mondragone Castle, Italy. Among the texts was a manuscript written entirely in code. It became known as the Voynich Manuscript.

For a century, academics tried to break the code. But not a single word or phrase in the 245 pages of the Voynich Manuscript has been read.

In 1944 a group of code-breakers working for the US government formed a Study Group to try and decipher the text. They failed. Between 1962 and 1963 a second Study Group was formed. Eventually Americans joined with British code-breakers based at Bletchley Park Mansion. They failed.

In 1969 the manuscript was donated to Yale University and registered simply as 'MS 408'. It is kept hidden from general view in the Beinecke Rare Book and Manuscript Library. Since that day, the secret code has remained unbroken.

UNTIL NOW ...

Also by H. L. Dennis

SECRET BREAKERS

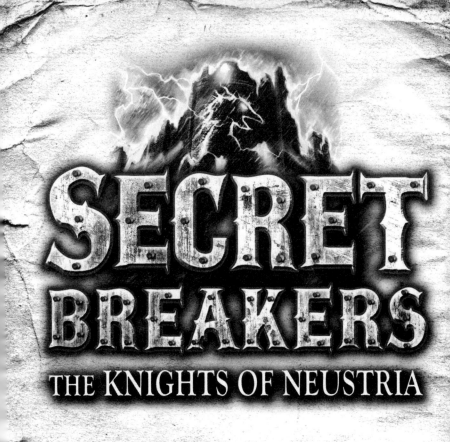

SECRET BREAKERS

THE KNIGHTS OF NEUSTRIA

H. L. Dennis

Illustrations by Meggie Dennis

Hodder
Children's
Books

A division of Hachette Children's Books

A Catalogue record for this book is available from the British Library

ISBN 978 0 340 99963 9

Typeset in AGaramond Book by Avon DataSet Ltd,
Bidford-on-Avon, Warwickshire

Printed and bound in Great Britain by
Clays Ltd, St Ives plc

The paper and board used in this paperback by Hodder Children's Books
are natural recyclable products made from wood grown in
sustainable forests. The manufacturing processes conform to the
environmental regulations of the country of origin.

Hodder Children's Books
a division of Hachette Children's Books
338 Euston Road, London NW1 3BH
An Hachette UK company
www.hachette.co.uk

For three special *Secret Breakers* supporters,
David Dennis, Ella Lewis and Melanie Botting

We can easily forgive a child who is afraid of the dark; the real tragedy of life is men who are afraid of the light.

Plato

1

The Listening Post

There was a storm brewing.

Black clouds hung heavy in the sky.

Brodie Bray hadn't slept for nights. Now she could hardly breathe.

She knew what she had to do. She needed to remind herself what the struggle was all about. She needed to see the code.

The wooden trunk was on the centre of the table. She unlatched the lock and unbuckled the straps. Then she eased back the lid. The trunk was filled with shimmering gold. It must have been just as Voynich saw it exactly a century before when he hoped his find would change his life forever. It had. And it had changed Brodie's life too. Made her part of a chain throughout history of people determined to break the secret it contained.

Slowly, she reached inside and lifted out the golden bundle. She turned it gently, unrolling the folds of fabric. Finally, freed from its wrapping, she held the tatty leather manuscript in her hands. The cord tying it shut was loose. She slipped her finger underneath it and the cover of the manuscript fell open. The pages fanned in the stifling air. Page after page, turning as she watched. Their story still, after five hundred years, untold. The secret of every single coded word of MS 408, unbroken.

Brodie searched for the folded section. The map of the unknown islands. She extended it out and the shadows formed by the light spewed across it. Then the shadows stilled and the unknown islands glowed.

Brodie took a breath and folded the map away. She rewrapped the manuscript and put it back in the trunk. It still mattered. She only had to see the islands.

She closed the lid and refastened the straps.

'Are you ready?' Tusia was standing by the door.

Brodie didn't answer. Instead they walked together out into the dark.

Hunter and Sheldon were waiting for them. The sky pressed down but there was no rain. The four of them ran together towards the mansion.

The front door was open. Smithies stood in the

porch. 'It's time to tell you everything,' he said.

Kerrith Vernan had worked in the government Black Chamber, where codes are made and broken, for years. She enjoyed working on secrets. But recently she'd become involved in a secret inside a secret and she was loving every moment. She'd been promoted to Level Five of the Black Chamber. And Level Five had a mission. To stop anyone making sense of MS 408, the most mysterious manuscript in the world. Kerrith's personal mission was to stop Jon Smithies. He'd worked at the Black Chamber up until a few months ago but now he was running some ridiculous scheme involving freakish children and MS 408. Smithies had become the enemy. Three thoughts banged together unpleasantly in Kerrith's mind: a banned book, a banished man, and children. She felt slightly sick.

Kerrith's new office was bigger than her last one. That was because she'd done well. She'd pleased the Director and he wasn't an easy man to please.

The Director was happy because Kerrith had caught Robbie Friedman. Since Friedman had been thrown out of the Black Chamber he'd been on the run. Kerrith's research had connected him to the outrageous scheme Smithies was operating from Bletchley Park Mansion. With the precision of an expert angler,

Kerrith had reeled Friedman in. She could still remember the joy of watching him squirm in front of her. A fish without water.

She'd made those no-hopers at Station X think the authorities were going to charge Friedman for leaving Brodie's mother dying at the side of the road in Belgium. They thought this was all about law and justice. They had no idea. Right now Friedman was supposed to be out on bail waiting to be charged with something like negligence. That made her laugh. Charging *him* with not caring. Those meddlers at Station X thought he was a free man again for a while. Kerrith wondered if they'd worked out why he hadn't come back to them. Did they blame his shame? Perhaps, even better, they thought now the truth was out, he'd changed sides.

No wonder the Director was pleased with her. Her plan was working nicely!

Which was why she was here. Out of her new, airy office and seated in the dingy side-room of the detention centre.

'Miss Vernan?' The nurse's voice broke through Kerrith's reverie. 'Are you ready to sign the papers?'

'Excuse me?'

'The transfer documents for Mr Friedman. I understand the place they're sending him to will be able to deal in a more specialist way with his problems.'

Kerrith looked down at the pages in front of her. 'It'll be a totally secure unit?' she said, trying hard to mask the delicious hint of pleasure playing on her lips.

'Totally secure, ma'am.'

'And he'll have no chance of release?'

'Absolutely none.'

Kerrith lifted the pen. 'And contact with the outside world?' she added, as the nib hovered in the air above the page.

'They'll still allow letters in and out,' the nurse said, 'although we can insist he's denied that privilege now, if you prefer?'

A droplet of ink dripped from the pen on to the paper. 'No. Let him think he's writing to them,' she said mockingly, 'but monitor every word.'

'They call this place Station X,' Smithies said. 'They're wrong.'

Brodie was confused.

'It's not accurate to call the whole of Bletchley Park Mansion by that name. Station X really refers to a specific part of the building. "The Listening Post." The place where enemy messages were overheard and intercepted during World War Two. The time has come to show you.'

Miss Tandari led them through the mansion to a

small curling staircase. Not the main staircase they'd used before, but a hidden stairway that corkscrewed up through the building.

'The Listening Post is in the turret of the mansion,' Sicknote explained. 'It had to be high up above everything so the radio messages from the enemy could be received clearly.'

'And it's because we want things to be clear to you that we're taking you there,' added Smithies. 'It's time to know exactly what you're dealing with.'

Brodie was scared. It's what she wanted. What she'd begged for. To have everything explained so all that had happened to them made sense. Now, as they reached the top of the stairs, she was suddenly unsure.

In front of them was a door. A notice tacked up with rusty pins. 'STATION X. NO ADMITTANCE.'

'Ready?' said Smithies, and he turned the handle and stepped inside.

The room was small and square. Windows looked out on the gathering storm. Old-fashioned radio equipment lined the tables. Wooden steps stretched up into the eaves and water pumped into a huge overhead tank groaning through greened copper pipes. Brodie tried to take all this in. But it was hard to concentrate because of the walls.

Every vertical surface was covered in pieces of paper. Not patterns or colours. But words. Cuttings from newspapers, letters and articles. Pinned and stapled so there were no gaps. In places the writing overlapped. New sections tacked over old. Yellowed pieces faded and torn, partially covered by new crisp white.

'This is *our* Listening Post,' said Smithies. '*Our* Station X. Everything is here.'

For the second time that night, Brodie was confused. 'What is it all? What does it say?'

'The truth of what we're really involved in.'

Brodie peered closer. Articles about book burnings and riots. Pictures of prisoners. Reports on missing persons.

'But all this,' Tusia said quietly. 'How does any of this have anything to do with what we're trying to do here?'

'It has to do with Level Five,' said Miss Tandari.

'But this is worldwide stuff. Disasters. Huge news events.' Tusia was staring at a report about an international space accident. 'I thought Level Five was involved with codes.'

'Level Five is concerned with truth,' said Smithies. 'Hiding truth and controlling truth. Sometimes they use codes to do that. And sometimes . . .' he considered how best to go on, 'they use other things.'

7

Brodie scanned the walls.

'We've tried to warn you that you were involved in something far bigger than you knew. And this place is where we listen in. It's where we monitor the work of the enemy. Because we are up against an enemy that's very real. They're watching us. We know that now. It's important we watch them.'

'But how d'you know all this is the work of Level Five?' Brodie was pointing at an article about a train crash.

Smithies steered her towards a section nearest the window. 'Years of listening. Years of knowing how they work.'

By the window frame, a news article flapped in the slow-moving air. It was about an explosion months before. Brodie's house turned to rubble. She remembered the ornamental dragon that had been put on the doorstep moments before the blast. She remembered the code sprawled across the dragon's stomach. She knew the explosion was a warning. And she knew Level Five had been responsible.

She lifted the edge of the article. Behind it was an older piece. The paper yellowed. It showed the carcass of a car, crushed beside a foreign roadside. And then another photograph, smaller, yellowed too. A funeral scene. People dressed in black. And a small child holding the hand of an older man. The child was crying.

Brodie's throat tightened so she could hardly swallow. The photo was of her, gripping tight to her granddad's hand on the day they buried her mum. The crushed car the one her mum had died in.

'I didn't bring you here to upset you, Brodie.'

She stared at the photograph.

'But to remind you that Friedman may well have been there when Alex died. But Level Five were involved. You know that. Kerrith told you in Brighton when she followed us to the Royal Pavilion. And the accident. Your mother's death. It was part of something bigger.'

Brodie looked away from the picture of the crying girl. But the next article made it worse. A recent photograph. A man walking from court, released on bail, awaiting trial.

'All this,' said Smithies, 'is the work of the enemy and we can't go on unless we understand that whatever Friedman did, he had to have a reason.'

Brodie choked back the anger that burnt in her throat. She jabbed at the picture of Friedman with her finger and then balled her hands into fists. 'So where is he? They let him go. He's out there somewhere. Why doesn't he come and explain?'

'Would you listen if he did?'

Her knuckles whitened.

'I don't know where he is,' Smithies said slowly. 'But there's this.' He held out a postcard. It was addressed to Brodie. A phone number printed across the back. 'It's a number you can reach him on. I've tried. A woman answered and took my name.' He hesitated. 'I guess it's you he wants to speak to.'

Brodie didn't move.

'I'll leave it here,' Smithies said softly. 'For when you're ready to listen.' He put the postcard on the table and then on the top he put a small round disc. The phoenix medallion that had been tucked inside the copy of *Morte d'Arthur* from the restricted section of the Guildhall Library. The book they'd struggled so hard to find because they were sure it would help them with the code. Hans of Aachen's medallion.

There was a flash of lightning. In the glow, the phoenix on the medallion seemed to burn. There was silence. Brodie counted in her head. Then the thunder came. The storm was still miles away, but it was getting closer.

She looked back again at the image of the crying girl.

Outside the rain began to fall.

* * *

'I'm sorry to disturb you, sir.'

The Director spun round on his chair.

'This better be good, Wheeler.'

The man at the door hesitated a little. It was clear he was unsure. 'It's just you said if ever we received anything, you know, sent special delivery, then we were . . .' He was struggling to make himself clear.

The Director didn't have time for this. Indecision, hesitation, unpolished shoes. All these things were a source of great irritation to him. He snapped his fingers as if summoning a waiter. There was really no need to waste words in such situations.

'I just felt you would be . . .'

Now the Director was more than cross. 'Give it here, Wheeler!'

The visitor stretched out his hand. At first it was difficult to see what he held. A tiny paper tube, a container of some sorts? The Director squinted to see. And then his heart thudded near the base of his throat.

It was a scroll. Tied with a thin strand of black ribbon.

'It's just you said that if ever—'

The Director lurched forward. He grabbed at the scroll. 'Yes, thank you, Wheeler. You did well.'

'So I did right to—'

'That will be all, Wheeler.'

11

The Director heard the door click. He didn't see Wheeler leave the room. He was focusing on the scroll and the thin black ribbon.

He took a moment to lean back in the chair. To savour every second. But it was hard to keep waiting. He'd waited so long.

He took the scroll from the desk and let his finger move across the ribbon. Should he untie it? Should he slip the scroll free? He wasn't sure. In all his imaginings he'd focused always on what was inside.

The untied ribbon moved like a snake across his hand and the scroll took a moment, an age, to lay flat on the table. He tried not to rush the reading. To allow his eyes to take in every detail.

The scroll was plain. Crisp white, not old or yellow. In each corner was an embossed design. Four of them of course, as he'd known there would be. He let his fingertip brush across each one. A small planet spinning on its axis: earth. A circular swirl: wind. A flame: fire. And finally a wave: water. The Director linked his fingers together and took a deep breath. Then he leant forward and read the words written across the scroll. There were few of them. But there were enough for him to know things had got serious.

You must watch them, for we are watching you.

The Director lowered his fingertip one final time to the scroll and this time he pressed not the signs in each corner, but the embossed letter at the base of the scroll.

The letter 'T'.

'You gonna ring the number, B?'

Brodie was staring at the postcard.

'Wouldn't it be better if you just let Friedman explain?'

Brodie pushed her hands into her pockets.

Hunter picked up the medallion and twisted it in the air. The feathers of the phoenix caught the light. 'It's your decision.'

'He left my mum . . .' She couldn't finish the sentence.

'I know, B.'

Brodie's throat hurt. The words stuck in her mouth. 'I thought he was my friend.'

Hunter looked at her a long while before he answered. 'We don't know he wasn't. We can't be sure.'

Brodie picked up the postcard. Then she tore it in half.

They stood for a moment with only the sound of the water sloshing in the storage tank above their heads breaking the silence.

'I reckon we should keep this with us now,' he said, slipping the phoenix medallion into his wallet. 'It feels wrong it being in here.'

They'd talked about how the room made them feel and it wasn't good. But the four of them had come to the Listening Post every day for the last three days. Brodie felt her mind was fit to burst. Smithies had promised them everything and here it all was. Stories of lives changed by the work of Level Five. Her own picture was still there. A tiny girl crying at her mother's funeral. She tried not to look at it again.

'Things are changing,' said Tusia, peering out of the window.

'Of course they're changing, Toots. We're a man down. We know more than we ever wanted to know. Things can't be the same. You can't squeeze the ketchup back in the bottle. Once it's out, it's out.'

Tusia scowled. 'I mean, changing at the mansion.'

Brodie joined her by the window. They could see the sentry box by the back gate. The fencing had been raised. Barbed wire stretched along the top now.

'Total lockdown,' said Sheldon. 'That's what Smithies said. Museum closed. No one in or out.'

'Odd that,' mumbled Tusia.

'What, odd that Smithies wants to keep us safer than ever?'

'No. Odd that if no one's allowed in or out that they're letting *that* in.'

Brodie pushed her way to the window to have a closer look.

She decided odd was definitely the right word to use in the circumstances.

Godfather of Cryptology

Brodie skidded to a halt at the entrance to the mansion and peered to check she was really seeing things right.

Some sort of carriage was shrouded by the thick morning mist. Brodie shielded her eyes and squinted. There were no horses. It was being pulled by a team of zebras.

The carriage stopped and a tall man, in a long leather coat and sharp red leather boots, lowered the reins and bounded down from the driver's seat. A golden tooth glinted in his smile.

'Fabyan,' beamed Mr Bray, stepping forward to shake his hand. 'So great to see you again. I thought you were caught up with issues stateside.'

'I was.' There was a hint of sadness in his tone. 'But I figured you needed me.'

Without Fabyan's help the work at Station X would have ground to a halt long ago. Brodie's grandfather had contacted him a few months earlier when the government tried to ban the team from Bletchley. Clever use of the law and a serious amount of cash from the American billionaire meant Mr Fabyan was now the main owner of the Bletchley Park estate, and the team had been using his money to survive. But billionaires are busy people and he'd made only the briefest of visits before returning to Illinois.

'If I could have a hand in with a few of my things that'd be awesome,' said Fabyan. 'Some of the stuff I've brought is old and valuable, so a little bit of care would be greatly appreciated.'

It took nearly an hour to unload the carriage and make sure the zebras were safely stabled.

'What *is* all this?' asked Mr Bray almost nervously. 'You didn't bring your egg collection or the Egyptian mummy did you?'

The American rocked back his head in laughter. 'No. I travelled light, my friend. But before I show you what I've brought, I need an update on my investment. A rundown of all Team Veritas has been up to. And I don't want anything missed out. I need you to explain things from the very beginning so I'm totally up to speed. Presume I know nothing. That way you won't miss out any important details.' He scanned the room. 'So come on then . . . who's going to remind me what the work at Station X is all about?'

Brodie was aware everyone was looking at her. 'Me?' she said. 'You want me to explain?'

'Absolutely,' said Fabyan. 'I'm all ears. I need to know everything.'

Brodie took a deep breath. 'OK. I'll try.'

She began with Voynich. 'This Polish book collector found an ancient manuscript in a trunk. It was hidden in Mondragone Castle, Italy.'

'And it was a hundred years ago,' cut in Hunter. '1912. Times and dates are important, B.'

'It's over two hundred pages long,' she said, adding the page number to make sure Hunter was happy. 'It's totally in code and loads of clever code-crackers have had a go at working out what it says. But they've all failed. Worse than that, Level Five of the government Black Chamber made rules stopping people trying. Voynich's manuscript has a code-name, by the way. I forgot that bit. They call it MS 408. And it's banned.'

'Which is why Smithies formed Team Veritas in secret,' said Tusia. 'And why we're here. And without your money, Level Five could chuck us out. So we're really grateful.'

Fabyan seemed to appreciate the thanks.

'Smithies started all this because there was something new,' continued Brodie. 'A message called the "Firebird Code".'

'We called it that because the message came in an envelope sealed shut with the mark of the phoenix,' said Tusia.

Brodie nodded and ploughed on. 'The Firebird Code was written by this professor called Van der Essen. We thought he'd rescued a code-book for MS 408 during World War One, and that he'd hidden it. We thought that's what we'd find if we broke the Firebird Code.'

'Which is why we went to the Royal Pavilion in Brighton,' explained Tusia. 'But we didn't find a code-book. We found a music box instead.'

'That's where I came in,' said Sheldon. 'I'm new.'

Fabyan smiled a broad welcome.

'They got me involved because I know about music,' said Sheldon. 'The music box played a tune by the composer Elgar. And I knew Elgar had written all sorts of codes.'

'And we connected these to MS 408,' said Brodie. 'We solved a coded message Elgar had written.'

'It's all to do with shapes on a map,' blurted Tusia, keen to cover every detail.

'And anyway, the answer to Elgar's code gave us the name of someone called Hans of Aachen.'

'He lived way back in the 1500s,' said Hunter.

'And all the writing in the history books about Hans, called him an Orphan of the Flames,' said Brodie. 'It's because his dad died trying to keep a book from being burnt. We were sure this book must be the code-book to MS 408.'

'And we tracked it down,' said Tusia proudly. 'We found it hidden in a library basement in London. The book's called *Morte d'Arthur*.'

'It's all about King Arthur,' said Brodie. 'Thomas Malory wrote it.' She paused for a moment, checking she'd mentioned all she needed to.

'You have to say about the glyphs,' hissed Tusia.

'What about the glyphs?'

'Well, there's these strange shapes in between the letters all through that copy of *Morte d'Arthur*.'

'They look like the writing in MS 408,' caught on Brodie. 'So that made us sure MS 408 and *Morte d'Arthur* were connected. But we haven't really worked out how yet.' She'd enjoyed telling all these parts of the story. Up until then, things had been going well. But she knew she'd got now to the part where things had gone seriously pear-shaped.

Hunter smiled at her. 'Shall I take it from here, B?'

What we know so far...

Voynich Manuscript

Where's the code book?!

Van der Essen's Firebird Code

Phoenix Constellation

Number 88 Piano Keys

Royal Pavilion - Brighton

Dorabella Cipher

Elgar

Firebird Music Box

Maps

Orphan of the Flames

Hans of Aachen

Morte D'Arthur

Guildhall Library - London

?

Fabyan leant in closely to hear more clearly.

'There was a chase. Underground in London. Workers from Level Five of the Black Chamber took Friedman away. It wasn't good.' Hunter hesitated but Brodie nodded for him to go on. 'We all knew Friedman had been friends with Brodie's mum when they were younger. We knew they'd both tried to work out what MS 408 said long before we all got together here. But we didn't know he'd been there on the day she died. Or that he hadn't done anything to help save her.'

Fabyan looked horrified. 'But surely there was—'

'Friedman didn't deny it,' Brodie said quietly. 'He left my mum when she was dying.'

'It's been a bit difficult since then,' said Tusia.

'But we haven't given up.' Brodie's voice faltered as she finished speaking.

The American tapped her gently on the arm. 'And you all still believe it's important you find a way to read the most mysterious manuscript in the world?' he said gently.

'Yes.' Somehow Brodie felt that more than ever now. They'd been chosen. All of them charged with making sure that whatever MS 408 had to say it was kept safe. That the knowledge wasn't destroyed, or corrupted or lost. That when the time was finally right, the secret was broken.

'OK,' said Fabyan. 'So we carry on then. And I may have some things here that will be of help.'

Fabyan stepped his way between three large round hatboxes, an ornamental golden birdcage and a selection of patterned umbrellas, then made his way towards a large wooden trunk which had been near to the back of the carriage.

The trunk had caught Brodie's eye from the start. It was made of a dark, warm-coloured wood. There was an intricate hinge system and a fancy black iron lock. The lid shone like polished glass. It looked just like the sort of trunk she'd read about in pirate stories.

She sat down beside the trunk and Sheldon came to sit beside her. 'I feel I should play some sort of drum roll,' he said.

Fabyan took a large iron key from his pocket and turned it in the lock. Then, in a fluid, arching movement, the lid swung open to reveal the contents.

It was packed with papers and magazines, pamphlets and books. A treasure-chest of words.

'Great. Some more reading for us to do,' said Hunter sarcastically. 'I can't wait.'

Fabyan showed no signs of having heard and began to unpack the trunk carefully in front of them. 'It's like a time capsule,' he explained. 'Things in here date back to my great-grandfather's time.'

'This stuff belonged to the original Colonel Fabyan?' asked Granddad.

'Was he a very rich guy too?' asked Hunter.

'Colonel Fabyan was more than a rich man. He was the godfather of cryptology. He gave code-cracking its first real American home. George was a collector. He collected animals. I get my love of zebras from him, but *he* even had time to build a miniature zoo at home. Kept bears and a troupe of monkeys in the house. He collected things: Egyptian mummies, Samurai armour, even ostrich eggs. But most importantly to our cause here, he collected mysteries.'

Brodie let the phrase circle in her head. *Mystery Collector*. The story possibilities thrilled her.

'He was totally unable to walk away from a puzzle.'

'And he worked on the puzzles alone?' asked Brodie.

'No,' said Fabyan. 'He employed others to work with him. The very best minds in the country. If Fabyan was the godfather of cryptology, then those he employed became the parents of the code. Three incredible code-crackers really. Elizabeth Wells Gallup and a young couple who met while they worked for him. They fell in love and eventually married. Elizebeth and William Friedman.'

Brodie felt a sudden uncomfortable tightening in her stomach.

Fabyan looked a little awkward. 'I know things have not gone well here with Friedman's grandson. But William Friedman was one of the best code-crackers America ever produced until he died in December 1969. His work on codes helped shorten World War Two. I think it may be important we think about him.' He looked at Brodie as if asking permission to go on. She bit her lip and nodded slowly.

'William Friedman worked at Riverbank with Colonel Fabyan. And this trunk of goodies contains some of the things he worked on.'

'So it's all to do with MS 408?' said Hunter.

'Ahh, well, that's the good bit. I've broadened the net. I've brought to you a world of things to do with code-cracking and the quest for knowledge. There's a chance the things I've brought may not *entirely* relate to Friedman's work on MS 408. But I think that's the beauty of the scheme.' He clutched to his chest a large album of sepia photographs. 'I've brought everything,' he said with an obvious sense of relief. 'Anything I could find to do with secret non-war-based code-cracking at Riverbank. Fabyan set up the first Study Group on MS 408 and Friedman the second so I hope there'll be stuff about the original Veritas work in here.

the American Link

Riverbanks Lab

Known as Fabyan villa. (Geneva, Illinois)

Owned zebras!

Colonel George Fabyan

Godfather of Cryptography

Born 1867
Died 1936

Had a troupe of monkeys in his loft!

Had 2 bears in his house!

Parents of the Code

William F. Friedman

Born 24th Sept. 1891
Died 12th Nov. 1969

Elizebeth Friedman

Born August 26th 1892
Died Oct. 31st 1980

Was born 'Wolf Friedman'!

Wow! Great name

Worked with Elizabeth Wells Gallup on the cipher wheel.

And there might be some other stuff too.'

'Other stuff?' asked Tusia.

'On Shakespeare.'

Hunter's sighs of exasperation sounded as if he were in extreme pain.

'What's Shakespeare got to do with MS 408?' asked Tusia.

'Absolutely nothing,' admitted Fabyan. 'But I couldn't leave the stuff behind. That's how Elizebeth and William first got together working for Fabyan. They thought there were all sorts of secrets hidden in Shakespeare's work. Mrs Wells Gallup even thought there was a coded message on the front page of his collected works. She reckoned there was an anagram about a secret being hidden at a place called Chepstow. Never proved, of course. But anyway, the most exciting secret's really who the writer of Shakespeare's plays was.'

Tusia's shoulders sagged. 'Isn't the clue in the name?' she said. '*Shakespeare wrote Shakespeare?*'

'My great-grandfather was sure he didn't,' said Fabyan. 'He thought the real writer left a code about his identity for somebody to find. That's the first puzzle Friedman Senior worked on with Fabyan. So I brought along some of his work on that too.' He undid the buttons on his cuffs and rolled up his sleeves. 'Besides, it was when I was packing all the stuff Friedman and my great-grandfather had on Shakespeare that I remembered.'

'Remembered what?' asked Granddad.

'Remembered Riverbank Labs was in possession of an extraordinary thing. A truly awesome thing which for decades had been forgotten. And I knew if I could bring to the new Team Veritas the thing that's been forgotten, there was a chance a breakthrough could be made.' He turned dramatically towards a large plain wooden crate which had been unloaded last from the zebra-drawn carriage. 'So, I bring you this.'

The Shakespeare Mangle

The Director mulled the words of the scroll over again and again. He was being watched. The thought thrilled him. He'd waited so very, very long to be noticed. The Chairman would be happy. But he mustn't rush things. Mustn't tell the Chairman too soon. He would bide his time.

He opened the desk drawer and looked again at the flattened scroll. The four embossed emblems seemed to sparkle. But it was the letter 'T' that excited him most. It would excite the Chairman too. When he told him.

Fabyan wielded a shiny hammer in his hand. 'Mind your backs. Coming through,' he ventured, before ripping off the side of the packing-case with the claw of the hammer.

'What the banana sandwich is in there?' asked Hunter, as the team peered at the shaking packing-case. 'And how the sherry trifle did you get that through customs?'

'It's not alive, is it?' whispered Sicknote, clutching Miss Tandari's arm.

Brodie wasn't sure it was such a crazy question. The American had, after all, shipped a pair of zebras into the country.

'Nothing alive,' wheezed Fabyan, swinging the hammer again. 'Just special.'

The side of the packing-case creaked free and clattered to the ground. There was a cloud of dust. Then the fog lifted and the contents of the case became visible.

'What on earth is it?' asked Smithies, wiping his glasses on his sleeve.

'A cipher wheel,' Fabyan said.

'Looks like two wheels to me,' quipped Hunter.

Tusia jabbed him forcefully in the ribs.

In front of them was a huge box-like contraption like an upended wardrobe or rather deep coffin. Inside were two huge wheels positioned side by side. Each was as big as a tractor tyre. Stretched across the two wheels was a thick linen fabric and sticking out from the centre of one was a stubby handle.

'And this belonged to Friedman?' asked Tusia, running her finger cautiously along the rim of the nearest wheel.

'Sort of,' said Fabyan. 'Elizabeth Wells Gallup had more to do with the machine itself. It was invented by someone called Dr Orville Ward Owen. Lots of Friedman's work centred round the secrets this wheel revealed.'

'What secrets?'

'Hidden identities. Stories of deceit. Betrayal.'

'All that from something which looks like two snare drums without the skins?' offered Sheldon. 'How did it work?'

'Like this. Books and pamphlets were cut up and their pages glued across the material stretched across the wheels.'

Brodie flinched at the idea of books being cut up but still leant in closer to hear more.

'When the big wooden wheels were rolled backwards and forwards it was possible for lots of pages of the book to be seen at once.'

'Why did they need that?' whispered Hunter. 'Suppose it gets the reading over with more quickly.'

It was Brodie's turn to poke him in the ribs.

'The advantage of spreading the pages like this,' carried on Fabyan, 'was that any codes and messages hidden in the writing on the page could be clearly seen. People at Riverbank used the cipher wheel to look for messages in things written in the fifteenth century. They worked on the idea that the real writer of Shakespeare's plays and poems left coded messages in other writings of the time. That got me thinking.'

Tusia's finger slowed to a stop. Her eyes widened as if she'd processed a really painful thought. 'You think we should cut up MS 408 and spread the pages on the cipher wheel?' she whispered.

'Well, as you seem to have come to a bit of a dead-end, I just wondered if it might be worth a try,' said Fabyan. 'I know you were led to the copy of *Morte d'Arthur*, but you obviously haven't managed to make it work as a code-book to help you read the manuscript yet, have you?'

It was true. None of their attempts to use Malory's text as a code-book for MS 408 had left them with anything more than sore eyes and headaches.

'It's a bit extreme,' mumbled Sicknote. 'But I suppose we're dealing with *a copy* of MS 408 after all. There's no reason why we can't try with the facsimile.'

'I think we should give it a go,' said Miss Tandari. 'What d'you all think?'

'Let's do it,' said Hunter.

The idea of trying something new was a good one.

But Brodie just couldn't shake the nagging feeling something was wrong.

'You all right, BB?' asked Hunter, later that evening.

'Yep. Totally fine.'

'You don't look like we're on the brink of discovery. I mean, don't you see? We might be an onion slice away from a casserole. This might be all it needs. A magic machine from the past to help us read MS 408. Imagine!'

She'd done little else than imagine for the last few months. This was why she was here. It was everything she wanted. Everything her mum had wanted.

But something just wasn't quite right.

'You like it?' The Director was leaning forward in his chair, his fingers steepled together.

Kerrith followed his gaze to the ornament on his desk. A bronze casting, of a rock, with a sword plunged in deeply so only the hilt was visible.

'You know the story it represents?' the Director continued. 'Of Arthur. And the sword marking him out as king.'

'The sword in the stone,' Kerrith said, reaching forward and tracing along the grip. The bronze was cold.

'No other man could draw the sword from the stone, Miss Vernan.' This thought pleased him intensely. 'It was a way of selecting those who'd be great and those who'd fail.' He folded his arms and rested them on the desk. 'So? What have you got to tell me?'

'Friedman's been transferred as you requested,' said Kerrith quietly. 'And I was wondering what else you wanted me to do now. As regards the happenings at Station X?'

'I think now, we simply wait.'

She was unsure how to respond.

'They'll expect us to keep pursuing,' said the Director. 'They'll expect us to bring them down as we've done Friedman. So we'll wait.'

'For what, sir?'

The Director considered his answer. 'It's become clear to me that the team at Bletchley are very thorough in their examination of the evidence. Got me thinking it would be a shame to waste such hard work.'

'Waste, sir?'

'MS 408 is banned, Miss Vernan, because of where it may lead. But I say now, let them follow that lead.' He laughed and there was a sense of mania about the laughter which scared her. 'Let Smithies and his ragbag team of has-beens and wannabes follow the breadcrumb trail to the cottage in the wood.'

'So you want us to leave them alone? Let them get on with trying to translate the document?'

The Director nodded.

'And do nothing to stop them? Just wait?'

'Until they're so close to an answer the smell of success burns in their nostrils.'

'And then?'

'Oh, then we bring them in. But let them walk close to the edge of discovery first,' he said.

'And why do we do that, sir?'

'Because it's so much more pleasurable to see hope built up and *then* destroyed,' he said, emphasising his words with care.

Kerrith stood up from the table.

'There's still a need to watch them carefully, Miss Vernan,' he said. 'And while you're watching, there's a few things I want to teach you.'

'Teach me, sir?'

'I believe your training about the historical work of the Suppressors is an area which needs extending,' he said.

Kerrith turned back to face him.

'I'll let you know when we should begin,' he said, and then he rested his hand on the sword trapped deep in the stone.

The cipher wheel had been set up in the ice house although, if anyone had any doubt about where it had been placed, they only had to stand still for a moment and listen to the sound of arguing coming from beside the mansion.

Brodie rounded the corner to find Sicknote and Hunter struggling with what looked like a long, unrolled section of stair carpet. Tusia was in the middle of the courtyard, outside the ice house, looking dishevelled, the pencils in her hair lopsided and a generous glob of glue shining on her cheek.

'I told you,' hissed Sheldon. 'It doesn't look pretty.'

'Well, it may not look pretty, but at least it looks now as if there's a chance of it working,' snapped Tusia. 'You lot are just in time to help us get it on the wheel.'

They spread themselves along the length of the linen and, walking backwards at Tusia's command, they snaked their way into the ice house and fed the length of pages across the huge wheels of the machine. Then, rolling up her sleeves despite the cold, Tusia stepped forward and began to turn the handle.

The pages stretched across the material, moving slowly round the surface of the wheels.

Eventually, Brodie was brave enough to speak. 'What exactly are we supposed to be looking for?' she asked.

Hunter wiped his hand across his face and a tear of glue dripped from his eyebrow. 'Well, according to

The Cipher Wheel.

66 Take your Knife and cut all our books asunder
And set the leaves on a great firm wheel
Which rolls and rolls, and turning the
Fickle rolling wheel, throw your eyes upon FORTUNE,
that goddess blind, that stands upon
A spherical stone, that turning and inconstant rolls
In restless variation. Mark her the prime mover;
she is our first guide. 99

=Steps for Use:

1) Attach ⚉ the pages of the book across linen

2) Stretch the linen across the wheel

3) Look for guide Words!

4) Read hidden message by guide words!!

Mrs Wells Gallup, when books were stretched across the cipher wheel, it became easier to see a "guide word" hidden in the text.'

'Oh.' Brodie peered in closely.

Hunter blinked anxiously. 'Mrs Wells Gallup found the guide word and then she focused in on those certain sections of the text and they gave her hidden information.'

Hunter looked away and silence returned, broken only by the gentle click of the wheels and the quiet hum of the handle.

'When shall I mention it?' whispered Brodie to Sheldon, under the careful disguise of her cupped hand.

'Mention what?' he hissed back.

'*That MS 408 hasn't got words we can read,*' she said. 'That's the whole problem!'

'Wouldn't mention it at all,' said Sheldon, who was looking in Tusia's direction where she'd taken on the colour of a well-cooked lobster after the exertion of repeatedly turning the handle. 'Not if you value your life.'

It took about ten minutes before Tusia's hand slowed on the handle. 'OK,' she said. 'I suppose it's time we faced it.'

Brodie bit her lip.

'We're not going to find a guide word, are we, in a

manuscript written entirely in code.' She wiped a ribbon of sweat from her forehead. 'I don't know what I thought would happen. Maybe we'd see a pattern of something forming in the glyphs as they turned.'

Brodie stepped forward and rested her arm supportively around Tusia's shoulder. 'It wasn't a bad idea,' she said quietly. 'Everything's worth a try.'

'But it just felt like the cipher wheel could be the answer, you know.' Tusia was obviously trying to smile. 'And I don't know what to look at next.'

It was a good job Brodie did.

'Seriously, BB? You want us to look through all of these?'

'Yep! Every single one.'

Hunter ran his fingers through his hair in desperation.

Brodie had to admit that the stack of *Philological Quarterly* probably didn't look like the most exciting read in the world. But it was a start, and they needed to begin somewhere. She sat down beside the huge wooden trunk and handed everyone a few magazines. 'This was edited by someone called Curt Zimansky. He was American but in the war he worked here at Bletchley solving codes.'

'I remember him well,' said Mr Bray, smiling as he got up to leave the four younger members of the team to begin their research. 'He was a perfectionist. One of the most hard-working men I ever met.'

The reference to hard work didn't do much to improve Hunter's mood.

'Let us know what you come up with,' added Mr Bray as he turned to shut the door. 'I've things to check at the Listening Post.'

Brodie nodded encouragingly at her granddad and then turned back to the open trunk. 'Zimansky put together this magazine on languages in the fifties and sixties and there's all sorts of interesting stuff in here.'

'*Really*, B?'

'We might find something. You don't have to be so negative.' She wished she felt as confident as she sounded.

A while later it seemed Hunter may have had a point. 'There's nothing here on MS 408,' whined Tusia, dropping her magazine on to the discard pile. 'It's all to do with Greek and classical languages and . . .'

Sheldon had stood up. He was flapping his magazine in front of him. 'Hold on! Hold on!'

'What? You got something on MS 408?'

'Not really.'

'You swatting flies, then?' asked Hunter.

'No!'

'So what, then?' Brodie was struggling to stay calm.

'OK. There's this article . . .'

'There's lots of articles, Fingers. That's the problem. I've read seventy-two of them and—'

'Will you let me finish!'

Hunter nodded an apology.

'OK. There's this article. It's not very big but it talks about Friedman. William Friedman,' Sheldon added quickly. 'Apparently Zimansky asked him to write something in the magazine sharing his theories about MS 408.'

'Well, that's great! So where's what he said?'

'Ah. Now, that's the problem.' Sheldon took a deep breath. 'According to this piece here, Friedman had ideas about MS 408 but he wasn't totally sure. He was still doing research.'

'So?'

'So, he gave Zimansky a sealed envelope with his theory about how to read MS 408. Friedman said when he'd proved his theory he'd let Zimansky print his prediction in the magazine . . . but until then Zimansky should keep his theory safe.'

'Brilliant,' said Tusia. 'So what's the date of your magazine?'

'1959.'

'OK. So that's perfect, then. We know we need to look in all the magazines printed after then.

Somewhere in the later magazines.'

'Perfect,' said Hunter, tossing his 1957 magazine to the side. 'Let's get this problem narrowed down. 1959 and beyond.'

'Are you asleep, Hunter?'

'No, no! Just resting my eyes!' Hunter hadn't turned a page in his magazine for over twenty minutes.

'This is ridiculous,' said Tusia. 'We're up to 1970. Why isn't Friedman's theory in here?'

'You sure you didn't miss—'

The glare Hunter gave her convinced Brodie it was best not to push things.

It was dark outside. Long past midnight and even Brodie's eyes were itchy and tired.

'Let's carry on tomorrow,' said Tusia. 'We're not getting anywhere and we'll miss things if we're not focused.'

'Yep. We'll stock up on mint imperials and carry on in the morning,' said Hunter. 'Your turn to buy the supplies, B.'

'Fine,' said Brodie dejectedly. If she had her way they'd keep reading all night but she supposed things might look clearer in the morning.

Things became a whole lot clearer before then though.

4

A Message from Zimansky

'He's dead!' The voice was coming from outside.

Brodie sat bolt upright in bed, her heart thumping so hard against her ribs she could hardly breathe.

'1969. I remembered. He was dead!'

Tusia stumbled to the window and pulled back the curtains. Sheldon and Hunter had their faces pressed to the glass.

'What in the name of—'

'Let us in, you doughnuts! It's freezing out here!'

'But we're not allowed—'

'Do you want to know what we've worked out or what?'

Brodie didn't bother answering. She ran to open the door to the hut.

Hunter paced backwards and forwards at the end of

the beds as Brodie fumbled to do up her dressing-gown. 'What have you worked out? When? Who's dead?' she gabbled.

'Friedman,' said Sheldon.

Brodie's heart thumped frantically again.

'Friedman Senior,' he added quickly. 'William Friedman, not the other one.'

Brodie's heart slowed a little. 'Well, we know he's dead.'

'Yes. But he died a long time ago, we mean.'

'1969!' said Hunter confidently. 'Fabyan told us.'

'How d'you remember the date?'

'It's what I do, Toots,' grinned Hunter, tapping the side of his nose.

'But how does that help us?' said Brodie, sinking to the end of the bed and trying to steady her breathing.

'It means Friedman's answer won't be in the magazines, B.'

'We've looked through every magazine since 1959 right up to when Friedman died, so if there's no answer in the magazine then the answer can only be in one place.'

'Where?' pressed Tusia.

'With Zimansky!' said Sheldon. 'Or Zimansky's family or solicitor.'

'Like Van der Essen's Firebird Code. Kept safe until

it was passed on to us "worthy alchemists of words" here, remember?' said Hunter.

Sheldon looked a little confused.

'So what do we do?' said Brodie.

'Well, I reckon we write to Zimansky care of the publishers of the magazine, and see what happens.'

'Oh, I don't know,' said Tusia. 'I mean, we're in lockdown, aren't we? Not supposed to involve anyone else.'

'Well, I wasn't in on things at the beginning, was I?' said Sheldon, suddenly looking more excited. 'You involved me.'

'But that's different.'

'Why?'

'You had information we needed.'

'So does Zimansky!'

'I'm not sure,' said Brodie.

'You don't have to be sure,' said Sheldon. 'I can be the one who writes the letter. Trust me. It'll be fine.'

'Where is he?' Brodie wasn't sure which watch to look at. 'He should be back by now. We should never have let him do this.'

Hunter took another mouthful of toast. 'You worry too much, B. It'll be fine.'

Actually, it wasn't fine.

Brodie had never seen Smithies this angry before. Bright-pink blotches blazed on his cheeks and a bead of sweat glistened on the top of his lip. 'We have rules, Sheldon! Clear rules and you should not have tried to leave the station without permission. The last time you all went without checking with us first, things went very wrong with Friedman.'

Sheldon was scowling. 'That wasn't my fault!'

'But this is,' said Smithies. The guard was standing in the doorway, an envelope in his hand. Sheldon was standing moodily beside him. 'Thank you,' Smithies said to the guard and gestured for him to leave. 'We can deal with this now.'

Sheldon folded his arms defiantly.

Brodie waited for Smithies to speak. He was choosing his words very carefully. 'I think you need reminding,' he said at last and strode towards the doorway. 'Well, come on then! All of you.'

The four of them followed Smithies towards the mansion. He led the way up the back stairs and pushed open the door to the Listening Post. Granddad was already there attaching a new cutting to the wall.

'It's all here, Sheldon,' said Smithies. 'To remind you we aren't involved in a game. This is dangerous stuff!' He gestured frantically to the articles all around them. 'You weren't there in the explosion at Mr Bray's house. I get that. But you have to understand that we need to be careful.'

'I was being careful!'

'You should not have involved other people. We have rules!'

'And didn't you involve me because I was prepared to break the rules?'

Smithies floundered for a moment. 'What? No! We included you because you understood music and . . .'

'And because I was prepared to break the rules to solve the code,' Sheldon said. 'That's why I'm here.'

'But—'

'You knew I was a risk taker from the very beginning. And what is all this if it isn't taking risks?'

'But you can't just go asking people things! You don't know what side they're on. You don't know if it's safe.'

Sheldon turned to look out of the window. 'We don't know anything!' he snapped. 'That's the problem.'

Smithies pushed his glasses up on to his forehead as if he was concentrating very hard on trying to keep his temper.

'We can't wait here forever, hoping the answer's going to come to us. It's out *there* somewhere.'

'But I'm worried about you all!'

'Yeah. Well, that's all very nice and everything but

you should be worried that we're not getting anywhere. And just let us try.'

Brodie looked down at the floor. She wasn't sure where else to look.

Smithies took a deep breath. 'I know you were trying to help. But we stay at Bletchley and we don't involve other people without permission. Understand?'

If Sheldon did understand, he didn't say so aloud.

The guard put the letter on the table. He reached for his phone. This would be good. Great to have a letter going out of the place rather than postcards coming in. Head Office should be pleased he was so observant. It was about time they said something positive.

He was just pressing the last digit when the door opened. 'Mr Bray. Nice to see you. Time for a cuppa?'

Mr Bray nodded.

The guard put away his phone. He liked the old man. Had a lot of time for him. He knew his stuff and he knew Bletchley. And he enjoyed their chats.

He didn't enjoy the fact, though, that when Mr Bray left the gatehouse he could no longer find the letter. He'd hidden it when the old man came in. He must have done. Put it somewhere safe and now he couldn't find it. He supposed it was a good job he'd never made the call, then. What Head Office didn't know wouldn't hurt them.

'Wholemeal flapjack?' said Tusia quietly.

Sheldon shook his head.

'Smithies'll come round,' she said. 'You should have seen Miss Tandari once. She got so cross with me about my normal lessons I thought she was going to burst a blood vessel.'

Sheldon grinned.

'They just want what's best for us, you know. And it was a great idea.'

'It was the only idea we had,' said Sheldon. 'So what do we do now?'

No one said anything for a moment. They watched the water feature splutter and spray.

'If you don't want that flapjack, Fingers, it's a shame to waste it.'

Brodie rolled her eyes at Hunter. She had no idea what to say to him.

And she'd even less idea about what to say when the wooden spoon arrived.

'It's from Zimansky.'

'What?'

Mr Bray was blushing. 'I know I shouldn't have

done it but I got to thinking and . . .'

'You sent Sheldon's letter! And this is the reply? About Friedman's views on MS 408. But . . .' Smithies was spluttering to find the right words. 'Eddie, how could you have . . . ?'

Brodie hardly ever heard her granddad called Eddie. It made him sound younger.

'Oh, come on, Jon. The kid's right. We're getting nowhere. The cipher wheel, the *Morte d'Arthur*, it's leading nowhere. And when you get to my time of life you can't keep waiting.'

'But . . .'

Mr Bray seemed to pull himself up straighter. 'I've lost my home, Jon, not to mention my daughter, and I'll do anything, anything at all, to keep everyone else I love safe. But I can't keep waiting. We have a choice. We let Level Five keep us captive here or we take control again and we start getting out there and searching.'

Brodie could tell Smithies couldn't find an answer.

'We all feel bad about what happened in London.' Brodie noticed her granddad didn't mention Friedman's name. 'But I'm not going to let Level Five stop us finding answers. I say if we find a lead, we follow it.'

Smithies turned to Miss Tandari. A tiny smile flickered across her face.

'You agree too, Oscar?'

Sicknote shuffled a little where he stood but he was nodding.

'And you?' Smithies turned to look at Fabyan.

'We're here to do a job, Jon.'

Smithies took a deep breath. 'OK, Granddad. Show us what you have.'

Mr Bray put the wooden spoon down on the table.

The spoon had a long handle and the number twelve had been carved over and over into the wood.

'So what does it mean?'

'No idea.'

Tusia picked up the spoon. 'What's this?' There was a picture of a closed book scorched into the bell of the spoon.

'Guess it's to do with MS 408. A picture of it. Closed. Unreadable.'

Tandi was shaking her head. 'That's not MS 408. That's the book of Cambridge.'

'Excuse me?'

'From Cambridge University. That picture of the book is on the university crest along with the motto. *Hinc lucem et pocula sacra.*'

'Which means?'

'Something about *"from this place, we gain*

enlightenment and precious knowledge".'

'Oh great. You reckon Zimansky or Zimansky's solicitor or whoever you sent the letter to has an answer for us, but we've got to go to Cambridge University to collect it.'

'It's Zimansky's solicitor,' explained Mr Bray. 'I checked with my own. Hackett, Pout and Gurr put me on to her. The woman's called Miss Jarratt.'

'But Cambridge is a big place, right?' mused Tusia. 'How do we find who we need?'

'And when?'

'I think the when's easy, B. It's in all those twelves! Must be twelve minutes past twelve on 12 December this year. 2012.'

'Seriously? You worked it out that quick?'

'It's what we do, isn't it? I'm getting good!'

'OK. Maybe you're right about the time. But we still don't know where.' She twisted the spoon in her hand. 'Why would this Miss Jarratt send a message on a wooden spoon?'

'I thought wooden spoons were for people who came last at things,' said Sheldon.

Hunter's eyes widened. 'They are, Fingers!' he yelled. 'Well done!'

'Why well done?'

'Because now I know where we need to go. Seriously,

I'm *more* than good today! I'm chocolate waffles wonderful!'

'Hold on a moment,' said Smithies. 'Following leads is one thing . . . but leaving Station X. That's something else. That's a risk too far.'

'But it could take us to an answer,' pleaded Miss Tandari.

Smithies looked at Sheldon.

'It's your call, sir.'

'I can watch things here,' said Mr Bray.

'And I can help at the Listening Post,' added Fabyan.

'Please, sir,' Brodie pressed gently.

Smithies waited a moment before he answered. 'Where do you think we need to go, Hunter?'

The Mathematical Bridge

The Mathematical Bridge at Cambridge stretches across the River Cam between two sections of Queens' College. Students talk about it connecting the 'Dark Side' of the college, the old bit, with the 'Light Side', the new. Brodie loved this story. It fitted with everything they'd learnt before, even if the 'Light Side' was really only a student name for what was officially called 'The Island'.

'There's another story apart from that one, B,' said Hunter, as the Matroyska wove its way towards the Corn Exchange car park, 'that the bridge was built by Sir Isaac Newton and that he didn't use any nails to keep anything in place. It's just held up because of the force on the sections.' He tried to show them what he meant by linking his hands together. 'It's an urban myth, of course. The bridge was built after Newton died. But it's a great story. Maths supporting the whole structure.'

Brodie wasn't sure how much longer she could listen to Hunter going on and on about the wonders of tangents and arcs. She had to admit, though, it was amazing that he'd worked out that the clue led to the bridge. Apparently, wooden spoons were traditionally given to people who came last in their maths exams at Cambridge. The Mathematical Bridge had to be the place to meet. She looked at her GMT watch. 10.16. She remembered waiting on another bridge once. It seemed so long ago now.

They'd made good time through the traffic and Smithies insisted they waited somewhere out of sight until it was nearly midday.

'He wants us to wait in Trinity Chapel?' moaned Hunter. 'There must be some good cake shops round the place. Couldn't we wait there?'

Brodie could tell Smithies was still shaky about leaving Bletchley so she wasn't going to push things and Tusia said nothing because she was so excited about the patterns inside the chapel. 'The ceiling's incredible,' she said, gazing up.

Brodie could see why Tusia liked it, with all the wooden panelling fitting together like some enormous chessboard, but Hunter just sniffed. 'Could still do with a slice of carrot cake,' he moaned. 'That guy's got the right idea.' He leant his weight against a huge statue of a seated man who looked so relaxed he seemed to be sleeping.

'Hunter, please show some respect!' tutted Sicknote.

'The guy's dead! Like I will be if I don't eat soon.'

'*The guy* is Sir Francis Bacon,' scowled Sicknote. 'A total genius.'

'A *dead* genius,' whispered Hunter, rubbing his stomach.

Brodie tried to change the subject. 'Just under two hours,' she said, thrusting a map of Cambridge under Hunter's nose. 'That's all there is to wait and then we'll have some answers.'

Hunter's groaning reminded her this wasn't the first time they'd hoped that.

The nurse took the stack of papers and slid them one by one into the shredder. This job was getting slightly tedious. Friedman had done nothing but write. It seemed she'd done little else than shred what he wrote. Still. It was her orders. Let Friedman think his messages were getting through. It was all designed to add to his despair.

The nurse took one of the pre-prepared postcards

Zimansky's Spoon ?!

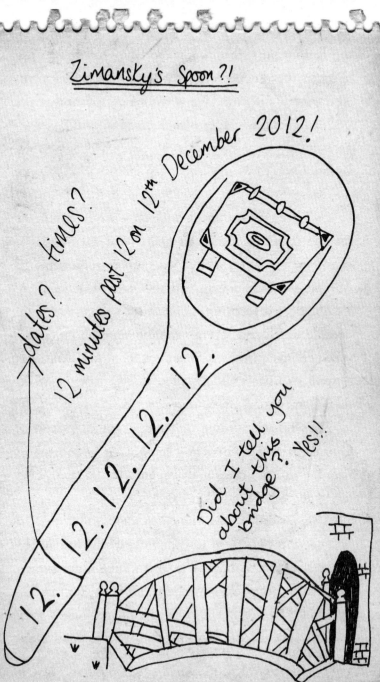

dates? times?

12 minutes past 12 on 12th December 2012!

12. 12. 12. 12.

Did I tell you about this bridge? Yes!!

the facility sent as if they were from Friedman. She checked the phone number on the back and smiled. The letters she shredded were addressed to lots of people. This Smithies guy was obviously supposed to get a lot. But the postcards only ever had one name. Brodie Bray.

Sicknote led the way through the city. Brodie had never seen so many cyclists. The roads were narrow, lanes running into lanes, and it was almost impossible to work out which college entrance was which. There were notices advertising various meetings, concerts and open lectures, and several warning signs about 'rising road bollards', whatever they were. They had little time to take it all in. It was nearly noon when they reached the Mathematical Bridge.

The woman appeared from a doorway in the side of Queens' College. She had a heavy coat pulled round her, the collar raised high to hide her face, and an unopened umbrella in her hand.

'Miss Jarratt?'

The woman walked to the centre of the bridge but she didn't answer them. She took a large dusty brown stone from her pocket and balanced it on the wooden frame of the bridge. Then she turned and looked back towards the college. 'The number twelve gives more than time,' she whispered. 'The chosen ones need you to understand.'

'Excuse me?' Brodie tried to make sense of what the woman said.

'There are all sorts of underground forces you need to be mindful of,' she said and her eyes flashed from side to side.

'Miss Jarratt, please.' Smithies reached out to touch her arm but she pulled away. 'We believe you had something to tell us. Information to help us. About MS 408. And Friedman's sealed message he left with Zimansky.'

The woman's eyes twitched. 'I've left you all you need.' Then she held out the umbrella.

Sicknote's face turned grey. 'Careful, Smithies. Remember Georgi Markov.'

'Who?' Now Tusia was struggling to keep up.

'A Bulgarian killed by a poisoned umbrella on London's Waterloo Bridge in 1978.'

'What?'

'The umbrella had a poisoned tip. Markov was stabbed in the leg. Died three days later. Terrible business.'

'And a business I had nothing to do with,' snapped Miss Jarratt. 'But . . .' Her words petered away. 'There are those who would do you harm and this,' she held the umbrella out again, 'is the means of your protection.'

Smithies still looked cautious but the old woman's eyes were steely now. 'You wanted my help,' she said. 'So here it is.'

Smithies took the umbrella.

'Don't forget the number twelve,' Miss Jarratt said. 'There are several pieces to my puzzle.'

'Number twelve. Chosen ones. What's she going on about?'

'Number of days of Christmas? Months of the year? They're all twelve.'

'They're not *chosen ones* though, are they, B?'

'Apostles,' blurted Sheldon. 'Twelve apostles. Chosen by Jesus. You reckon? Elgar wrote a piece of music called *The Apostles*.'

Brodie was impressed. 'Maybe. But how does that help us with her stone or this umbrella?'

They were waiting alone now on the centre of the bridge and Tusia was holding the dusty brown stone in her hand. 'Come on, Brodie. Anything in all those stories about apostles that mentions stones or rain?'

Brodie racked her mind. 'Don't throw stones? Don't cast the first stone? Don't plant your seed on stony ground?'

'Lovely stories, B. But how the treacle pudding do they help?'

Brodie wanted to point out that Hunter hadn't come up with any ideas of his own but that seemed a bit mean.

'Let's focus on the apostles and not the stone, then,' said Sheldon. 'What did they do? These apostles?'

'Preached; told stories; baptised people . . .' A thought was forming in Brodie's mind. 'Let me see.'

She grabbed for the stone. The dust left marks on her fingers. It needed to be washed. Made clean. And the umbrella. That was to do with rain. And water. So it fitted. Maybe.

She ran along the bridge towards the side where the bank was highest.

'B! Please. With the running away. Where are you going?'

Brodie scrambled down the bank. She crashed to her knees and rolled up her sleeve.

'Oh, what the bacon bagel is she doing now?' yelled Hunter. 'B, please!'

Brodie didn't look back. She plunged her hand into the river. The shock of the cold was scary. For a moment she thought she'd lost the stone. Her fingers floundered and her teeth locked with the chill, but when she lifted her hand from the river, water dripping down to her elbow, she was smiling.

The stone was perfectly clean. The dusty coat

washed away. And the message painted across the stone was clear to see.

What was also clear to see was that the rest of the team were no longer alone.

It was the shoes. Long and pointed at the toe. They reminded Brodie of the Child Catcher from *Chitty Chitty Bang Bang*. She'd seen them before. At the Royal Albert Hall. And in the lift of the Guildhall Library. And she'd seen the suited man who'd worn them.

Two men stood on the dark side of the river. They were watching.

'Open the umbrella!' screamed Brodie. 'And run!' Her arms pumped as she ran back along the bridge.

'What?'

'Run!'

Hunter looked behind him and suddenly understood. He stretched the black umbrella upwards. A rectangle of plastic dangled from a central spoke.

'Our protection?' blurted Sheldon. 'Really?' He grabbed the plastic tag and it came free in his hand.

'Our protection's speed,' said Hunter, and he grabbed Brodie by the arm and steered her back the way she'd come. 'Keep up!'

They thundered along the bridge, Sicknote's breathing coming in short sharp gulps. The suited men hurried after them, but where the bridge joined the shore there was a gaggle of people huddled round a student who was giving a guided tour of the area. 'Of course, when the bridge was first built there were no rivets or nails,' said the student, 'and during restoration it was difficult to rebuild the bridge the same way because—'

'Sorry! Coming through!' boomed Hunter. 'And he's wrong, you know. About the bridge.'

'Focus!' begged Sheldon, pulling the umbrella like a wild circular kite. 'And this thing . . . we have to lose it. It's like a flag telling them where we are!'

'Not yet,' said Brodie. 'There must be a reason.'

They careered down Queen's Lane and as they rounded into King's Parade, Tusia gasped. A host of tour groups waited, bunched together in the street, each group circled around a different umbrella.

'Perfect,' said Hunter, steering them towards a group bustling behind a man striding ahead armed with a stripy umbrella. Sicknote's breathing was coming in rasps.

'Merge!' said Sheldon, collapsing the black umbrella and joining the throng. 'Try and look like we belong.'

Brodie wasn't sure this would be possible as they had a man wearing pyjamas in their group, but as she glanced around the tourists she could see, Sicknote didn't actually stand out too badly. Cambridge tours obviously drew together the unusual. She lowered her head and tried to keep in step with the tour group, her eyes focused firmly on the pavement, terrified to look behind her.

'Are they there?' she whispered. 'Did we lose them?'

'Not sure,' hissed Tusia, matching her stride to Brodie's. 'Just keep your head down.'

'Cambridge is a place of secrets and history. Secret places, secret societies,' said the guide, 'and as we near the end of our tour of the hidden city, I'd like to thank you in advance for joining with me today.'

'Great!' blurted Smithies. 'The group's going to break up. What now?'

Brodie dared to turn her head. She was sure she could see the suited men just metres behind them. They weren't safe yet.

'Bikes!' exclaimed Sheldon, pointing at a bunch of cyclists waiting patiently at the traffic lights.

'You want us to steal another bike?' groaned Brodie, remembering how Sheldon had caught up with them once before on a bike stolen from the Elgar Museum. 'Once might be OK but twice would be pushing it.'

Sheldon had run ahead. 'We use the bikes! We don't steal them!'

Brodie had no idea what he was talking about.

'Trust me!' he added, darting across the line of cyclists and crouching down beside the road in an archway that led into some sort of cloister.

They had no choice. The men in suits were closing in.

Sheldon directed them all to crouch behind him out of sight from the road. 'OK!' he said. 'Let's hope the next batch of cyclists are good.'

Brodie held her breath. Sheldon lowered his head and straightened his arms. The black umbrella quivered a little. And the footsteps of the suited men got nearer.

Sheldon darted forward. There was a surge of black fabric. The umbrella canopy opened like a billowing sail right in the path of the next group of advancing cyclists. The air trapped inside cracked like gunfire.

There was a muddle of cyclists trying desperately to keep on track. The suited men stumbled. The first lurched from the kerbside, his child-catcher shoes splashing in the gutter.

There was a screech of tyres. A flurry of bags and paper and books. Cyclists careering onwards, screaming obscenities as they tried to right themselves. The suited men didn't stand a chance.

'Dear Lord! I hope there's no broken bones!' yelped Sicknote, covering his eyes.

There was one very broken umbrella. The skin

flapped free of the crushed spokes as the handle wrapped around the leg of one of the suited men. It would have been hard to tell which one it was from his position in the gutter if it hadn't been for the shoes.

'Hurry!' said Sheldon, leading the way across the cloister.

'Oi! This is college property. No right of way!' yelled a college porter.

'Sorry!' called back Hunter. 'We're avoiding a cycle pile-up.'

Brodie would have reminded him about their unicycle crash way back when they first met if she hadn't been so scared.

They raced across the grass and towards an entrance in the far wall.

'Oi! Come back!'

'No chance!' yelled Tusia. 'We're out of here!'

'And you two!' came the porter's voice. 'Where are you blokes going? This is college—'

Brodie didn't hear if the porter got an answer. It was clear from what he said though that the suited men were still after them. They'd won a little time perhaps, but not much. And now the men would be angry.

'Corn Exchange,' panted Smithies, looking up at the street signs. 'The Matroyska. We need to get away.'

Tusia took charge. 'Come on!' she urged.

'I'm sorry. I really can't keep . . . my knees . . . my feet . . . !'

'Come on, Mr Ingham. Please!'

Brodie's eyes were blurring. Sweat ran down her forehead into her eyes. But she could see it now. The orange bonnet of the Matroyska. They were nearly there.

Smithies flung open the door and they piled inside. Miss Tandari grabbed the keys and threw the vehicle into first gear. It lurched forward, a cloud of chip fat belching from the exhaust.

'Take a left!' yelled Tusia, scrabbling to keep the map flat as the Matroyska shuddered onwards. 'We need to head for Silver Street.'

Tandi threw the Matroyska around the corner. White pompoms from the edge of the curtains bashed against Brodie's face. She spilled across the seat and crashed into Sicknote's lap. 'My motion sickness!' he yelped. 'I need to keep my eye on the horizon!'

'Well, I'd keep your eye on that!' yelled Tandi, waving madly at the rear-view mirror. A sleek Mercedes was so close behind them it was practically in the back seat.

'No!' squealed Brodie. 'What do we do? What do we do?'

Help!

Brodie could almost see the whites of the driver's eyes. She didn't need to see his shoes now to know who it was. His headlights flashed. The engine roared.

'This isn't good!' said Tandi.

Brodie knew it wasn't good. They were being followed by men from Level Five and they were closing in. 'We have to get away from them!' she shouted, straining over her shoulder to see behind.

'No. I mean *this* isn't good!' blurted Tandi, her hands waving madly at the signs beside the street.

Brodie read the words aloud. 'WARNING! RESTRICTED ACCESS. VEHICLES MUST BEAR ELECTRONIC TAGS. What? I don't understand!'

'We won't get through!' said Tandi as the Matroyska swung into Silver Street.

'But why?' groaned Hunter. 'The road's clear.'

'Oh no it isn't!' exclaimed Tandi, the gears grinding under her hand as she tried to slow the van.

Across the centre of the road were two pillars. They weren't that tall. Maybe up to the level of the windscreen. But they were thick and heavy and they were in the way.

Brodie strained to look over her shoulder. Behind them the silver Mercedes was drawing closer, its lights blazing. In front of them the road was barred. They were trapped.

'This can't end well!' said Tusia. 'There's no good way out of this storm!'

Sheldon's eyes widened. He scrabbled in his pocket, swaying in his seat.

'What do I do?' squealed Tandi. 'We're going to crash! The road's blocked and I can't stop with them behind me!'

'Here!' yelled Sheldon, scrambling towards the front of the van. 'Take this!' He held out the small rectangle of plastic that had been suspended inside the spokes of the umbrella. 'Our protection.'

'What?'

The bollards were getting closer. The Mercedes closing in.

'It's our protection!'

'It's a piece of plastic!'

The bollards were metres away. Moments from the bonnet.

Sheldon clambered over the seat and slapped the plastic against the dashboard. There was a flash of light from a roadside traffic camera.

The bollards were closer. Centimetres away. And then—

The bollards began to lower. They sank into the ground so the metal pillars disappeared.

'Electronic tagging!' yelped Sheldon. 'We saw the signs. Miss Jarratt knew!'

The Matroyska ploughed forward, the bollards safely lowered below the chassis of the van.

And for one tiny moment it looked as if the Mercedes would clear them too. But the bollards rose. They screeched and thumped below the undercarriage of the car and lifted it from the ground, crumpling the floor and throwing the passengers against the windscreen as if they had been fired from a catapult. The car horn sounded from the weight of the driver's body against the steering wheel.

Brodie could still hear the ringing of the car horn in her ears when the Matroyska was miles away from Cambridge and back on the open road.

* * *

'What d'you mean, you lost them?' the Director thumped his fist down on the desk. A pile of papers toppled on to the floor.

'Sir, it was busy! Hard to be unseen!'

'But you weren't unseen, were you!' Now the Director was flapping a printout of a breaking news story wildly in front of them. 'It was a Black Chamber car! How could you have been so careless?'

The two men in front of him thought it best to say nothing.

The Director took a deep breath. He put the news report on his desk. He picked up the papers from the floor and restacked them in front of him. 'But what did you find? Why were they there?'

There was still no answer.

The Director felt his toes curling inside his particularly well-crafted Italian shoes. 'It's no good watching if you don't see what they see!'

'Understood, sir.'

The Director just wished he could understand what had taken the team from Station X to Cambridge in the first place.

'That's it! We're not leaving here again! Smithies was right! From now on we do everything from inside the station!' Sicknote was pacing beside the dinner table, his roast dinner hardly touched. He'd been pacing for quite a while.

'They didn't stop us, though,' said Hunter quietly, serving himself with another portion of creamed potato. 'They didn't find what we found.'

'But they were there. Watching. It isn't safe!'

'But we can't find the answers unless we go out,' said Tusia. 'That's the point, isn't it? The answers we need are hidden in the real world?'

'It might be *the point*, Miss Petulova. It's also the reason my blood pressure's sky high and my arms have broken out in hives! Lockdown means lockdown. We're safer here.'

'But the answers we need are out there,' said Tusia.

Mr Ingham sank down into the chair.

'We just have to be more careful. More aware next time,' said Miss Tandari.

Ingham groaned and held his head in his hands.

'There may not need to be a next time,' said Brodie, 'if we can make sense of this.' She pointed to the stone in the centre of the dining table.

'Come on then,' said Sheldon. 'What did Zimansky leave behind for us to know?'

Brodie read the message on the stone aloud. '*The Voynich MSS was an early attempt to construct*

an artificial or universal language of the a priori type.
– Friedman.'

'D'you understand that?' whispered Sheldon.

'Not a cookie crunch of a clue, mate.'

Brodie read the sentence again as if this would magically help them. 'What's "a priori" mean?'

Sicknote went to explain but before he could organise his answer, Tusia rushed to get a dictionary and flicked frantically to the right page. 'I've got it! Let me! It means the language of the document isn't based on any other vocabulary. It's a totally new way of putting words and letters together. It's a language anyone could learn and it's not connected to, say, French or English or Latin.'

'A new language. Not like any others.' Brodie thought hard for a moment. 'So does that help us? I mean, does it make things easier?'

Hunter scooped up another mouthful of creamed potato. 'It must do. We just don't know how yet.'

Tusia pushed the dictionary across the table. 'I don't think it does help us at all,' she said slowly. 'I don't think it can be a good thing.'

'Really?' said Sheldon. 'Why?'

'It might mean that finding a code-book written in a known language won't help us read MS 408,' she said.

Hunter looked up from his plate, his hand hovering on the way to his mouth. A forkful of potato slopped into a mountain of cabbage.

'So what on earth was the point of the Firebird Code which led us to Elgar's music and then eventually to *Morte d'Arthur*?' groaned Sicknote. 'If the book can't be used to read MS 408 then why was there all that fuss about leading us to it? All that work to find a book written by Malory and you're telling us it was never the code-book for MS 408? It would never have worked to help us read it?'

Tusia sipped from her glass of water.

'So it was all a waste of time, then?' continued Miss Tandari. 'All the code-breaking we did before to send us to Malory's work, just a game. No wonder we couldn't make the two things work together.'

Sicknote sat down at the end of the table. 'Seems Malory's book is as useless to us as the cipher wheel. Both of them a waste of time.'

The mood around the table was sombre. Not so much of a celebration of a message received. More like a wake. Finally, in black and white it seemed, they'd got proof of the reality they'd been trying to avoid for weeks. All the searching for the code-book for MS 408 *had* been a waste of time.

* * *

Cambridge. The Director circled the word on his notepad. He wrote the word again, then underlined it. Why Cambridge? What secrets did the city have to hide? And how did they connect with MS 408?

He turned the page and wrote something new. *Station X.* How close were the team of has-beens and not-old-enough-to-be-anythings getting?

He tore the two pages from the notepad and placed them on the desk side by side. Then he leant down and opened the desk drawer.

The scroll was where he'd left it. Easy to access but out of sight. He put it on top of the pages from his pad. He traced the letter 'T' with his fingertip. Then he prodded each of the four raised emblems.

Where was this all leading? And would he be quick enough to stop them when he knew?

He took a deep breath. Then he looked at the ornament of the sword in the stone on the front of his desk. It comforted him.

Suddenly, Hunter stood up from the table.

'Hunter?'

His eyes bulged.

'Hunter. You OK?'

For the first time since Brodie had known him, he left the plate of food in front of him half finished, and hurried from the room.

'Should I go after him?' she said keenly.

Before anyone had time to answer, Hunter had returned grasping the *Morte d'Arthur* in his hands. 'I've got it,' he yelled.

'Yes. We can see you've got it,' tutted Tusia.

'No. I mean. I've GOT it,' he said, waving the book. 'Artificial universal language, Tusia says, with no possible code-book. So why were we led to discover something as useless as this?' His eyes were wide, and then, with an enthusiasm he usually reserved for eating, he picked up his knife from the table, wiped the gravy on his jumper and in front of them all, in a swelling terrified silence, he began to cut the pages from the book and let them fall like autumn leaves one by one on to the floor.

Finding Fortune

The wind was biting through Kerrith's coat as she stood outside number 23 Leinster Gardens, Bayswater. It seemed an odd place to meet. The Director had been very specific though. Number 23. She looked up at the windows and the shiny wooden door. There was no letterbox.

'Nice place, don't you think?' A silver saloon car pulled up alongside her and the Director stepped out. 'Property prices are high in this part of town. How much would you pay?'

Kerrith began the calculations in her head, but before she could answer, the Director had begun to walk.

'A coffee, to warm up?' he said, leading the way down the street.

Kerrith hurried to keep in stride.

They turned the corner and the Director led the way into a small hotel called 'Henry VIII'. 'They have a conference room we can use,' he explained.

A waiter took their order for coffee as the Director took off his coat and draped it round the back of the chair. Then he strode towards the window and pulled back the curtain.

'Sir, I'm a little confused,' said Kerrith quietly. 'I thought you had wanted to begin my training on the work of the Suppressors,' she said.

The Director laughed. 'Oh, but I have.' He gestured for her to join him at the window. 'The house,' he explained. 'Where we met. You were going to tell me how much you'd pay to live there.'

Kerrith could feel the edges of her brain fuzzing. 'Erm, I suppose millions if I had it,' she said.

'Well, then you'd pay an awful lot of money for a shell,' he said, and pointed out of the window.

From their position on the fourth floor, Kerrith presumed they were behind Leinster Gardens now. Directly behind the house she'd seen from the street. But what she saw from the window made no sense.

Where there should have been a house, there was a gap. A railway line running instead between the houses either side. No million-pound property at all. It was just a panel painted to look like the front of a house facing the road and hiding an enormous space behind.

'It's a facade,' explained the Director, obviously enjoying the confusion wrinkling her face. 'It's not what it seems.'

'But?'

He held his hand up to stop her. 'A space was needed to allow the steam to escape the underground. But no one wanted the line of houses spoilt. So they put up a board with the front of the house painted on it, like a panel of theatre scenery. The board hides the gap behind and if you walk down the street you'd never notice.' He laughed. 'You *didn't* notice. It's important the public sees what it needs to see. Appearance is everything, Miss Vernan. Everything.' He moved across the room and took a seat at the table. 'Now, you may find it hard to believe what I'm going to say, but you must pay attention and remain focused.'

Kerrith walked across the room and sat down opposite him.

'Good. I'll begin.'

He took from a small briefcase two maps of the London Underground and slid them across the table.

'Look carefully in the area around Tottenham Court Road,' he said, moving his finger like a pointer across the papers. 'What d'you notice?'

Kerrith peered in closely. Apart from the obvious

age of the first map she didn't notice anything.

'Look at the stations shown,' added the Director, the slightest note of annoyance lacing his voice.

Kerrith screwed her eyes up and peered with more determination. Then she looked up. 'The British Museum station. It's not on the second map.'

Sun glinted from the ring on the Director's hand. 'Well done, Miss Vernan. First a house that's not a house and now a station that's not a station.' He drew in a deep breath. 'The map shows the stations as they were listed at the beginning of the century, but around 1933 there became reasons for certain stations to disappear.'

'Disappear?'

'From public view at least. The British Museum station still exists, of course, but the trains never stop there. Except, of course, when they have special need to.'

Kerrith could feel the skin on her neck prickling.

'Tonight, at exactly 11.57 p.m., you'll board an eastbound train on the Central Line.'

A bead of sweat settled in the hollow at the base of her neck.

'That train will stop at the British Museum station. You'll get off the train. I'll be waiting for you.'

* * *

'What's the matter with you?' yelped Sheldon, as Hunter continued to slice page after page from *Morte d'Arthur*.

'Lots of things, if you ask Tusia,' Hunter snapped in reply, not taking his eye off the fluttering pages of the book. 'But I know what I'm doing!'

'So do I,' called Brodie, jumping to her feet.

'We all know what he's doing, dear,' snarled Sicknote, before downing two tablets from a jar he kept on the table. 'He's destroying a five-hundred-year-old manuscript which we spent ages searching for, and which has survived the fires of Savonarola!'

'I mean, I know why he's cutting it up,' added Brodie.

'Finally,' said Hunter. 'Surely anyone can see I don't give up the best roast parsnips known to man for nothing.'

'It's the wheel, right?' continued Brodie, bending to retrieve the scattered pages as they fell.

'Of course it's the wheel.'

'Any time you're willing to let us know the reason for your madness would be good,' snapped Tusia, 'or you could just keep cutting up great chunks of history without letting us in on your secret.'

'The wheel,' said Brodie again, exasperated the others were taking so long to catch on. 'Mr Ingham said *Morte d'Arthur* was as useless as the cipher wheel.'

'I didn't mean that was a reason to cut the thing up,' pleaded Sicknote from behind the serviette which he was now dabbing frantically on his forehead.

'But we need to cut the thing up to make it work,' argued Hunter.

'You're going to put it on the cipher wheel,' Tusia blurted.

'Took your time,' groaned Hunter, but he smiled appreciatively. 'Of course we're going to put it on the cipher wheel.'

Smithies lowered the end of his tie which he'd been frantically curling around his fingers during most of the slicing. 'The cipher wheel was used to look at ancient texts and we took that to mean MS 408.'

'But,' interrupted Mr Bray, 'because the book was all in code we couldn't find a "guide word". And now we think the language used is a totally new language, any patterns we found in the shapes of glyphs wouldn't help us either.'

'And so,' Sheldon went on, 'you think if we put the pages of *Morte d'Arthur* on the cipher wheel we'll be able to find something to help us.'

'Exactly.'

At the end of the table, Sicknote was finally looking more composed. 'So our quest to solve the Firebird

Code and follow Elgar's song wasn't a waste of time, then?'

'No waste at all,' encouraged Hunter.

'We need to look for a guide word, remember.' Tusia was taking control. 'Mrs Wells Gallup said they found a whole hidden message in Shakespeare explaining how to look for a certain word. Find this word and then you look beside it and get sentences to make a hidden message.'

'Got you. What's the guide word again, Toots?'

'In the Shakespeare, it was "fortune".'

'OK. So we're looking for the word "fortune" in a story about King Arthur,' beamed Brodie. 'Do we stick the cover down?' She held up the discarded leather front piece with its handwritten request to '*let Sir Bedivere be your guide*' scrawled inside.

'No, just the pages, I guess,' said Hunter. 'We only need the printed words.'

'And if we find this guide word, then what?' she asked.

'We look in the sections around it and "collect" the sentences nearby.'

'What do we do with those sentences?'

'Read them!' Tusia was getting anxious. 'Mrs Wells Gallup and Dr Owen found that when they put these sentences together they found new "hidden" stories. The sentences told something different to the Shakespeare stories everyone knew. One time Dr Owen found a description of a huge sea battle just by arranging sections of Shakespeare across the wheel and looking for the guide word.'

'OK. Let's get looking. "Fortune", where are you?' encouraged Sheldon. 'And what story are you hiding?'

It seemed the answer was that 'fortune' was hiding nothing at all. It had taken them hours. They listed every sentence next to the guide word. It gave them nothing. Just a jumble of nonsense.

An awkward silence settled over the group. Behind them, the cipher wheel groaned forward.

'It would seem,' said Smithies at last, breaking the silence, 'we've sliced up and glued down a unique and precious document which has absolutely no secret to tell us.'

'Whoops,' said Brodie.

It was only as the final traces of December sun were bleeding into a frosty sky that Granddad got up and walked over to where Brodie sat. 'Why are we here, sweetheart?' he said quietly.

Brodie wasn't really in the mood for one of his games.

'Seriously. Why are we here?'

'To solve MS 408?'

'But why are *we* here?' he said. 'I mean, us lot. Why us?'

Brodie shrugged.

'I know why you're here. You're brilliant. But I guess I'm a little biased. But us . . . I mean Oscar and Jon and me. Why are we here?'

She had absolutely no idea what he was getting at.

'We're all past our best really, aren't we? Some of us even more so than others.'

For a moment, Sicknote looked a little offended but then his face softened into agreement.

'We've all been rejected from past searches.'

Not only did she have no idea what he was going on about, but she now had no idea what to say to him.

'I'm just glad you young ones have realised we're not ready for the scrap-heap yet.' He winked. Brodie felt a surge of excitement.

'*You're* brilliant, Granddad!' she said. 'Absolutely brilliant!' She stood up and scrabbled for the discarded leather cover of the book then held it up so everyone could see. 'It's Sir Bedivere,' she yelped.

'Pardon?' said Miss Tandari quietly.

'We need to "*let Sir Bedivere be our guide*",' said Brodie, emphasising her words.

Smithies clapped wildly. 'The words written by hand inside the cover of the book,' he said. 'Let Sir Bedivere be your guide. Of course!'

Tusia stood up and gripped the handle tightly. 'Well done, Mr Bray,' she said as the cipher wheel began to turn. 'Well done.' The pages clicked and turned. 'Now, everybody concentrate. Every time we see the word Bedivere in the text, we have to mark it. Sir Bedivere will lead us to the message we need to find.'

Brodie was asleep almost before her head hit the pillow, the slow rhythmic ticking of her two watches reminding her of the turning cipher wheel, as she dreamt of deep green caverns and crystal waters.

In the morning, Smithies got them to write down the highlighted sections thrown up by the guide word 'Bedivere'. Once this was complete, the sections were read in various orders to try and find a hidden story.

'Discovered any sea battles?' Smithies laughed, prodding their notes as they worked. 'Any battles at all?'

'Only one,' said Hunter despondently, 'and that's the one written about in the story the book's really about. It's hardly hidden. It's the battle of Camlann, Arthur's final battle. Surely we should be finding a *hidden* story, not one that's there all along.'

Sheldon tried to lift their spirits by launching into a rather raucous sea shanty but the glare from Tusia made it clear this was not the time for singing.

Finally, three days later, Brodie groaned loudly and thumped her fists down on to the windowsill. 'I can't do it,' she said. 'It's impossible. I'm giving up.'

She lowered her head and rested it on her arms, lifting it only when Fabyan entered the room carrying a tray of pies.

'Oh, not more pumpkin,' whispered Sicknote. 'It really doesn't agree with me. Plays havoc with my digestion.'

Fabyan batted away the negativity. 'Not pumpkin, no. We've moved on to mince pies. Don't you realise it's only seven days till Christmas?'

Sheldon exhaled loudly. 'I reckon it'll take us till *next* Christmas at this rate, to find the hidden message.'

Hunter leapt up to take an offered pie and blew a cloud of icing sugar across the room as he bit into the pastry.

'Careful,' yelped Tusia, brushing the sugar away. 'You'll ruin the manuscript.'

Brodie felt it would be mean to point out that cutting the book up with a knife and gluing its pages down on to long strips of linen had pretty much done that already, and then, because she felt bad for thinking it, she jumped up to stand beside Tusia who was frantically wiping at the manuscript on the cipher wheel. A tiny frosting of sugar rested over a glyph drawn in the margin; one of the many glyphs in the work which had convinced Brodie the book they'd taken from the Guildhall Library was the right one to reveal the mysteries contained in MS 408. 'If only we knew what these weird shapes meant,' Brodie sighed, running her finger along the twisted form. 'I mean, you say the Voynich shapes don't represent letters in a known language. I just wish we had a clue about what they could mean.'

Tusia lifted her finger. 'The glyphs were obviously put in this version of *Morte d'Arthur* so eventually someone would connect the two books together and figure out their story. But I'm beginning to think we'll never work out how.'

'Pie?' offered Hunter. 'There's plenty.'

Tusia turned and launched into an inquest about whether or not the mincemeat used was vegetarian. Brodie wiped the sticky sugar from her fingers. They felt tacky. A trace of the sugar was left behind. And it was this stickiness that took Brodie's last thought and wouldn't let it go. How could they connect the two books together?

The rush of inspiration which followed reminded Brodie of what it felt like to burn your hand in a cloud of kettle steam. It crept up on her, innocent at first, and then scalded her mind.

She hurried back to the pages and pages of notes they'd taken from the wheel and scrabbled to find the first section.

'Brodie. You OK?' Sheldon was looking up from his seat in the corner, the pencils he'd been drumming against the window ledge stationary now. 'Seriously. You don't look right.'

'It's the glyphs,' she yelped, flicking the pages backwards and forwards then running back to the cipher wheel and cranking the handle to make it spin. 'It's the placement of the glyphs that's important. Bedivere shows us that.'

Miss Tandari cast a rather worried look in Brodie's direction. 'Lack of sugar, maybe,' she whispered to Smithies. 'Or exhaustion. We've been working on this pretty intensely. It's bound to take its toll.'

'It's the glyphs, I tell you,' Brodie called again, turning the wheel as if she was cranking the handle of a slot machine at an arcade and was sure any minute soon she'd win the jackpot. 'It's Bedivere's glyphs.'

Tusia turned from the half-empty plate of vegetarian-friendly mince pies and hurried to stand beside her friend. 'I can tell you're on to something, Brodie. But for us to catch up, you need to speak slower.'

'No! We need to look quicker.' She shook her head and laughed. 'This is perfect. Look. I can see it already. A story inside a story and all we have to do is read it.'

8

The Most Faithful of all the Knights

As the wheels spun, Brodie pointed out the pattern she could see forming.

Scattered across the pages were glyphs. Small, letter-sized shapes, like the symbol writing used in ancient Egypt, but known to them all as the letter shapes from MS 408. At first glance they were almost missable, like the dusting of icing sugar from the top of the mince pies. But peering in closer, you could see how they broke into words and phrases, standing next to regular letters, like unexplained printing errors, or smudges on the page. Brodie pointed to where, in places, the glyphs were close to the word 'Bedivere'. 'We need to combine the two!' yelped Brodie. 'Look for places where the glyphs are near the guide word. Then we'll know which sentences we need and we can ignore the rest. It's the combination that's important! And then we need to focus on the letters next to the glyphs . . . not the words. It's more precise than we thought.'

Brodie collected letters as the wheels spun.

A message was emerging. Hidden over time.

Then he called to him Sir Kay and Sir Bedivere, and commanded
Tæhoem secretly to make ready horse and harness for hirtmystelf and
them twaisn: for after evenszong he would ride on pilgrimage witrhit
theom two only unto Stfaint ℋ Michael's mosunt

THEN the king did do call Sir tf Gawaitfnes, Sir Borrs, Sir Lionel, and
Sir Bedivwere, and commanded twxhsewrm to go straight to Sir Lucius
and say ye to him that hastily he remove out of my land; and if
he will not, bid him make him ready to battle and not distress
the poor people

To the which tent our ksnzizgtfhstzs zrozde toward, and fHull
Ordaintewwd Sir Gawaine and Sir Bors to do the message, and left in
a butfsaawdhment o Sirwwd Lizonel atfhd Sir Bedivere.

92

Tusia chewed the end of her pencil, as Brodie took the paper and began to read the letters the guide word had led them to.

THIS IS THE STORIE OV THE KNIGHTS OF NEUSTRIA.

'The Knights of who?' asked Sheldon.

'Neustria,' repeated Brodie.

'But this book's the story of King Arthur's Knights of Camelot,' said Miss Tandari.

'On the *surface* it is,' said Brodie. 'But there's another story *hidden* inside.'

Brodie turned the handle of the cipher wheel again and began to read out more letters highlighted by the guide word and the glyphs.

It took them all night to find the story.

It took them only minutes to read it.

This is the storie ov the Knights of Neustria.

And so it was that Arthur's most trusted Knight returned the sword Excalibur to the waters from whence it came. Then, tending to the dying King, Bedivere, his most beloved, was rewarded by the gift of precious tales and knowledge that Arthur had kept till thence, only unto himself. And so it is that Bedivere and those who follow in his blood line, protect the stories and the truths that Arthur shared before he departed. And this they do under the cloak of deepest secrecy, this being the pledge of each of the brother Knights of Neustria.

'It's incredible,' said Hunter, not for the first time the next morning. 'The whole idea's amazing.'

'A secret society, hidden from the pages of history,' added Sicknote. 'It doesn't get more exciting than that.'

'There's really nothing about the Knights of Neustria in the history books?' Tusia asked. 'Nothing at all?'

Sicknote puffed out his chest. History of the code was his thing. He relished talking about what they'd discovered using the cipher wheel. 'There's not a word about such an organisation. Of course, if a society's really secret then there wouldn't be, but many societies which begin in secret, eventually, over time, become known about.' He puffed out his chest once more. 'Take the "Rosicrucians" or the "Skull and Bones".'

Tusia grimaced.

'If the Knights of Neustria have no recognised recorded history,' he continued, 'we've got to ask what was so important that they had to keep their group secret.'

'Something dangerous?' said Sheldon with a glint in his eye. 'Something risky?'

'Which might explain why Level Five are so keen we leave MS 408 alone,' said Granddad.

'Is Neustria a real place?' Tusia's voice cut strongly into Brodie's troubled thoughts.

'It was,' said Sicknote. 'In about the year 500, the word "Neustria" meant most of the north of present-day France.'

'And what was Bedivere's connection with Neustria?' asked Fabyan.

Brodie raised her hand. 'I found a book in the library,' she offered.

'Don't tell me,' laughed Hunter. 'You've done some research already.'

She pulled out the wad of notes she'd made from her reading. 'Like Mr Ingham says, there's nothing in the history books about a group calling themselves the Knights of Neustria. But I did find out some interesting stuff about Sir Bedivere. It might be helpful.'

'Go ahead, sweetheart,' encouraged Granddad. 'If you've discovered something, let us know.'

Brodie organised her notes. 'We all know Bedivere was one of King Arthur's knights.' she said. 'Arthur gave Bedivere his sword when he was dying. Wanted him to throw it back in the lake.'

'Mad to throw the thing away if you ask me,' whispered Hunter.

'We didn't,' muttered Tusia. 'Ask you, I mean.'

Brodie chose to ignore their bickering and ploughed on with her explanation. 'After the final battle at

Camlann, Bedivere got made Duke of Neustria because he was so loyal.'

'Great,' said Miss Tandari. 'So there's the connection to the story we found.'

'He lived for a bit as a hermit, maybe while he got over the shock of Arthur dying and everything.' She remembered for a moment how she'd wanted to be on her own and had escaped to Station IX for a while, after hearing the shock of Friedman's betrayal. She could understand how Bedivere might have felt. 'Anyway,' she looked back at her notes, 'then Bedivere went on fighting battles. Got his hand chopped off in one of them.'

Sicknote's eyes flickered a little and he rubbed his wrist enthusiastically, checking for signs of injury.

'Things weren't all bad for him, though,' went on Brodie. 'He had two children: a son called Amren and a daughter called Eneuvac.'

'I'd have to do something with those names,' groaned Hunter. 'Let's say we call them "Ren" and "En".

'You can call them what you want,' said Brodie. 'But here's the interesting thing. Every time Bedivere's mentioned in the history books, they go on about how he escaped death. They say it was a bit of a miracle. Like he was a phoenix, rising again from a fire.'

'Perfect,' declared Tusia. 'All our work on the

Sir Bedivere

• King Arthur

asks his most trusted ~~his~~ Knight to return his sword, Excalibur, to the Lake

Twice Bedivere says he has - but Arthur ~~know~~ knows he is lying. On the third attempt the sword is returned.

After battle Sir Bedivere becomes 'Duke of Neustria'

He lived for a while as a hermit

He had a son, Amren

He had a daughter, Eneuvac

He loses a hand in battle

→ He got the name 'the phoenix' because he didn't die!

Is MS408 the book of secrets of the knights of Neustria?!

Firebird Code leads us to the discovery of a story about a man they called "the phoenix". So you see. Everything *was* connected after all.'

Brodie loved the connection. The most perfect of stories. A loop back to the place where they'd begun. Like a circle.

'This is good,' said Smithies. 'All good. Let's go through all the links we've made. Firstly, we've followed a code which led us to a book about the story of King Arthur. We've used an ancient cipher wheel to find a story hidden inside a story and the tale talks about a secret organisation called the "Knights of Neustria". And we know the organisation must have really existed and that Bedivere and his son and daughter were the original members.'

'All right so far,' said Tusia, who'd taken it upon herself to scribble a flow chart of their findings on a flip-chart on the wall.

'The story of the Knights of Neustria,' went on Smithies, 'is all about a quest. A search really. But we're not sure what it was the Knights were searching for.'

Tusia drew a large question mark on the chart.

'And finally, we're not really sure how all this connects with MS 408. I mean, we know the two *are* connected because the codes we solved link them. But it *still* doesn't make it clear what MS 408 is really about.'

Sheldon leant back on his chair. 'Do you think MS 408 is the story of the Knights' quest? The story of what they searched for?'

Tusia's eyes widened. 'Or the story of what they found!'

'Makes sense,' said Miss Tandari. 'The manuscript must be the book of the Knights' secret. Perfect.'

'It *could* be the book of their secret,' said Smithies, in a tone of warning. 'But we have to be careful. We can't jump to conclusions.'

Brodie tried hard not to let Smithies' note of caution dampen her excitement. The idea of a book of secrets was so full of story possibilities she could barely contain herself. 'Look, I have this idea, but it's just a small idea. It's not really clear in my head, but it might be worth thinking about.'

'Go on,' said Smithies. 'We're listening.'

'OK. Now, I've shown you that the books go on about Bedivere being like a phoenix, right?'

'Go on.'

'Well, we followed a phoenix code from Van der Essen to lead us to Elgar and that led us to Malory's book.'

'OK.'

'So d'you think then, Van der Essen and Hans of Aachen, the guy who protected the copy of *Morte d'Arthur*, and even Elgar were all Knights of Neustria?'

'Sort of modern-day Knights?' asked Sheldon.

'Well, members of the same organisation at least, protecting the same idea. The hidden message we found said there were brother Knights who pledged to keep the secret. And it talked about the line of Knights continuing. Supposing it continued right up to the modern day?'

'And you think all the modern Knights are called phoenixes?' said Sheldon.

'Maybe. Or firebirds. I just like the idea.'

'It's great. But where does that lead us?' asked Miss Tandari.

'Well, if there were other Knights of Neustria who helped protect the secret then we need to look for things written by them to help us piece the story together. That'll help us read MS 408.'

'So we need to find more Firebird Codes?' asked Hunter. 'Is that what you mean?'

'Maybe,' said Brodie. 'Other things written by other Knights of Neustria.'

'OK,' said Tusia enthusiastically. 'But how exactly are we going to find this hidden stuff?'

'The mark of the phoenix, I guess,' suggested Brodie.

'We could look for things marked with firebirds. Or . . .' She was aware that she looked a little awkward. It was a stretch, she knew, but surely one worth taking. 'We could look for other marks too.'

'Others?' said her granddad. 'What d'you mean, sweetie?'

'Maybe the Knights had other crests.'

'Like the book on the crest of Cambridge University?' said Fabyan.

'Kind of.'

'So what crests d'you think we need to look for, then?'

'Well, in the time of Arthur everyone important had their own crest. Amren, Bedivere's son, had a griffin on his and Eneuvac, his daughter, had branches, like a tree.' She took pages of notes she'd copied and passed them to Tusia who tacked them to the flip-chart. 'Maybe all three symbols are marks of the Knights of Neustria? If we can track down writing with these marks on, we can add them to what we know. The best way to keep a secret, after all, is to break it into pieces which must be put together.'

'Like pieces of a puzzle?' said Tusia, scribbling the idea on the flip-chart.

'Exactly. Pieces of a puzzle which, when we connect them, give us the whole picture.'

'And you think the whole picture will be us reading MS 408, the book of the secrets of the Knights of Neustria?' asked Hunter. 'Well, that's the sort of puzzle I could enjoy, B.'

'Great,' said Smithies. 'So where do we start our hunt?'

'No idea,' said Brodie. 'No idea at all.'

Tusia put down her pen. 'I do,' she said. 'Follow me.'

9

Sign of the Wild Boar

'Bacon,' called Tusia, as she hurried over to Hut 11.

'OK, Toots,' called Hunter. 'I mean, it's never too late or too early for a bacon butty, right? But I thought you were off the bodily products, what with being a veggie and everything.'

'Yes. Unlike you, I have morals about eating the flesh of dead animals,' retorted Tusia. 'But I'm not talking about the food "bacon",' she explained. 'I'm talking about the person.'

Hunter did little to hide his disappointment.

They waited for Granddad to catch up with them and then Tusia led the way inside. 'OK,' she said, putting her hands on her hips decisively. 'It might be nothing . . . or it could be just the clue we need.' She turned to point to three towering stacks of papers in

103

the corner of the room. 'Stuff from Fabyan's trunk,' she explained. 'I thought it needed ordering. I sorted it all into three piles.'

'Whoa, great maths,' whispered Hunter.

'Based on,' Tusia continued, obviously trying to ignore him, 'three main ideas.' She waved towards the largest pile. 'Pile one is cryptology magazines which were stored at Riverbank Labs. They led us to Zimansky.'

'And the clue on the spoon and the stone we had to wash. Perfect,' said Brodie.

'The second pile's stuff about the cipher wheel.' Tusia moved along the line to point to the third pile, the smallest of the three. 'And this is stuff about Bacon. The person.'

'Go on,' said Miss Tandari.

Tusia needed little encouragement. 'Well, at first I thought this pile was the least important. We hardly looked at it. Didn't see how it could link to MS 408.'

'So why's it here?' asked Smithies.

'I can explain,' cut in Fabyan. 'Sir Francis Bacon was born in the fifteen hundreds. Fabyan and Elizabeth Wells Gallup thought Sir Francis really wrote everything Shakespeare gets credit for. Loads of people think Shakespeare was just a name for another writer and using Dr Owen's cipher wheel,

Mrs Wells Gallup was sure she could link the plays with Bacon. You see, Sir Francis was known for being great with codes. He even made up his own coding system. It's called the bilateral cipher and it's where some letters are written darker than others to hide secret words.'

'Is he going anywhere with this?' whispered Hunter. 'Or just trying to confuse us?'

'I'm not trying to confuse you. I'm trying to explain that Sir Francis Bacon is important in the world of codes. But, like Tusia said, I'm not sure how he helps us.'

'Well, if he was the man who really wrote the Shakespeare stories then he gave us loads of fabulous writing,' said Brodie. 'That's helping!'

'I mean, helps us with MS 408!' said Fabyan. 'But anyway, William Friedman *didn't* think he was Shakespeare. He and his wife wrote a book about it called *The Shakespearean Ciphers Examined*, and they went through everything Mrs Wells Gallup said but in the end they disagreed with her.'

'So why did your great-grandfather keep all this stuff?' urged Brodie, looking at Fabyan.

'I'm getting to that.' Tusia hurried over to the windowsill and picked up the logbook. 'I made a sketch,' she said.

'Oh nice,' groaned Hunter. 'She makes neat piles of magazines and papers and now we have to look at one of her spacial puzzle things.'

'It's not a puzzle,' said Tusia. 'It's a picture of a family crest.' She gestured to her drawing. 'Bacon's crest.'

'Appropriate, don't you think?' laughed Sicknote. 'For someone with a name like Bacon.' The page fluttered a little but Sir Francis Bacon's family crest was clear to see. A wild boar.

'She just keeps making me hungry,' groaned Hunter.

'And you just keep making me annoyed,' snapped Tusia. 'Now be quiet and listen.'

Hunter said nothing more as Tusia passed the sketch around.

'And so the boar was Bacon's crest, but then something about that wasn't right.' She rummaged through the third pile of papers. 'Like I say, I haven't looked at all this properly yet. But in this piece of writing about Sir Francis, look, there's a picture of a crest.'

'Another picture of a wild boar?' moaned Hunter, clutching at his stomach.

'Not a boar,' Tusia said, 'but this.'

She passed the document around so everyone

could see. There, clear and precise, drawn in thin ink lines, beside some writing about Sir Francis Bacon, was a different crest and this one was a picture of a griffin.

'So d'you think, then,' said Brodie, holding the page as it came to her last, 'that this Sir Francis Bacon, the person who Fabyan Senior thought was the real Shakespeare, was also a Knight of Neustria?'

'Yes!' encouraged Tusia. 'Bacon was interested in codes. He left hidden messages for people to find, and, in some of his work, for no apparent reason, he used the wrong crest. You said earlier, one of the original Knights of Neustria, Bedivere's son Amren, had a griffin as a crest.' She paused and then added almost apologetically, 'Maybe there's a connection. It's got to be worth thinking about. Don't you think?'

Smithies looked over in Sicknote's direction. 'See, Oscar. Yet more proof, if we really needed it, of how brilliant these kids are. They just *see* things, you know.'

Sicknote looked surprisingly chirpy as he nodded in agreement.

Smithies opened his hands. 'So, I guess that pile of papers towering behind you is the place to start.'

Brodie felt a ripple of excitement surge through her at the prospect of more reading as, beside her, Hunter let out a long and audible groan.

* * *

The guard in the mansion gatehouse picked up his mobile. His *work* mobile. His *home* mobile hadn't rung for weeks. His wife hadn't been keen on the new tattoo. She didn't like dragons.

'No. She's not responding to the postcards, ma'am.'

The line was crackly. Part of the security measures.

'But yes, I pass them on. All of them. Every single day.' He felt slightly awkward about the mention of mail. He still hadn't found that letter the kid with the harmonica had been trying to post.

He held the phone away from his ear. There really was no need to shout. He was doing his best. This was a thankless task. Like he was invisible to them, stuck out here away from the action. Just there to do what they wanted. 'Yes, ma'am. I'll keep trying.' He pressed the button and the lights on the phone died. Trying was what he did. But sometimes it didn't make him feel the same as it had.

'So what do we know now about Sir Francis Bacon?' asked Smithies, who'd taken a place at the front of Hut 11 and, as usual when concentrating very hard, was wearing his glasses on his forehead and peering at everyone in front of him as if he was looking through a thick fog.

Miss Tandari had given them two days. Forty-eight

hours to discover all they could and feed back to the team. Tusia was once again at the front of the room with the flip-chart ready, pen poised for writing.

'I'll start if you like,' said Brodie, glancing down at the notes she'd made.

'Go ahead,' said Smithies. 'And, Tusia, if you record the most important snippets.' He lowered his glasses to the bridge of his nose. 'Mind you, we won't really know what's important. So perhaps you should just write everything.'

Brodie took a deep breath. 'Bacon was born on the 22nd of January 1561 and died in 1626. His family crest was the boar, but he didn't pass this crest on to anyone because he had no children.'

Tusia scribbled this frantically on the chart.

'He was very clever! Went to Cambridge University at the age of twelve!'

Sheldon made a whistling noise between his teeth.

'He'd have been chosen for Team Veritas then,' chipped in Hunter.

'Definitely,' went on Brodie. 'He did loads of travelling when he was younger. To Europe. Spent some time in Seville,' she said. 'Then his dad died so he came back to England.'

'To work?' asked Miss Tandari.

'Sort of. He was really into science. But here's a

weird thing. He was actually killed by his own experiment.'

'Burnt burgers! What'd he do?'

'He was in London and it was snowing. Fridges hadn't been invented and he suddenly had this crazy idea that keeping things cold could stop them rotting. So he stopped his carriage and went to a house near Highgate, killed a chicken and asked this woman there to pluck it. Then he filled the chicken carcass with snow.'

'And that killed him?' whined Sicknote, who'd turned a little grey.

'The cold did, so the story goes. He got pneumonia and died in his friend's house a few days later.'

Tusia added the words *'died as the result of chicken experiment'* to the notes page.

Smithies winced a little. 'But did you find anything else which would connect him to the Knights of Neustria?'

'Not really, apart from his use of the griffin crest for no obvious reason.' Brodie thought for a moment and scratched her head. 'Bacon's written loads of things. I've been really good, though, and only read his factual stuff and theories.'

'Really good?' quizzed Hunter.

'Well, there were stories and poems I could have

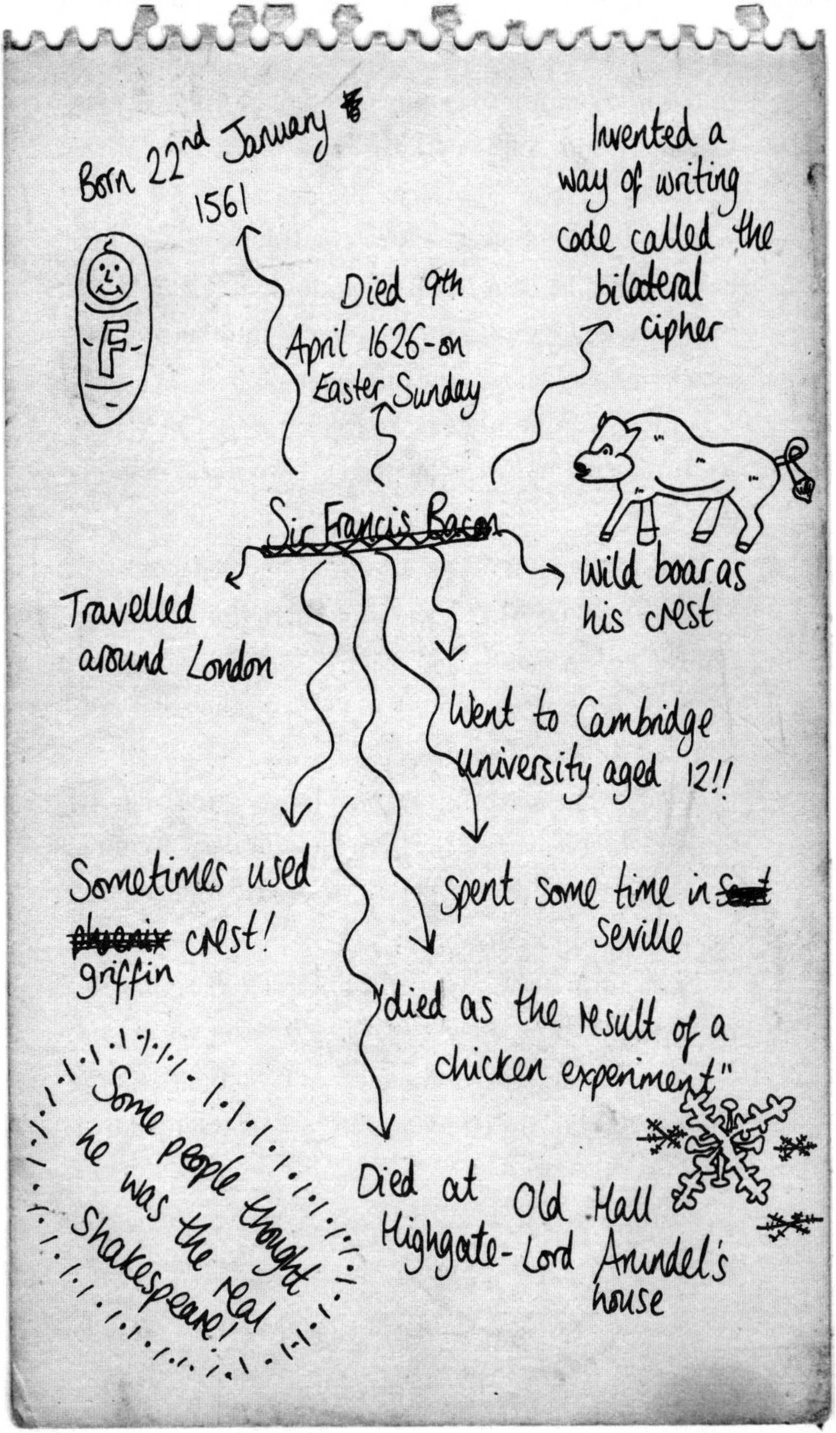

Born 22nd January 1561
Invented a way of writing code called the bilateral cipher
Died 9th April 1626-on Easter Sunday
F
Sir Francis Bacon
Travelled around London
Wild boar as his crest
Went to Cambridge University aged 12!!
Sometimes used griffin crest!
Spent some time in Seville
"died as the result of a chicken experiment"
Died at Old Hall Highgate-Lord Arundel's house
Some people thought he was the real Shakespeare!

read but I tried not to get distracted.' She knew she was looking rather pleased with herself but the others obviously failed to appreciate the sacrifice she'd made. 'It's hard stuff. Bacon was fascinated by codes. Like Fabyan said, he even made things look different on the page by writing some letters darker than others to hide secret messages. That's the bilateral cipher. It's a bit like how the glyphs hiding next to the letters in the Malory book worked. The code makes you notice certain letters.'

'But is there anything else to connect Bacon with MS 408?' asked Miss Tandari. 'Apart from that idea and the griffin crest?'

'If there is, I can't find it yet.' Brodie knew she sounded disheartened.

'Well, what about other people we think may be Knights of Neustria?' suggested Granddad. 'Is there any way some of the people we've looked at in the past are connected to Bacon?'

Tusia turned the pages on the flip-chart and added another title. '*The Knights of Neustria: connections.*'

Miss Tandari looked thoughtful. 'OK. We think the original Knight was Bedivere and he's represented by a phoenix.'

Tusia sketched a quick firebird above Bedivere's name.

'And we think we've come across other Knights who are protecting the secret contained in MS 408, and they're Van der Essen, Elgar and Hans of Aachen.'

Tusia made a quick chart and added these names.

'Then,' continued Miss Tandari, 'there were Bedivere's children, Amren and Eneuvac.'

Tusia sketched first a griffin and then branches in the sections of the chart.

'And we think Sir Francis Bacon counts in the griffin section,' offered Brodie, 'because instead of using that pig symbol all the time, he sometimes used a griffin.'

Tusia added the name.

'But we've no suggestions of people to put under Eneuvac's name yet, have we?' Brodie looked round the room to see if anyone knew something different. No one spoke.

'But there must be a time connection,' offered Hunter. 'If the story of the Knights was passed through time, from person to person, then there must be names in the gaps.'

'Exactly.'

'Malory was in a gap,' blurted Brodie. 'We nearly forgot him. The glyph coding system meant we found the story of the Knights of Neustria hidden in the book written by Thomas Malory. Remember?'

'So, Thomas Malory must have been a Knight of

Neustria, then,' said Sicknote.

'A most trusted member if he was allowed to write the story down in code,' added Smithies.

'I think I've got it,' said Tusia slowly. 'Perhaps Sir Francis Bacon taught Malory how to use the code of hiding glyphs by the letters. Malory wrote the story down using Bacon's code and hoped one day it'd be discovered and read.'

'No,' said Hunter. 'If Malory died in 1471 and Bacon was born in 1561 they can't have met. That can't have been how it worked. If anything, Malory must have had the idea for the "glyph between the letters" code and Bacon found out about it. Seeing that code helped Bacon think up the bilateral cipher.'

'But there's still a gap, isn't there?' said Miss Tandari. 'Bacon and Malory can't have met because of the dates. So if there's a gap in the dates then there must be a missing Knight of Neustria. Someone who lived in the time between Malory and Bacon and was the bridge between what they knew.'

'And perhaps,' said Tusia, 'that person was someone we've already thought about.'

'Who?'

'Hans of Aachen, our Orphan of the Flames.' She let out a sigh. 'Maybe he lived in the time between the two men. His father was a gaoler when Malory was in

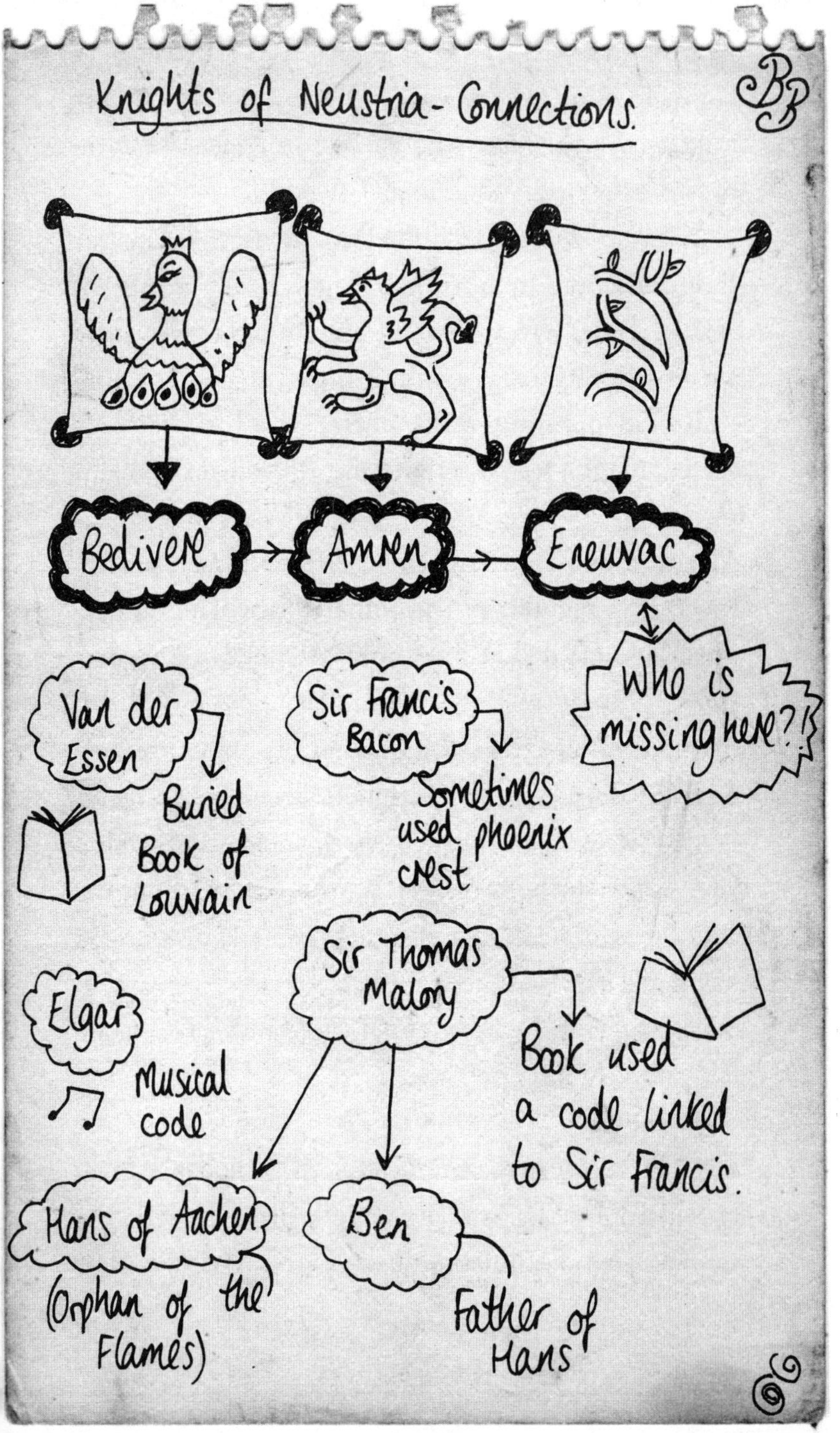
BB
Knights of Neustria - Connections.
Bedivere
Amren
Eneuvac
Who is missing here?!
Van der Essen
Buried Book of Louvain
Sir Francis Bacon
Sometimes used phoenix crest
Sir Thomas Malory
Book used a code linked to Sir Francis.
Elgar
Musical code
Hans of Aachen
(Orphan of the Flames)
Ben
Father of Hans

Newgate Gaol. We know Malory's book was passed on to Hans. Maybe Hans told Sir Francis Bacon about the coding system the book used.'

'OK. So we need to find a link between Sir Francis Bacon and our Orphan of the Flames then.' She looked around hopefully. 'After all the things we've done already, I can't imagine it'll be too hard.'

Brodie looked up at the chart Tusia had drawn on the board. She wasn't so sure she agreed.

Kerrith didn't enjoy travelling on public transport. It was the 'public' bit which bothered her. The thought of sitting next to a builder from Hackney or a student from Toxteth made her shudder. She pulled her Christian Dior coat tighter round her shoulders and, finger by finger, ensured her gloves were fitted correctly.

Her concern for hygiene was, today, unfounded. The 11.57 eastbound train on the Central Line was entirely empty. Until she stepped on board. She wondered if the Director knew the train would be deserted. She began to wonder, in fact, if the Director had arranged for it to be so.

As the train pulled out of Tottenham Court Road, she glanced up at the overhead map. Holborn was the next listed stop. She watched as the walls of the darkened tunnel swept past the grubby windows. Then the train juddered slightly. There was a hissing of brakes. And the train stopped.

She wasn't at Holborn.

From the window, Kerrith could just make out a sign for 'British Museum'.

The doors slid open. Kerrith felt a rush of exhilaration. Then she stepped off the train on to the platform.

The light was dim; the air rank and stale. Kerrith pulled her pashmina over her nose, trying desperately not to inhale. Behind her, the train rattled on the tracks, and then with a grinding click, it pulled away from the station.

She was now totally alone.

As her eyes became used to the lack of light, she could just make out a single doorway peering at her. She stepped forward, reached out and pushed. The door swung open.

'Miss Vernan.' The Director's voice boomed as if he was in possession of a megaphone. 'Welcome, welcome. I hope the journey was in no way unpleasant.'

Kerrith lowered her pashmina from her face.

'Please, please, come this way,' he said, turning and gesturing towards a long dimly lit corridor stretching in front of him. 'There's lots you need to see.'

'What *is* this place?' she called as she followed his lead.

He relished the moment which saw her hovering between a state of ignorance and knowledge. 'This,' he said, pushing open the door in front of him, 'is the real Black Chamber.'

Kerrith held her breath as another door swung open. And for just a moment time stood still.

In front of her, stretching further than the eye could see, were rows and rows of shelves arranged like vertebrae along a spine. The space was clean, clinical and airy, and the ceiling high. The air was filled with the sound of a gentle humming, an air filtering system she presumed, and all around the space, of which she could see no end, people in white coats walked and waited, like customers in a library, searching for a perfect read.

'I don't understand,' she said quietly.

'Ah well. That's why we're here,' he laughed. 'To help aid your understanding.'

Kerrith peered at the shelving. It held rows and rows of books and documents. Thousands, stretching out of sight.

'What are they all?' she said.

'They are "the suppressed",' he said, and the words excited him. 'The banned and the prohibited. The unsafe and the unsound. They're all that shouldn't be. They're the real reason Level Five exists.'

Kerrith stepped forward, closer towards the shelf. 'Can I?' she said, reaching out towards the nearest volume, a leather-bound book, faded and worn with age.

The Director didn't object.

Kerrith took the book from the shelf. *Les Miserables* by Victor Hugo. She knew her face showed her confusion.

'Go on,' he said gently. 'Open it. Look inside.'

Kerrith turned the cover. Inside, marked across the front page, was a stamp.

'You recognise it?' said the Director.

'It's the mark of the Suppressors,' she said. 'I've seen it before.'

This answer pleased him.

'All over the world, in every corner where words are committed to the page, there're writers who've woven together stories that corrupt, harm and destroy. Throughout time, there've been those who've fought to keep our world safe from those who'd do us damage. Organisations which have sought to maintain goodness and truth.' He was enjoying his speech. 'We are the heart of those organisations. The pulse behind the work of all those who wish to maintain order and structure. We're the life-blood of all that's good.'

'Level Five is?'

'Of course. Our work also extends to cracking codes and reading hidden messages. But only so the job of suppressing all that's wrong and corrupt can continue. Those who work in the code-cracking wing of the department are important to us. Valuable even. But those who uphold *this* work are the true heroes of our organisation. The real secret workers.'

Kerrith looked around at all the seemingly ordinary people who scurried backwards and forwards between the shelves.

'But all these books,' she said. 'All of them need "suppressing"?'

'Every one of them,' he said, 'capable of corrupting innocents.'

'But this book?' Kerrith said, holding out the copy of *Les Miserables* she'd taken from the shelf. 'You can buy this book now. Read what's written. Why's this book here?'

The Director ran his finger along his chin. 'The book you hold was on a forbidden list until 1959. The list no longer exists now, officially. But the work to protect continues.' He steepled his fingers together. 'It's our job to suppress the totality of the text. The version you can buy above ground is a shadow version of the words you contain in your hands,' he said proudly. 'For the very best type of suppressing is when people believe they've been given all there is. A house that's not a house. A station that's not a station. Give the people what they think they should see and you have social order.'

Kerrith's head was beginning to throb. 'And where does MS 408 fit in with all of this?' she said, waving towards the shelves.

The Director folded his arms. 'We believe whatever MS 408 contains will be dangerous, with the potential to destroy the lives of many. Our aim was clear. A simple D notice. A ban on its research. Discredit all those who spoke about it. Ridicule everyone who claimed to know what it said. Yet in recent months our strategy has encountered some complications.'

'Smithies?'

'And those ridiculous children who have the tenacity of a dog with a bone. They seem unresponsive to threats. Even undaunted by the removal of one of their number.' The Director straightened his back. 'And so our plan now has been to let them explore. Let them experiment. Let them, if they must, find the answers.'

'And then?'

'Then, we suppress the knowledge they find and make it totally inaccessible to anyone else. Ever.' His eyes glinted. 'In the past, writers of forbidden works have been thrown into the flames or punished. We don't know who wrote MS 408. But soon, we may have those who can read it.' He waited and watched her, wondering if she'd reached the conclusion he was about to verbalise. 'And when we do, our opportunity to punish will arise.' A bubble of spit glistened on his lips. 'When they can read MS 408, we eliminate them all.'

Searching for a Father

'We need to think about fathers,' said Hunter in a matter-of-fact way.

Brodie felt her stomach tighten. As far as she was concerned, fathers were the last thing to consider, bearing in mind she didn't have one or even know who her father had been. She shot a look in her granddad's direction but he lowered his head awkwardly. He was probably remembering the last time she'd asked him to tell her about her past. Not that it had been much of a conversation. He'd told her it wasn't the time to discuss things. Apparently, it was never the time.

'Not *our* fathers,' he blurted, suddenly understanding her look of disapproval. 'No way should we be considering *them*.'

Brodie flicked a speck of dust from her arm defiantly.

What did Hunter have to be precious about? At least he knew who his father was. What could possibly be worse than not knowing?

Hunter pointed to the flip-chart. 'We've got to try and fill in the gaps in the dates,' he said.

Brodie turned to a new page in her logbook and wrote the title 'Dates' and underlined it.

'We're trying to work out connections between Knights of Neustria. That might give us a chance of being able to read MS 408. So let's start with the code we solved last. Malory's.'

Brodie wrote the name Malory under the title.

'Malory died in 1471. And Francis Bacon wasn't born until ninety years later. Hans of Aachen's father, Benjamin Barge, was the gaoler in Newgate, remember? He must have spent time with Malory. He got the special version of *Morte d'Arthur* and kept it safe from Savonarola's fires. Then his son Hans brought the book back to England. We know all that because Brodie found the book in the Guildhall Library in London.'

Brodie's stomach squirmed again at the memory of that particular day. This was turning into quite an uncomfortable session.

'So if we reckon that somehow this guy called Sir Francis Bacon knew about the coding system Malory used in his book,' he looked hopefully round the room, 'then we've got to work out how he learnt about that secret.'

Sheldon raked his fingers through his hair. 'Maybe,' he said ponderously, 'Hans of Aachen came to London and explained the system to Sir Francis Bacon *before* he left the book in the Guildhall Library.'

'Possible,' said Hunter. 'But I don't think so.'

'Why?' snapped Tusia. 'Seems logical to me.'

Hunter let out a sigh. 'You keep wanting things to fit when the dates don't work,' he said, with a definite tone of annoyance. 'We know Hans was fourteen years old in 1496 when his dad escaped Savonarola.'

'We do?' groaned Tusia.

'It was in the Aachen town records!' Hunter reminded her. 'We used that information to solve the Elgar puzzle.'

'We did?' she groaned again.

Hunter's eyes rounded with exasperation. 'Yes! We knew the Orphan of the Flames was fourteen when the town took care of him. Keep up,' he added forcefully.

'But there's too many numbers,' whined Tusia.

Brodie feared for a moment Hunter would implode. 'How can there *ever* be too many numbers?' he wailed.

Tusia at least knew better than to push the argument.

'Anyway,' said Hunter, after he'd composed himself,

'if Hans met Sir Francis Bacon, then Hans would have been getting on for his late seventies. Sir Francis was just a baby. Doubt they sat down and had chats about codes together.'

Granddad cleared his throat and raised his eyebrows. 'Are you saying Hans would have been too old?' he said curtly.

'Or Sir Francis too young?' snapped Tusia.

Hunter rolled his eyes. 'Things were different then. Age isn't important now.' He seemed to be particularly emphasising this for Granddad's benefit. 'But I'm not sure it would have made sense then. There's got to be a more logical answer.'

'Like what?' asked Miss Tandari.

'Fathers. Like I said.'

'Just explain why you think fathers are important,' Smithies said softly.

'Because of the law,' Hunter said. 'We've got to link Hans to Sir Francis Bacon somehow. So, we've got a prisoner – that's Malory. He's writing this book to hide a secret. Then we've got a prison officer – that's Benjamin. He takes the book from Malory to keep it safe. Course, that's hard what with Savonarola wanting to burn it and everything. But he manages and eventually he gives the book to his son – that's Hans. Then somewhere along the line this guy Sir Francis

Dates 📅 📅 📅

Connections between Knights of Neustria

Malory → Wrote Morte D'Arthur
        Was in Newgate Gaol!

died 1471 ~~1582~~ RIP.

What's the link?

Francis Bacon → Born 90 years later

Hans of Aachen → Orphan of the Flames

Dad was a jailor at Newgate
(Benjamin ~~Boot~~ Barge)

He got books from Malory

Kept safe from Savonarola

Passed onto son

Bacon gets involved. There's a missing link and the link's *the law*. Or more precisely, *the lawyer*.'

'Go on,' pleaded Brodie, whose head was thumping with the effort of keeping up.

'I think it happened like this. Malory wrote a book in code, passed it to his gaoler. Then the book comes back to England to keep it safe. Hans could have chosen lots of people to help him when he got here with the book. He'd need someone he could trust. And if your dad was a prison guard, why not get the law to help you?' He blew out a breath elaborately. 'And *there's* the link. The link between Hans *and* Malory *and* Bacon.'

'Where?'

'*Sir Francis Bacon's father was a lawyer.* He was called Sir Nicholas Bacon. He's the link we need. The dates work. When Hans came to England, I bet he asked Sir Nicholas to help him. Sir Nicholas could have been a Knight of Neustria and so knew all about the secret in *Morte d'Arthur*. And then, when the time was right, Nicholas told his son Francis all about the secret and the code.'

'Sir Nicholas Bacon,' said Miss Tandari. 'A man trusted with the story of the Knights of Neustria who passed the story on to his son just as Bedivere passed the story to his children and Benjamin passed the story on to Hans.'

128

'It's how stories pass through time,' said Sicknote. 'Generation to generation.'

'It's a great idea,' said Brodie. 'We're not jumping to conclusions, are we?'

'Don't think so,' said Tusia. She flicked the pages on the flip-chart back to the notes they'd made before and pointed to the pictures she'd sketched. 'There's the whole griffin thing,' she said. 'Bacon *has* to be connected, otherwise why the griffin on his work?'

'If Sir Nicholas Bacon is a missing Knight of Neustria,' said Miss Tandari, 'then let's prove it.'

'Look, I didn't mean to upset you.' Hunter was hurrying after Brodie, failing not only to catch her up, but also to avoid a good soaking from the temperamental water feature. 'What the fig biscuit is the *matter* with that thing?' he yelped, running his fingers through his dripping-wet hair.

Despite herself, Brodie couldn't help but slow down and wait for him.

Hunter caught up and then shivered violently. 'Seriously, BB. I didn't mean to upset you.'

'It wasn't you,' she said. 'I don't know what's wrong with me at the moment.'

'What, more wrong than usual?' he said, and then jumped defensively out of the reach of her hand.

'I just feel weird. You know. These postcards from Friedman are getting to me, I guess.' She'd had another one only this morning and as usual she'd thrown it away, but they played on her mind, like an insect bite irritating the skin. 'And it's coming up to Christmas. I just feel like the whole family thing's getting me down.'

'Your family's here, B,' he said quietly.

'Oh, I know my granddad's here and that's great. And it must be awful for you not seeing your family at all.'

'That isn't what I meant,' he said.

Brodie tried to work out what he was thinking.

'I meant *we're* your family. And don't feel bad for me not seeing my parents. I'm cookie-dough cool with that.'

'Really?'

'No. But it sounds better to say it. I mean, I can't admit to you I'd like to spend time with them and that I'm annoyed they're not even popping by for a quick visit. Admitting that would just be way too sad, wouldn't it?'

Brodie wasn't sure how to answer.

'No, seriously. I'm used to it. They're always busy. You adapt, like you had to adapt to having no mum or dad at all.'

'No one adapts,' she said.

They'd been walking as they talked and were now at the front door of the mansion. Hunter sank down to sit on the steps. 'Will you ring him?' he asked at last.

'Friedman?'

'Give him a chance to explain. What he did. Why he hasn't come back.'

'It's because he's not on our side. Because he never was.'

'You don't know that.'

Brodie blew out a breath and it fogged on the air. 'Talking to him wouldn't help.'

'Listening to him might. If you knew the truth, wouldn't that be better? Isn't that why we're here, to find answers? Can you really be better off not knowing?'

'Not sure,' she said. 'I mean, it's like with MS 408. Sometimes I want to know so badly what it's about, it hurts. Then sometimes, I think the truth must be dangerous and so we should give up searching.'

'I reckon knowing is always better than giving up, whatever the danger.'

'Maybe.'

He leant against the weathered stone griffin guarding the entrance to the mansion.

'Don't let Sicknote see you do that. He's got a thing about you leaning on statues.' She remembered Ingham's desperate plea to show more respect when

Hunter had leant on a statue in the chapel at Cambridge. Her mind began to whirl. She was trying to remember who that statue was of.

'Seems ages ago, doesn't it?' said Hunter.

'What does?'

'When it all started here, with that message tucked under the griffin's feet.'

Brodie smiled at the memory. 'Yeah.'

'It took us a while to cotton on, but we got there in the end,' he said, tapping the statue firmly.

'You're right!' she said.

'What, about everything?' Hunter laughed.

'No! About Sir Nicholas.'

'Really?'

'Yes!'

'And why am I right?'

'The griffins,' she laughed.

He wrinkled his nose in confusion.

'Come on,' she said. 'We need to get the others together and tell them you were right all along.'

11

The Golden Griffin

'OK,' said Tusia. 'What's the evidence?'

'Griffins, apparently,' said Hunter, shivering because he was still wet from the water feature.

'You should really go and get dry clothes on,' interrupted Miss Tandari. 'You'll get pneumonia sitting in those wet clothes.'

'Actually, pneumonia's an infection,' explained Sicknote. 'It's caused by a virus. It's not the result of the cold. That would be hypothermia.'

Smithies clapped his hands together. 'Erm, if it's not too much trouble with everyone, Brodie says she's got some information and I for one would like to know what it is.'

Brodie smiled appreciatively. 'I think Hunter's right about Sir Nicholas being the missing link and the missing Knight of Neustria,' she said. 'And I'm trying to show you why.'

At last, after rejecting several papers and building a pile of discarded texts resembling a heap of dirty washing, which seemed to cause Tusia a fair degree of distress, she pulled a particular document from the stack and waved it victoriously. 'Hunter told us Sir Nicholas was a lawyer in London. And that was great. But this document tells us where he trained and lived. I knew I'd read something about those griffins,' she said, glancing at the pile of rejections. 'And it was here.'

'Go on.'

'Sir Nicholas lived and trained as a lawyer at a place called Gray's Inn in London. It's still where some lawyers train.'

'And?'

'And the crest for Gray's Inn is . . .' She held out her hands like a pantomime star waiting for audience participation.

'My goodness,' mumbled Smithies, taking the sheet of paper from her. 'It's a griffin.'

Brodie beamed.

'Baked bananas brilliant!' said Hunter, shivering so much his teeth chattered. 'So what do we do now?'

Brodie looked across the room at Smithies. 'Well, I suppose we read up all we can on Sir Nicholas Bacon.

See if he or his son left anything behind to help us with MS 408.'

'But what about this Gray's Inn place?' asked Sheldon.

'What about it?'

'If Sir Nicholas lived there and that's where you reckon he may have met with Hans of Aachen when he needed *Morte d'Arthur* to be kept safely, then perhaps there's things at Gray's Inn which may help us.'

'Oh no. Not this again,' said Smithies cautiously. 'We have to remember we still have Level Five on our backs. We don't want them to know we're making progress. We took a risk in Cambridge and look how that turned out.'

'It turned out fine,' said Hunter quietly. 'Well, fine for us anyway.'

'We were lucky.'

'We were quick. And we got away. And you can't keep us locked up here and not let us follow leads when they come up. Can you?'

Smithies folded his arms.

'Isn't that what Level Five do? Make it impossible to follow up leads by banning things?'

'Now hold on a minute!'

'Sorry. I'm just saying. Are we in this to find answers or what?'

Smithies' face softened a little.

'Break the rules to break the code and all that,' said Sheldon sheepishly.

Smithies was obviously wavering. 'We got away with it once. Supposing this time things go really wrong? Suppose Level Five find out what we're searching for?'

'Have you ever thought,' asked Brodie nervously, 'that perhaps Level Five are searching too? And perhaps they'll get to the answers before us.'

The air crackled with tension. Smithies' jaw tightened. He looked across at Sicknote.

'I can stay and manage things at the Listening Post,' said Mr Bray. 'Make sure we keep up to date with what Level Five are up to.'

'I'll help with that again,' said Fabyan.

'OK,' Smithies said at last. 'We'll take a chance. A covert trip down to London in the Matroyska. But we'll be extra careful. And we'll be back in a week whatever we find.'

'I hope you'll be back in three days,' laughed Fabyan.

Brodie looked down at her Greenwich Mean Time watch. The minute hand had just ticked past midnight. Three days till Christmas. That was sort of exciting.

But not as exciting as the thought of taking the search down to Gray's Inn in London.

* * *

'Whoa, nice place,' called Sheldon, putting his harmonica down on his knees and rubbing a hole in the misting on the window behind the bobble-edged yellow curtains.

Brodie was strangely disappointed Sheldon's tune had finished. She turned to peer through the window beside him.

'Bet they have cream *and* custard with their crumble,' laughed Hunter, as the Matroyska came to a shuddering halt and belched a cloud of chip fat in the air.

The camper van stopped at the place where High Holborn and Gray's Inn Road crossed, and Smithies jumped out to deal with the parking meter.

The rest of the team clambered down from inside and took in the view.

After a moment, a small, squat-looking woman hurried over the grass to meet them, long black robes fanning out behind her and on her head a wispy, grey curled wig balanced precariously.

Sicknote steered his way nervously through the waiting party and embraced the woman in a tentative hug.

'Oscar. My dearest Oscar. How long's it been?' She pushed him away with her hands still clasping his in an attempt to scan him fully then drew him back again into another bear hug. 'It's been far too long.'

Sicknote, when he was finally released from her vice-like grip, began to make introductions.

'I met Bessie at Trinity,' he said. 'Oxford,' he added, in case those who listened hadn't quite understood they'd met at university. 'We were both in the amateur dramatic society as I remember,' he added, his face reddening a little.

'And weren't you just the star?' the woman said in a girlish giggle. 'Quite the old drama queen.'

Sicknote looked undecided about whether or not he should be offended, but ploughed on with the introductions anyway. 'I remembered Bessie came to finish her legal training here at Gray's. I was pretty sure she had her office here.'

'One of the few who do,' she said, winking off-puttingly. 'Can't keep away from the place.'

'Seemed a good idea to call on Bessie to be our guide,' Sicknote added.

The woman straightened her wig rather forcefully. 'It'll be my delight to,' she said. 'But please excuse my get-up. Having alterations made to my court robes. Seems I've been a little too welcoming to the fine food we're offered here.' She patted her tummy and Brodie noticed Hunter's eyes glinted at the mention of food. 'Well, come along then,' she said keenly. 'No time like the present.'

The party probably made an odd sight leading across the grassy forecourt. The children were dressed in their Pembroke uniforms and Sicknote, perhaps as he thought he'd better make a special effort, had swapped his usual slippers for trainers which actually made the paisley pyjama trousers look even more odd than usual. Miss Tandari and Smithies followed in last with Smithies mumbling quite loudly about the parking charges as he walked.

'So,' said Bessie, after she'd shown them to her rather cramped chambers. 'Take a seat. Take a seat. And tell me what brings you to Gray's?'

Brodie looked round at the shelves of documents, each neatly tied with red ribbon. In spaces between the shelves were impressive oil paintings. Brodie guessed they were past residents of Gray's Inn. She leant forward in her chair. She was looking forward to hearing Smithies explain this one.

'Pembroke has asked some students to put together a project on famous fathers of the law,' he said without a moment's hesitation, suggesting to Brodie he'd practised what to say before leaving Bletchley. 'Our team is particularly interested in the life and work of Sir Nicholas Bacon.'

Bessie re-straightened her wig. 'Well, it makes a change for people to be interested in Bacon Senior,' she said. 'His son Francis gets far too much air time if you ask me.'

Sheldon raised his eyebrows in Tusia's direction.

Bessie began to pour tea from a large spotted teapot then offered round a plate of rather sticky chocolate biscuits. 'Sir Nicholas was here in the mid-1500s,' Bessie went on.

Hunter winked at Brodie.

'He was a great man in my opinion,' she said, casting a girlish grin in Sicknote's direction. 'He was Lord Keeper of the Great Seal.'

Brodie had no idea what this meant, but it sounded impressive.

'It's a position of great honour,' explained Bessie, 'which came with symbols of office. It meant Sir Nicholas used the Great Seal of the Realm to stamp the monarch's approval on certain documents.' She paused for a moment. 'We don't know much about his time here. Apart from stuff about the library, of course.' She sipped from her bone-china teacup, her little finger raised, pointed in the air like an aerial.

'The library?' pressed Smithies.

Bessie lowered her cup on to the saucer. 'Oh yes. Gray's Inn has a very impressive library now, but this wasn't always the case. In the 1500s the library was housed in a single room in the chambers of Sir Nicholas.'

'So he was in charge of all the books kept here?'

Bessie's wig wobbled on her head. 'That's right. They didn't have a librarian here until 1646. Had to get one because books were being stolen. But until then, the library was quite a simple affair and it started life in Sir Nicholas's chambers.'

'Do you think it would be possible for us to see those chambers?' Brodie asked.

Bessie looked a little awkward. 'I'm afraid that isn't really possible,' she said. 'All the rooms in this place hold pieces of history.' She giggled as she said this and glanced rather girlishly again at Sicknote. He reached defensively for his asthma inhaler and took a deep gulp. 'I mean, I have a master key and everything,' she said, waving to a series of keys hanging on a wooden hook inside the doorway, next to an intricate map showing the layout of the building. 'But there's no way I can go round opening doors for people, however good friends they were in the past.' She giggled again and lifted the plate of biscuits from the table and thrust them in Sicknote's direction. 'Oscar, dear?' she preened. 'I'm sure you don't have to keep a watch on your cholesterol levels.' She pushed the plate further forward. 'Shame really,' she added after Sicknote weakened and took a biscuit from her plate. 'There was an interesting deed chest in the original library. You'd probably have liked to have seen that if you're keen on history.'

'Deed chest?' asked Miss Tandari.

Bessie tore her eyes from Sicknote's direction and glanced up quickly at Miss Tandari as if she were an irritating insect she'd like to swat away. 'Yes. Deed chest. A deed is a signed, and usually sealed, legal document giving certain rights to certain people. A deed chest is where the deeds are kept. Now, talking of deeds, did you ever do the deed and get yourself married, Oscar dear?' she asked simperingly.

Sicknote flushed so red he looked like he was suffering from scarlet fever.

'Shame,' she said, as he shook his head in answer. 'A criminal shame.'

'Well, I think it's a burnt toasted sandwich shame we can't get into Sir Nicholas's chambers and check out that deed chest,' moaned Hunter, as they made their way back to the Matroyska.

'Who said we weren't going to try and look in the deed chest?' Smithies said, swinging open the doors to the camper van and guiding them all inside.

Brodie froze mid-step. 'What d'you mean?'

'Well,' said Smithies, 'much against my better judgement you drag me down here from Bletchley as you all think there may be something here to find.

Now it looks like there may be a chest full of answers hidden by Sir Nicholas, and you all give up on me.'

'Give up on you?' said Tusia. 'What d'you mean, give up? That woman said she couldn't show us to the room.'

'I know she said *she* couldn't show us,' said Smithies, 'but she also pointed out to us where the key was and made it very clear how easily distracted she was.'

Sicknote blushed again, this time even more violently than before.

'You reckon we should go back and break into Sir Nicholas's chambers?' asked Sheldon, obviously relishing the plan.

'Oh, we wouldn't be breaking in,' said Smithies. 'I'm suggesting we use the key.'

12

Under Cover of Darkness

'I've *never* looked more ridiculous in all my life.'

Brodie thought this was a bit much coming from a man who usually walked around in his pyjama trousers tied up with a necktie!

Miss Tandari comforted Sicknote, who was wearing the starchy suit Smithies had picked up for him from the local Tesco.

'The trainers were one thing, but this is just too much,' Sicknote sniffed, downing two small tablets from a bottle which was near to empty.

'It's all part of the plan,' encouraged Brodie.

'Yeah. That Bessie woman needs to think you're serious,' urged Sheldon.

'Oh, this is serious, all right,' puffed Sicknote, running his finger between his neck and his collar. 'Deathly serious.'

The plan was simple. 'Now, remember,' said Miss Tandari as they clambered for the second time that day out of the Matroyska on to the pavement outside Gray's Inn, 'concentration is the key.'

'I think actually, that *the key*'s the key,' laughed Hunter. 'That's why we've come back.'

Miss Tandari frowned and locked her hands firmly on the steering wheel in readiness as the getaway driver.

Sheldon got sorted next. He leant against the lamppost at the edge of the green and put an open cap on the pavement in front of his feet. He dropped in a couple of pound coins just as a starter.

'Now, you're sure you can see the window to Bessie's room from here?' checked Smithies.

'We've gone over this,' groaned Tusia. 'It's the fourth room along on the first floor. This is a perfect location for him.'

'Brilliant,' relented Smithies. 'It's just I can't remember locations like you. I forget about your excellent shape and space thing.'

Sheldon took out his harmonica and skimmed his tongue across the holes in a quick warm-up. 'I play all the time the light's on in the room,' said Sheldon. 'If the light goes off, it means Bessie's on the move.'

'And once Tandi hears you stop playing, she turns on the lights of the Matroyska as a warning,' confirmed Smithies. 'And if Tusia's spacial skills have worked again, the place Miss Tandari has the Matroyska parked in should be directly in line with Sir Nicholas's chambers.'

'So you and I and Brodie will have the signal to get out,' said Hunter.

Smithies looked nervous. 'The only tricky thing should be the key transfer. Opening a window in December will take some explaining but I trust your flower idea will work. It's just down to you, Oscar. No pressure.'

Sicknote turned a little green. 'I know. I know. I'll sweet-talk Bessie.' He gulped back an obvious wave of nausea. 'I'll tell her all about how good it is to see her and how much I want to catch up.' The team nodded. 'Then, somehow, when Bessie's busy careering down memory lane, I'll get the keys.' There was more nodding. 'Then, I'll start reacting badly to the pollen in the flowers I've taken her. That'll be easy. How I haven't had a reaction already I really don't know. I'll get the window open and drop the keys down into the flower-bed where Tusia will be waiting. And she'll get the keys to you lot, and it's job done.'

'Exactly,' said Smithies with rather more confidence than Brodie believed he felt. 'Everybody ready?'

The next stage of the plan required more precision. CCTV cameras were positioned above the entrance to Gray's Inn, so Sicknote took one of the pompom-edged curtains from the Matroyska to drape over the camera. This meant Hunter, Brodie and Smithies could crouch in the porch without fear of being seen until Bessie opened the door to let Sicknote in. As he stepped inside, Sicknote jammed a roll of paper in the hinge to prevent the door closing fully.

The other three waited.

Brodie's knees were killing her. It didn't make it better that she could hear the gentle strains of Sheldon's harmonica lifting on the crisp December air. It was cold. It was dark. And they'd been waiting forever.

She glanced down at her New York watch but she was so cold she couldn't really calculate the time difference.

Suddenly, she was aware of a frantic hissing noise from the flower-bed beside the doorway.

A dishevelled Tusia peered up at her from behind a holly bush. 'Psst. I have the keys!'

Brodie's heart thumped.

'The flowers thing worked well, but I don't know

how much time you've got. I could hear that Bessie woman talking about the good old days with "Irresistible Ingham". Not sure how long Sicknote will be able to take it.'

Brodie reached out to take the keys, keeping her arm well behind the range of the blinkered CCTV beam just in case.

'And you're OK to stop the door from closing?' Smithies whispered.

Tusia pulled a large leaf from her hair. 'I'm fine,' she said, looking anything but.

There was no time to argue.

Brodie led the way into the building.

According to the map Bessie had showed them, Sir Nicholas's rooms were along the left-hand side of the building on the ground floor. Brodie hurried onwards and Hunter counted the doors as they ran.

'Here,' he said, skidding to a halt outside the fourteenth door. 'From what I saw on the map, I reckon it's this one.'

'You sure?' said Smithies.

'No! But I think we should try.'

Brodie took the bunch of keys and flicked through them. There were about eighteen keys. They had to find a way of narrowing it down. 'Shall I try them all in order?' she hissed.

Hunter shook his head. 'Try the fourteenth along from the key-ring.'

'Why?' His mathematical speed never failed to amaze her.

Hunter rolled his eyes. 'Because it's the fourteenth room.'

'Oh. OK.' She fumbled the keys and selected the fourteenth key, jamming it into the lock. Nothing. It wouldn't fit, let alone turn.

'Try the other end,' hissed Hunter.

Brodie knew she didn't hide her confusion well. 'The other end of the key?' she said in disbelief.

'No, you Pot Noodle. The other end of the bunch.'

'Oh, right.' Brodie turned the bunch and counted again from the other end. Key fourteen. It fitted. It turned. The door opened.

Smithies led the way inside and made straight for the window.

'Can you see the Matroyska?' Hunter asked.

'Just about.'

'And are the lights on?'

'No. That means Sicknote's managed to keep Bessie in the room so we still have time.'

Brodie felt it was at last safe to take a deep breath and as she did so she looked around the room.

It was very similar in size and shape to the chambers

Bessie used. Once again, the walls were lined with shelving stacked with rows and rows of scrolls, tied neatly with red ribbon.

'Nice place,' said Smithies. 'Now where d'you think the old deed chest is?'

They scanned the room. There was no sign of a chest.

'She must have made a mistake,' moaned Hunter. 'Perhaps they moved it out of here. Put it in a museum or something if the thing's so old.'

'But she said it was here,' Brodie mumbled.

'She also said Sicknote was looking well,' added Hunter ironically. 'She could have got it wrong.'

Brodie sank down dejectedly on to a velvet-covered bench seat in the corner. 'I just had a good feeling about it, you know,' she said. 'That we'd find something helpful.' She swung her feet backwards and forwards despondently and as they struck the wood of the bench seat, the air thudded.

'Stand up!' Hunter hissed.

'What?'

'Stand up.'

'OK. I was only sitting down to think, you know. I wasn't slacking.'

'Just stand up, BB.'

Brodie stood up rather more slowly than was

necessary. There was no need for Hunter to be mean to her just because the chest wasn't there.

She was just about to argue this point more forcefully when Hunter lurched behind her and began to tug at the velvet covering across the bench seat where she'd been sitting.

'What you doing?' Brodie yelped. 'Tell him, Smithies. We're supposed to be leaving the place how we found it so no one would know we'd been in. You made that quite clear, didn't you?'

Hunter was groaning behind her. 'And what's also most clear,' he said, wrapping the lengths of fabric round his arms as he pulled them away, 'is that *this* is *not* a seat. It's a deed chest. Look.'

The final folds of velvet fell free and Hunter stood back.

'I see,' said Brodie, staring at what had been hidden under the fabric. 'Now I understand.'

The chest was ornate and intricately carved around the lid, in a similar way to the trunk Fabyan had brought with him from the States. There was a wrought-iron lock too, just like the one on Fabyan's trunk. This trunk was much, much older though.

'We're as stuffed as a Christmas turkey if this thing's locked,' winced Hunter as Smithies scrabbled to lift the lid.

'Guess we're not turkeys then,' Smithies announced happily.

The chest swung open with ease and Brodie leant forward beside the others to peer inside.

Nothing. The chest was empty.

'No,' groaned Brodie, sinking back on to her heels. 'How can it be empty? After all that effort and planning and there's nothing.'

'Unbelievable,' said Smithies. 'I was sure this was an answer.'

Hunter let out a sigh. 'We should be getting used to it by now.'

'Sorry?'

'Empty boxes. Or boxes of things that were no good, like ash.'

Brodie put her hand down on the lid of the chest. 'Except they weren't, were they?'

'Weren't what?'

'Empty,' said Brodie slowly. 'There was something hidden.'

Suddenly the room was filled with light.

Smithies hurried to the window. 'It's the Matroyska,' he blurted. 'Tandi's put the lights on, which means Sheldon's stopped playing.'

'Which means Bessie's out of her room,' Hunter said. 'We have to go.'

'But there must be something. There's always something,' pleaded Brodie.

'But we haven't got the time,' snapped Hunter. 'Come on. We can't be caught.'

Brodie held tight to the lip of the chest lid as he pulled her.

The light from the Matroyska blazed in the room.

'BB, please.'

And as she pulled her hand away, a tiny section of wooden panel clicked open like a flap, to reveal a rolled scroll, tied up tightly with a crimson ribbon and sealed closed with scarlet wax.

Brodie grabbed the scroll and ran.

Kerrith drummed her bright-red fingernails against the arm of the chair and then pushed the plate with its barely eaten Eccles cakes towards the centre of the table. She detested Eccles cake. Sugar and caramelised fruit churned her stomach. There was no way of knowing how many calories lurked inside the puff pastry. But desperate times required desperate measures.

'Watch them all carefully,' the Director had said. One tiny deflection from the task in hand, involving Christmas shopping, and she'd lost them. So she was desperate.

'It's just, what with Christmas coming up, I really wanted to make contact.' She dabbed the corners of her mouth with the paper serviette. 'You know how it is, Gordon,' she simpered. 'You don't mind if I call you Gordon, do you?' she said, smiling at the name badge pinned to his lapel. Then she coiled the end of a long strand of hair around her finger and winked.

The befuddled man in front of her wiped his hands nervously on his apron and glanced around the nearly empty station café. 'No. Course not. Of course not.'

Kerrith re-twisted the strand of hair. 'If Smithies mentioned anything at all, anything you can remember, then I'd be able to catch up with them. It's the orphaned girl, you see.' She sniffed. 'It'd be such a shame if what I'd bought didn't get to her at Christmas. Awful, isn't it,' she added, 'how some people can be so totally alone in the world? So totally alone.' She let go of the end of her hair and the spiralled curl bounced on her shoulder.

The waiter's lips quivered nervously. 'But I sort of agree not to say things,' he said. 'Smithies is a friend. He just comes in for chats, you know, on his way from the mansion back towards home.'

'Oh, of course. Of course,' said Kerrith, straightening her back. 'I totally understand the tradition of secrecy between Bletchley Park Mansion and Bletchley Park Station. And of course I'd never want to see anyone violate a trust.' She glanced at the bulging bags of brightly wrapped packages beside her chair. 'It's just when you think of the children. And the idea of Christmas and the idea of them missing out. And the orphan,' she said, and something resembling a tear glistened in the corner of her eye.

Gordon thrust his hands into his pockets. 'I shouldn't be doing this,' he said. 'But like you said, it's all about the children.'

'All about the children,' Kerrith repeated, glancing once more at the brightly wrapped packages.

Gordon followed her gaze. 'Smithies mentioned doing some research. Down in London. They've been down to London before,' he added.

Kerrith said nothing, afraid speaking may break this train of thought.

'I know they stayed at the Carthorse Inn before.'

'Excuse me?'

'The Carthorse Inn. Apparently the food wasn't up to much. Smithies likes his food. You know, I often wonder if . . .'

Kerrith didn't hear what it was he wondered. She'd risen from the table and, hands laden with shopping bags, she made her way to the door.

'Thank you, Gordon,' she said, turning once more to face him. 'You've been very helpful. Very helpful indeed. It was certainly worth my time dropping in.'

She was sure he blushed as she closed the door behind her.

13

Lord Keeper of the Great Seal

'This better have been worth it,' huffed Sicknote, comfortable once again in his normal outfit of casual top and pyjama bottoms tied up with a necktie.

They'd made a rather speedy getaway from Gray's Inn and booked into the Carthorse Inn they'd used in the summer. The Polish chambermaid seemed very pleased to see them, but disappointed they hadn't brought Granddad this time.

Once Sicknote had changed, they all piled into his room and sat down to have a closer look at the document from the deed chest. Sicknote sat at the foot of the bed, breathing in heavily from a nasal spray and complaining that the flowers had, as he'd predicted, set off his allergies.

'So,' pressed Brodie, hardly able to wait a moment

longer. 'What is it? Any links to MS 408 or the Knights of Neustria?'

Smithies broke the scarlet wax seal which secured the scroll shut then untied the ribbon carefully, clearly worried the ancient paper might disintegrate. Then he peered in close.

'Ahh,' he said despondently, exhaling deeply. 'It's in Latin.'

Sicknote shuffled closer from behind and took the paper from him. 'No worries,' he said confidently. 'Leave it to me.'

There was a ripple of surprise.

'Latin's the language of medicine,' he said. 'I find it a rather useful skill to have a sound understanding, bearing in mind my constant need of regular healthcare.'

Even Hunter looked impressed as Sicknote began to make sense of the paper in front of him. Brodie scribbled down the words as he spoke them.

I, Sir Nicholas Bacon, as Lord Keeper
of the Great Seal, do hereby grant
licence and rights to the Knights
of Neustria for the continuation of
their quest.
I do hereby pledge that I will maintain
the honour of their secret, preserve the

sanctity of their knowledge and do all in my power to pass on the truth they protect to those deemed worthy to receive that knowledge.

I do this in the presence of Seeker Knight Hans of Aachen on this the fifteenth day of the ninth month of the year of our Lord, 1552.

Smithies took a breath. 'It was certainly worth it,' he said, smiling in Sicknote's direction.

'So we were right, then,' Tusia said. 'Nicholas *was* a Knight of Neustria. He knew the secret of the code in *Morte D'Arthur* and he told his son Francis all about it.'

'And then Francis invented similar codes like the ones invented by the Knights to protect their story,' added Miss Tandari.

'Everyone knew Francis Bacon had a huge secret to hide,' cut in Sheldon. 'But no one knew he was hiding the secret of the Knights of Neustria.'

'Quite right,' said Smithies. 'People were sure Sir Francis had a huge secret. Some thought he was Shakespeare. There's even the crazy idea he was the illegitimate child of Queen Elizabeth. And now we know, and can be sure, he was actually a Knight of Neustria.'

'So Francis and Nicholas and Hans were all Knights of Neustria. And the scroll from the deed chest said the Knights were searching for something important. But what was so important it had to be totally protected with code?' asked Brodie. 'We've still got no idea what the discovery in MS 408 is really about.' She reached up to cradle her locket. They were getting nearer, she could feel it, but it felt like swimming to the shore against a strong current. Land was getting closer but they were still surrounded by a wild and battering sea.

Sheldon wrapped the spare blanket around him. 'What d'we do now?'

'We get you warmed up for a start,' said Miss Tandari. 'You were outside for ages in the cold. We have to be careful about pneumonia.'

Sheldon jingled the hat in which he'd collected money while he busked outside Gray's Inn. 'Didn't do badly, though, did I?' He made a show of stacking the pound coins into a pile.

'No. You should have enough to buy yourself some flu remedy.'

Sicknote winced. 'I *have* explained this,' he said in a most aggrieved tone. 'Flu and pneumonia are caused by viruses. They've nothing to do with your body temperature.'

'Well, how come stuffing a chicken with snow was enough to give Sir Francis Bacon pneumonia and finish him off, then?' asked Sheldon. 'Isn't that how our Knight of Neustria popped his clogs?'

'You're right, Fingers. Stuffing the chicken stuffed him. Made mincemeat of him . . . and not the vegetarian type,' joked Hunter.

Tusia rolled her eyes.

'Strange, though, isn't it, that's the way he was finished off?' said Brodie. 'I remember thinking it strange he went to some friend's house to die.'

'Maybe the friend didn't do a very good job of looking after him,' suggested Sicknote. 'Caring for the ill is a tricky business. Not everyone's up to the task.'

'No,' said Brodie. 'That's the odd thing about it. Lord Arundel wasn't even in the house. Francis just went there to stay and died a week later.'

'That's weird,' said Hunter. 'What happened? Did the friend just come home and find him dead there?'

Brodie shrugged. 'No. That was odd too. Francis wrote him a letter.'

'What, when he was *dead*?' yelped Hunter. 'You bet your ready salted peanuts that's odd.'

'No. Not when he *was* dead. *Before.*'

'What! Telling him in advance he was going to die? That's even odder!'

'Suppose,' said Brodie. 'Hadn't really thought about that before.'

'So, hold on a minute,' said Smithies, pushing his glasses firmly up the bridge of his nose. 'You say you looked at all the academic writing Bacon did and you couldn't find any more clues about the Knights of Neustria.'

'I didn't manage to look at *everything* he wrote,' she said sheepishly. 'He produced a lot, you know.'

'But you read this death-bed letter he wrote?'

'I couldn't find it anywhere in the books or online. I've just read that he wrote one.'

Sheldon was deep in thought. 'If you could write just one last letter before you died, I bet you'd put in it all the things you hadn't managed to get around to saying while you were alive.'

'What d'you mean?'

'Well, most of the Knights we know about passed on bits of the story and how it needed protecting through their family, didn't they? Bedivere told Amren and Eneuvac; Benjamin told his son Hans; Nicholas told Francis. Elgar used Van der Essen, Dora Penny and Helen Weaver to make sure the story was still safe.'

'So?'

'Francis didn't have kids, did he? Who could he tell? He'd have to let someone he trusted know before he

162

died or the secret would die too.'

'So who did Francis Bacon trust?' Tusia's eyes widened.

'We don't know,' said Brodie, 'but I think Sheldon's right. If he knew he was going to die, that's probably when he wrote the secret down.'

'Popping popcorn, that's perfect!' said Hunter. 'Now we've got proof Nicholas and Francis were Knights of Neustria, we have to find that death-bed letter and see if it's got secrets in it.'

'Another excursion,' mumbled Hunter, as he munched his way through his third plate of scrambled eggs and mushrooms. 'Just as long as we don't bring home any more additions to the team.' He winked across the table at Sheldon.

Sheldon raised his glass of orange juice in a mock toast.

'Well, we won't have room in the Matroyska for more additions,' laughed Smithies, 'but I guess it's worth investigating the place where Sir Francis Bacon died before we go back to Bletchley, as long as we're really cautious.'

Sicknote downed his last dregs of tea, unclipped his chained mug from the radiator and led the way to the Matroyska.

'But we have to—' Smithies didn't get to finish.

'We'll be careful, sir!' Tusia and Brodie groaned. 'We get it.'

'We were fine at Gray's Inn,' said Sheldon. 'Perhaps Level Five has forgotten about us?'

Smithies seemed to turn a sort of purple colour and his left eye began to twitch violently. 'We presume nothing, you understand! Absolutely nothing! Level Five will be watching, you mark my words. We may not see them and we may not know they're there, but you never relax, you hear me? Never.'

'OK!' Sheldon raised his hands defensively. 'I was just saying.'

'Well, don't!'

They may have persuaded Smithies they had to leave Station X to find answers, but he was still looking out for them. He was still making sure they were safe.

It was about midday when they made it to Highgate. 'The Whittington Hospital's along there,' said Sicknote. 'Whittington. You remember? The man who sponsored Hans of Aachen's father?'

Brodie thought back to all their work on Elgar's code from months before and how they'd at last made the connection with Hans of Aachen and the *Morte d'Arthur*. She scored a circle in the mist-covered window.

'Nice houses,' said Tusia, leaning across her and peering through the condensation. 'Although places that big cost a fortune to heat. And the pollution that makes wrecks the ozone layer.'

Brodie pressed her nose against the window. The Matroyska pulled into a road called The Grove. 'How much d'you think one of them would cost?' she said.

'Millions,' said Hunter. 'Bet they're mainly owned by celebs now.'

'And famous people in the past too,' added Miss Tandari, looking over her shoulder from her position in the front. 'Look. That house has a plaque on it saying Samuel Taylor Coleridge lived there.'

Brodie focused hard. 'I love the poems of Coleridge,' she said. 'Do you know "Kubla Khan"?'

'Is that the name of a takeaway restaurant?' said Hunter. 'I'm feeling peckish.'

Brodie was just about to ask if he was ever anything other than peckish when the Matroyska turned a sharp corner.

'Look,' yelped Tusia, pointing madly from the window. 'Bacon's Lane. Must be getting close.'

The Matroyska juddered to a halt.

'Here we are,' said Smithies, peering for confirmation at the map propped on the dashboard. 'Number 17

South Grove. Now called "Old Hall". The place where Bacon died.'

They clambered from the Matroyska and hurried up for a closer look.

Two tall white stone pillars guarded the entrance. An iron gate was slung between them, firmly locked. Sheldon whistled. 'Very nice,' he said. 'Looks like a nice place to die . . . if you have to die, I mean.'

Sicknote seemed practically giddy with enthusiasm. 'Well, can we look inside?'

Smithies rattled the chain across the gate. 'Looks to me like the place isn't ready for visitors,' he said despondently.

'What d'you mean? We've come all this way and we can't get in?' huffed Tusia. 'Think of the carbon footprint we've made for no reason.'

Smithies raised his hand in an attempt to calm her. 'The place has neighbours. We're in London after all. And if my map's correct then there should be some people just a few doors down who'll be able to help us. As long as we are—'

'Careful! We know!'

Highgate Literary and Scientific Institution was only down the road.

'We're very interested in the life and death of Sir

Francis Bacon,' said Smithies to the keen-looking receptionist seated at the desk.

'His death in particular,' added Sicknote enthusiastically.

'I have already mentioned that,' hissed back Smithies. Sicknote folded the information leaflet he'd taken from the front desk and arranged it neatly into squares.

'Well, you've certainly come to the right place,' said the receptionist, leading the way towards the Exhibition Hall and pointing to a white bust which looked down on them.

'You'll find lots of Bacon fans here,' she said, smiling up at the statue. 'And of course the poor man died very near to here. Tragic,' she sniffed. 'Such a waste.'

'Yes, about the dying next door thing,' said Sheldon. 'Can we have a look at the place where he died?'

An older lady, her arms laden down with books, moved past them slowly, stumbling a little as she walked.

'Oh. I'm very sorry. I'm afraid the building now called Old Hall is a rebuild,' said the receptionist.

'Excuse me?'

'It's not actually the house Lord Arundel lived in. It's merely a building constructed on the same place in 1691, long after Sir Francis met his end.'

'So nothing he left behind is kept in the house,

then?' asked Tusia. 'Nothing he wrote?'

'My dear girl, no. All Bacon's writings have, over time, become property of the state. A mind like his couldn't be wasted.'

The old lady with the books hovered in the doorway, apparently considering the weight of the volumes she held.

'And so the death-bed letter Bacon wrote,' asked Hunter. 'Is there a copy anywhere?'

'Oh yes. I could get you a computerised copy of the letter if you'd like.'

'But you don't have the original?'

'Afraid not. If you want to take a walk around, I could rustle up a copy of the letter for you to take away.'

'Excellent,' said Smithies. 'That would be truly excellent. We'll have a little wander outside, then.'

The receptionist looked towards the window. 'Or, if it's too cold, you could take a look in the Coleridge Room or one of our libraries. We have an excellent range on offer here,' she said, waving towards a room crammed floor to ceiling with books.

'Oh, please,' begged Brodie, looking at Smithies longingly. 'You have to let me stay here.'

Smithies mumbled something encouraging but it did little to disguise the groans from Hunter and Sheldon.

'Not more books, B. Seriously, they can't be good for you.'

'And this from a boy who learns numbers from the telephone directory just for fun.'

'Fair point.'

Miss Tandari took control. 'Look, we'll stroll outside and get some air, while Brodie and Smithies wait in here for the printout of the letter. What do you say?'

Brodie didn't need telling twice.

Brodie could hardly contain her excitement. Why anyone would want to take a walk outside instead of looking at the books in the Coleridge Room was totally beyond her. Tusia stayed with them but the others set off for fresh air and food. Brodie felt she could easily do without both for a while. She stood for a moment, letting the silence wash over her. She closed her eyes and drew in a long, deep breath. The smell of aged leather and well-worn pages filled her lungs.

'You like Coleridge, then?' said Smithies, waking her from her reverie.

Brodie walked to join him and Tusia as they peered up at an oil painting on the far wall.

'He looks a little sad there,' said Brodie. 'I heard he had a complicated life.'

'Nice ring, though,' Tusia said, pressing gently against the canvas.

Smithies stepped forward to have a closer look.

It was as he lifted his glasses up to his forehead in concentration that Brodie became aware the three of them were no longer alone in the room. A strained, rather breathy voice, whispered close to her ear.

'I can do better than a computer.'

'I'm sorry?' Brodie turned to see the older woman she'd noticed earlier, struggling with the pile of books, standing close beside them, her eyes twitching nervously now and then towards the door.

'The computer printout. I can do better than that,' she said, and her eyes widened.

Smithies replaced his glasses on his nose and stared as if encountering an obstruction in the road and evaluating the best way to negotiate around it.

'And the house,' the old lady said quietly. 'I can show you that too.' She reached into a deep pocket and took out a copper-coloured key which glinted in the light when she moved it.

Brodie looked at Smithies.

'You can show us into Old Hall?' he said slowly.

The old woman had the look of a cheeky schoolgirl. 'I can do much more than that,' she said.

§14

The Deception of the Empty Tomb

'Are we totally sure about this?' said Smithies. 'I mean, we don't know even who this woman is and why she'd want to help us.'

Brodie hurried to keep up. 'She works at the Institution and at weekends she cleans Old Hall,' she said, repeating the information the woman had shared with them.

'She looks harmless,' said Tusia.

'Looks can be deceptive,' warned Smithies.

'True. And Level Five could be getting answers before us,' hissed Tusia.

By now the woman had opened the gate to Old Hall and was leading the way purposefully down the path. 'Keep up,' she called over her shoulder. 'I haven't got long, you know.'

Smithies turned to face Brodie and Tusia. 'OK. We give her a chance. But you keep with me and you keep alert. Got me?'

The girls agreed.

Once inside, the old woman leant against the closed doors and took a deep breath.

'And the owners won't mind?' questioned Smithies.

'The owners are away,' said the woman, in a way which suggested she wasn't particularly happy about this. 'Apparently celebrating Christmas and New Year in New York City is preferable to spending the time here,' she tutted. 'How anyone can leave this house is beyond me.'

'You're fond of the place, then?' he asked.

'It means everything to me,' she said.

'Now, I get that,' said Tusia. 'Places are important. They have souls of their own.'

Brodie looked at Tusia quizzically. She wasn't really sure what Tusia meant but the old woman pressed on. 'I took the job at the Institution so I could be near Old Hall and then, when the chance to clean here came up, it was an opportunity not to be missed.'

'But why are you so taken with the building?' asked Brodie, scanning the entrance hall.

'Because it happened here,' laughed the old lady. 'The Great Escape.'

'Love that film,' whispered Tusia. 'Steve McQueen's an absolute legend. But I thought it was set in a prisoner-of-war camp not a house in Highgate.' She frowned. 'That's not the "Great Escape" you mean, is it?' she said apologetically.

Wrinkled dimples appeared beside the old lady's mouth. 'No. I mean Bacon's escape.'

'We thought Sir Francis Bacon died in this house,' Brodie said. 'Well, not *this* house, but one built here before this one.'

'That's what everyone thinks,' she said. 'Apart from those who've bothered to do any research.' The old woman moved away from the doorway and stepped into the wide and open hall. 'Bacon didn't die here. He simply escaped to a new life.'

Smithies was clearly confused. 'He didn't die?'

'Not here, he didn't,' and with that she strode off down the hall and led the way into a large reception room with tall sash windows and a view out on to The Grove.

'It's true this isn't the actual house where it's claimed Bacon died,' she said, 'but its builders wanted to keep some of the most interesting characteristics of Lord Arundel's original premises.'

'And those characteristics were what exactly?' asked Tusia, with growing enthusiasm.

'Well, look,' she said. 'But mind you look with care.'

Brodie turned where she stood and peered around. She thought it looked very nice. A bit posh. Things were obviously quite old.

'Well?' pressed the old lady. 'Can you see yet?'

Brodie had no idea what she was talking about now and the others seemed as thoroughly bemused as she was, until Tusia bent down looking as if she was about to pick a daisy from a grassy meadow and yelped, 'The floor! The floor.'

The old lady beamed.

Brodie peered down to where Tusia was pointing. She had no idea why Tusia was so excited.

'The pattern of the wood runs under the wall on this side,' Tusia said. 'See.'

As far as Brodie could tell, there was nothing strange or unusual about the patterning of the floor, but Tusia was keen to show how the wooden bordering which ran round three sides of it was thinner on the fourth side and seemed to continue under the wall.

'And if the floor goes under the wall like that,' said Tusia, 'then I guess this wall,' she said, pointing at the one with a fireplace, 'is false.'

'Exactly,' said the old lady. 'Well noticed, young lady. Well noticed.'

Smithies mumbled approval as the old lady picked up a small silver-cased torch. She flicked it on and the light ringed her face like a Halloween pumpkin. Then she rested her other hand on the mantelpiece. 'And if there's a fake wall,' she said brightly, 'then there must be something hidden behind.'

With a gentle press against the mantel, the section of wall to the left of the fireplace began to slide backwards, revealing a door-shaped opening in the corner of the room. 'Would you like to see?' she said, pointing the torch inside.

Brodie felt very much like she'd done when standing in the Institution surrounded by all the ancient books. Her heart was racing full pelt. She followed the old lady's lead, the three of them stepping through the doorway into a room with a low ceiling. It was plainly decorated and empty of furniture.

'What on earth's this for?' asked Smithies, spluttering slightly from the dust lifting from the ground.

The old woman took a deep breath before explaining. 'The original house was designed to include lots of secret passageways and hidden rooms. Lord Arundel was a bit of an art collector and wanted to be sure there were ways of getting his artworks out of the building in secret.'

'And what's this got to do with Sir Francis Bacon?'

asked Tusia, who was batting away tendrils of cobweb tangled in her hair.

'Sir Francis came here, not to die, but to start a new life. It was the perfect plan. He waited in secret in the hidden rooms in the house until it was safe for him to get away from London.'

'But what about the pneumonia?' Tusia said, her hands now draped in cobweb. 'Bacon was supposed to have come here with pneumonia and died.'

The woman scowled. 'That old chestnut. Doesn't ring true, though, does it? Him catching cold so quickly and not even able to make it home.'

'Sicknote said that,' yelped Brodie. 'He said pneumonia is caused by a virus.'

The old lady's eyes sparkled suddenly, making her face seem much younger than before. 'Sir Francis didn't come to the Lord Arundel's house because he was dying. He was running away!'

'From what?' said Brodie breathlessly.

'Well, if you've heard anything about Sir Francis at all, you'll understand there are many theories about secrets in his life.'

Brodie looked at Tusia knowingly.

'Things got too much for him. So he wanted the world to think he died but instead he began a new life abroad.'

'Abroad?'

'Yes. France perhaps. Where he could be anonymous. The theories suggest he made his way to Chepstow to deal with some unfinished business there, and then made his way out of the country.'

'So you think Sir Francis used one of these secret passageways to get away?' asked Tusia.

'It was the perfect plan. Fake his death, and escape in secret. Sir Francis's life was all about secrets.'

Brodie's mind was spinning. Did this woman know about the Knights of Neustria? 'Do you know what secrets he was trying to protect?' she asked tentatively.

The old woman's shoulders sank a little. Her eyes dulled. 'I wish I did,' she said. 'I've spent my life wishing that. But I don't.' She paused for a moment and no one spoke. 'But I do believe the biggest secret is that he didn't die.'

'It sounds perfect,' said Brodie.

Smithies pushed his glasses once more up on to his forehead. 'I'm not so sure,' he said. 'I mean, you tell us Bacon faked his death, but surely there'd have to have been a funeral. I presume it'd have been obvious he wasn't dead if there wasn't a funeral?'

'Oh, there was a funeral,' said the old lady. 'But that doesn't mean there was a body.'

Brodie was finding it hard to breathe. 'Excuse me?'

'Who can be totally sure what's inside a coffin?' she

said playfully. 'I mean, who could tell what was behind this false wall without opening it?'

'But the death-bed letter,' added Brodie, remembering what had made the old lady talk to them in the first place. 'You said you could do better than a computer printout.'

'Follow me,' she said.

She walked across the room to a rickety door in the furthest corner. The door opened into a narrow tunnel which widened into a storeroom crammed with packing-cases. She opened the topmost case and rummaged inside.

'Here,' she said, unrolling a rather tatty-looking document, 'is the death-bed letter.'

Across the page, in careful, well-spaced writing, was the final message from Sir Francis Bacon.

Brodie read aloud.

'Certainly sounds convincing,' said Tusia.

'He was a writer, remember. It was his trade to convince,' said Smithies.

Brodie peered closer. Either she was tired and her eyes were playing tricks on her or there was something odd about the writing. It looked darker in some places than others. Her throat tightened.

'Do you see it?' hissed Tusia, behind the cover of her

My very good Lord,—I was likely to have had the fortune of Caius Plinius the elder, who lost his life by trying an experiment about the burning of Mount Vesuvius; for I was also desirous to try an experiment or two touching the conservation and induration of bodies. As for the experiment itself, it succeeded excellently well; but in the journey between London and Highgate, I was taken with such a fit of casting as I know not whether it were the Stone, or some surfeit or cold, or indeed a touch of them all three. But when I came to your Lordship's House, I was not able to go back, and therefore was forced to take up my lodging here, where your housekeeper is very careful and is diligent about me, which I assure myself your Lordship will not only pardon towards him, but think the better of him for it. For indeed your Lordship's House was happy to me, and I kiss your noble hands for the welcome which I am sure you give me to it.

hand, as the old lady replaced the things she'd rejected from the packing-case.

Brodie nodded. 'Bilateral cipher,' she hissed back.

'So we have to take it.'

'What! We can't take it! That's stealing!'

'The guy's dead!' urged Tusia. 'He may not have died here in this house but he's certainly a goner now. So we wouldn't be stealing. We'd be following his clues.'

'Oh, I don't know.'

'Well, I do,' said Tusia. She rolled the document and slid it up her sleeve. Then she walked back towards the packing-case, lifted the lid and made a show of sliding her hand back inside, all the while mumbling to the old woman about how kind she'd been and how amazing the building was.

'We can't do this,' mumbled Brodie as Tusia walked back to stand beside her.

'I just have,' Tusia grinned, tapping her arm.

'We're incredibly grateful to you,' said Smithies. His voice was shaking a little and Brodie guessed he'd seen what Tusia had done. 'I feel we've taken more of your time than we should have. We really should be joining our friends.'

The old woman blushed slightly, tiny pink circles lifting on her cheekbones. Then she led them towards the door and back outside into the busy London street.

15

Hiding in the Bilateral Cipher

The rest of the group had been waiting by the Matroyska, loaded down with steaming Cornish pasties.

Tusia steered them all into the van. 'It's the bilateral cipher,' she said.

'The what?' asked Sheldon. 'I thought you were waiting for a printout of the death-bed message.'

'We got ourselves much more than that,' Brodie said.

They pulled the door of the Matroyska shut, allowing the smell of potato and onions to fill the air.

Tusia explained their visit to Old Hall.

'I *knew* the pneumonia thing was suspicious,' said Sicknote.

'And so's this bilateral cipher,' said Hunter. 'So what did it look like?'

Tusia pulled the tatty document from her sleeve.

'You took the actual thing?' yelped Sicknote.

'Bacon's dead!' groaned Tusia. 'It's not stealing. He'd want us to find the message. We're either following the Knights' clues or we're not!'

Sicknote seemed to be convinced.

'So how's this cipher work?' urged Brodie, keen to get on with it now.

Tusia took a pencil from her topknot, and wiped it free of cobweb. 'OK,' she said. 'It's a space and shape thing. It's so obvious I don't understand why no one's read it before.'

'Well, I can't see it, Toots!'

Tusia jabbed the death-bed message with her pencil. 'Here. Look at this section.'

'I *am* looking! And all I see is words.'

'But look at *how* the words are written. Focus on the individual letters.'

Hunter peered in closer.

'Can you see?'

'Remind me what the jacket potato I'm supposed to be seeing?'

Tusia sighed dramatically and took a spare piece of paper from her pocket and began to write. 'Look, some of the letters are written straight and normal and some are bolder.'

Hunter shrugged. 'Darker, you mean?'

'Yeah. See?'

'Sort of. But not every letter's darker, is it?'

'No! That's the point. Some are and some aren't. That's what we need to focus on. If Bacon managed to build this code into his death-bed message, that surely proves something.'

'What?' asked Smithies, peering over the top of his glasses.

'Deciding which letters needed to be darker than others must have needed loads of concentration.'

'Which proves what?'

'If he was well enough to focus on writing in code, he really wasn't dying.'

'So you think the old lady's theory about him faking his death's true?' asked Brodie.

'Nice one,' laughed Sheldon. He'd reached into the bags of supplies they'd brought with them from Bletchley and pulled out all the books on Bacon that Brodie had packed for the journey. 'I think there's an explanation of the cipher in here.'

Tusia grabbed the book.

The page she found listed the twenty-six letters of the alphabet and beside each one was a series of five marks.

'It works like this,' Tusia explained. 'You write a normal everyday message, but in your head you have to divide the message into chunks. Each chunk is five letters long. So "Happy Birthday BB" would be made of three chunks, you see: HAPPY BIRTH DAYBB.' She checked to make sure everyone was following. 'Then each chunk stands for one letter in the coded message. If we took HAPPY that could stand for the letter C, for example.'

'And how do we know what letter each chunk of five means?' asked Sheldon.

'Because of how the chunk's written. Some letters in the chunk will be dark or bold and some will just be normal. Here's the key, look.' She showed the page listed in the cipher book. 'If we wrote HA**PP**Y like this, with the fourth letter darker than the rest, then the chunk would mean the letter C according to this key.'

Tusia put the book down so everyone could see the page clearly. Each letter of the alphabet was coded by five marks: * showing where the letter was written normally and B where the letter was written boldly.

'So, let's focus in on where the letters used in the note to Lord Arundel start being written in bold,' said Tusia. 'That must be where our code starts.'

Hunter moved the paper closer. 'I reckon it's those 150 letters,' he said.

Brodie looked at him in disbelief. 'How d'you count them so quickly?' she said.

BACON'S BILATERAL CIPHER

This cipher is a form of 'Steganography' where a secret message
is hidden in plain sight because of how the letters are written.

> **KEY**
> ★ means the letter is written in normal font
> B means the letter is written in bold

A=★★★★★	G=★★BB★	M=★BB★★	S=B★★B★	Y=BB★★★
B=★★★★B	H=★★BBB	N=★BB★B	T=B★★BB	Z=BB★★B
C=★★★B★	I=★B★★★	O=★BBB★	U=B★B★★	
D=★★★BB	J=★B★★B	P=★BBBB	V=B★B★B	
E=★★B★★	K=★B★B★	Q=B★★★★	W=B★BB★	
F=★★B★B	L=★B★BB	R=B★★★B	X=B★BBB	

'Well, how did you even notice there was anything
odd about them?' he replied. 'We can't all be chocolate
éclairs, BB. Some of us have to be plum crumbles.'

Brodie frantically wrote out the 150 letters Hunter
was pointing to. She divided the writing into chunks of
five and drew a circle round every letter that seemed
bolder than the rest.

them all three. But when I came to your Lordship's House, I was

not able to go back, and therefore was forced to take up my lodging

here, where your housekeeper is very careful and is diligent about me,

'OK,' Tusia said. 'Now we have to work out what each chunk of five letters stands for.'

'Right,' said Sheldon, rolling up his sleeves. 'Let's get going, then.'

It took ages. Brodie called out whether the letters were in bold or not, and Sheldon checked against the key in the book. Tusia wrote down what the key gave them.

After two hours, three cans of Coke and a break to share some Jammie Dodgers, Tusia put down the pencil and pushed the paper across the table. 'Perfect,' she said. 'Absolutely perfect.'

Brodie picked up the paper and read the coded message aloud.

KNIGHTS OF NEUSTRIA SERVE BEN SALEM

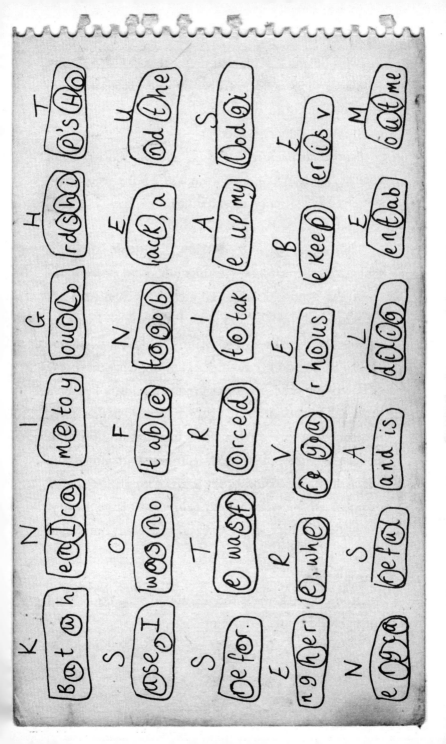

'So who the pig in a blanket do we think this Mr Salem fella was, then?' said Hunter, jabbing his roast potato with his fork and dunking it in his rather generous portion of cranberry sauce.

Brodie sat back in her chair and pressed her hand against her stomach. She wasn't sure whether, even if she did have an answer, she'd have the energy needed to speak.

They'd got back to Station X just in time for Christmas. Fabyan and Granddad had cut down a tree from the grounds and decorated it with ornaments from around the mansion. The Jumbo Rush Elephant took pride of place on the top.

Brodie couldn't remember spending Christmas Day with anyone other than her granddad. Tusia's parents came up from Cornwall to spend the day with them before flying off to visit her brothers in Fiji, but Hunter's parents had been too busy to come and Sheldon's mum couldn't leave the Plough Inn at her busiest time of year. She'd sent up a large turkey, though, for them all to share. Smithies promised to join them after lunch, which he was eating at home with his wife.

Brodie toyed with the handle of her knife and considered Hunter's question.

'I mean, my betting is, he's another Knight of

Neustria. Probably the leader, if they served him, don't you reckon, B? If we find out about him we should get more details on MS 408.'

'Perhaps there's another song we can decode,' said Sheldon hopefully.

'Or another story hidden inside a story,' said Brodie.

'Yeah. Perhaps this Ben Salem actually bothered to write us the story of MS 408 in a way we can easily understand,' joked Miss Tandari.

Brodie put her knife down and straightened the paper hat on her head. 'Wouldn't it be a wonderful Christmas present to know what MS 408 meant,' she said quietly. 'To know where that castle is and what those flowers are.' She reached up impulsively to her necklace.

'What's inside?' asked Tusia, straightening her own paper crown and leaning forward across the table. 'I've always wanted to ask you.'

Brodie had never shown anyone before, but it was Christmas, and they'd come so far together. She flicked the locket open to show the picture. It was a pencil drawing of the castle from MS 408. 'That's what I want for Christmas,' she said, pressing the locket shut when everyone had seen. 'To know where this castle is.'

The meal over, they moved into the ballroom for presents. Granddad and Fabyan had been busy. Miss

Tandari loved her new bracelet and Hunter seemed pleased with his three-dimensional sudoku game but he also appeared to have his eye on the chocolate chess set bought for Tusia. Sheldon played carols on a brand-new, three-level harmonica and Sicknote seemed thrilled with the game Operation.

Brodie felt the shape of her parcel and knew at once what was inside. 'With all the talk about Bacon and Shakespeare, I thought trying some of Bacon's creative pieces might be fun,' Granddad said. 'And I thought it was time you had a copy of the Master's complete works.'

The antique copy of Shakespeare's first portfolio must have cost her granddad a lot of money. She stroked the leather cover and turned to the first page.

About mid-afternoon, Smithies returned to Station X having left his wife sleeping in front of the Christmas specials on TV. 'Could I have a moment, Brodie?' he said softly.

Brodie left her book open on the arm of the chair, grabbed her coat and followed him outside.

'It's good for us all to be together at Christmas,' he said, as they walked briskly beside the lake.

She folded her arms across her chest to keep out the cold.

'Look, I don't want to spoil your day but it's just I can't get him to speak to me,' he said.

'I'm not ringing Friedman,' she said, her throat tightening around the words as she said them.

'Brodie, I don't understand why my messages don't get through. I don't know why he won't come back to us and explain. I've known Robbie for years and he was my closest friend and—'

'I thought he was my friend too.'

Smithies couldn't look at her.

She held out her hand reluctantly and took the postcard he offered.

'I'm taking it because *you* want me to. Not *him*,' she explained. 'And I'm not ringing him.'

As they stood in silence, Brodie could just make out the reedy strains of 'We Wish You a Merry Christmas' being played on the harmonica. As the song swelled, she crumpled the postcard and pushed it deep inside her coat pocket.

'Well, where have you put it?' called Sheldon, who for some obscure reason insisted on wearing his paper crown from the Christmas cracker not only all of Christmas Day, but all of Boxing Day too.

'I took everything stacked up next to the armchair over to our room,' snapped Tusia. 'If you'd tidied up your stuff yourself, when Smithics told us to, you wouldn't have lost things,' she added bossily. 'What've you left behind now, anyway?'

'*The Intermediate Guide to Concertos*. Evie from the museum gave it to my mum to send on to me with the turkey,' Sheldon grumbled. 'I swear I left it here.'

'Well, it's not here now, is it?' hissed Tusia, scrabbling under the chair to retrieve two walnuts, a tangerine and a box of dates. 'Go and check in our room. I may have put it with all those books Brodie got,' she added. 'And watch my sketches. I don't want you creasing any.' She tossed a stack of wrapping-paper on to the fire.

Sheldon marched out of the room purposefully.

'So, Ben Salem. Any ideas?' Tusia asked.

'None,' said Brodie. 'I'm just not sure where we go with this now. If the Knights of Neustria served Ben Salem, then how come not even Sicknote, with his obsession with history, has heard of him?'

Tusia started absent-mindedly peeling the tangerine.

'You don't think we've come to a dead-end, do you?' Brodie said nervously.

Tusia popped a segment of tangerine into her mouth and swallowed. 'We'd better not have!'

'Maybe we should just go and start looking back at MS 408?' Brodie offered. 'I mean, all this research seems to take us further away from the manuscript itself.'

Tusia wiped her hands together. 'I suppose,' she said. 'It's always worth a try. Let's go and get the pages out and just have another look.'

Brodie looked forward to seeing the unfolded page of the islands. They always made her feel better. So the two of them hurried over to their hut.

'This is totally ridiculous,' hissed Tusia. 'I told him not to move them. Some of these sketches took hours.'

Brodie reached out to pick up a large painting drying inside the door.

She put the painting back on the desk. It was excellent. Tusia had obviously copied from the front of the Shakespeare portfolio. He was certainly an odd-looking man, thought Brodie, if Shakespeare really looked anything like that. She reached across the table for the portfolio and compared the painting with the portrait in the front of the book. Tusia was good at what she did. You couldn't really tell the difference between what she'd drawn and the picture she copied. She'd even included the sharp line around the left of his face. From what Brodie had read, some people were so convinced Shakespeare was in disguise, they saw the sharp line beside his face as the edge of a mask. Brodie peered in closely. Tusia really had captured every detail. Except, of course, Tusia's picture didn't have the words written out below, because for her it was all about the shape and not about the words.

Brodie scanned the writing in the front page of the book.

This figure thou here seeft put:
O it was for gentler Shakespeare cut;

'Gentler Shakespeare.' That was odd. Gentler than who? And it was odd to think there was debate about who Shakespeare really was. Perhaps William and Elizebeth Friedman were wrong. Perhaps Sir Francis Bacon really was Shakespeare and that would mean the greatest storyteller of all time was a Knight of Neustria. Now, *that* could make things interesting.

'You OK, BB?' came a voice from the doorway. She turned to see Hunter standing there. 'Sheldon sent me over to try and find one of his books. He thought he'd found it but he's taken the wrong one.'

Brodie pointed to the pile just inside the doorway. 'It might be in there,' she said.

'Seriously, BB,' Hunter said again. 'You have that face on. You eaten too many of Fabyan's mince pies?'

Brodie tried to turn her face into a smile. But she

knew as she stood there she was failing. Hunter was right. Something was wrong. Or maybe very right. She wasn't sure. Her stomach was turning and twisting and somewhere deep in the recesses of her mind things were trying to make connections. Something else she'd read, or seen, or heard. To do with Shakespeare. And that front page. It was important, she knew it. But she just couldn't remember what it was.

The Man Behind the Mask

It never ceased to amaze Kerrith how particularly stupid people could be. The Polish chambermaid at the Carthorse Inn had been easy. A brief introduction, some mention of the geeky kids, and once the girl made the connection, she'd even brought leaflets from one of the rooms Smithies and the others had used. Kerrith took the leaflet stamped with the name 'Highgate Literary and Scientific Institution' the maid offered her and slipped it into her Burberry handbag. Why the girl expected a tip for being so careless about the secrets of guests who stayed in her hotel was beyond her. Besides, the girl probably didn't even have a work visa. She was lucky Kerrith wasn't reporting her to the authorities.

The next morning the guide at the Institution was even easier to tap for information. Yes, the team had made a visit. Yes, there was something in particular they were looking for. And in fact, they'd never collected the document they'd asked her to find because they'd disappeared. Kerrith could hardly contain her excitement. Of course the guide could pass the document to her. It'd save everyone a wasted journey.

And then there was the old woman. Kerrith ran the nail of her little finger under the nail on her index finger and flicked out a grain of dust. The old woman was particularly stupid.

Kerrith held the mobile and pushed the numbers on the screen with the stylus. Her nails were too long to use the touch-screen. The Director answered immediately. It was a long time since she'd had to dial the switchboard to get through to him. 'There's a woman here who was keen to tell me how she shared some particularly exciting information with the team from Station X.'

The Director said nothing. He waited for her to continue.

'I'm not totally sure she's really in her right mind, though, sir,' she whispered. 'She's talking about empty coffins and secret rooms.'

Another silence.

'And the document they asked for was something written by Sir Francis Bacon,' she added, almost as an afterthought. 'I studied him at university, sir. He wrote loads. Something about the island called Bensalem and lots about the reign of King Henry the Seventh.'

Kerrith ended the call and slipped the phone back into her handbag. She was still trying to process the details the Director had given her as she walked back to the old woman. 'My boss is very, very keen to hear the information you shared with my friends,' she said, forcing something she hoped looked like a smile to her face.

The old woman seemed to grow in stature. 'It's wonderful,' she said, 'to finally have the chance to share this information,' and she beamed.

Kerrith maintained her smile. 'Well, as I say, my boss is very keen to talk with you. He wants me to ask you to meet him at the following address on the day after tomorrow.' She offered the old woman a hastily written card. 'If, of course, you're able to.'

The old woman looked carefully at the card. 'And it would be to talk more about what we've discussed?' she said. 'My theories?'

'Won't it be wonderful to be taken seriously at last?' Kerrith said.

It seemed very clear from the old woman's reaction, she thought it entirely wonderful.

* * *

'Slow down, BB,' said Hunter. 'I can't keep up with what you're saying.'

It was the early hours of the morning and Brodie had been awake all night. Finally, she understood. It was, though, taking a little longer to make everyone else understand. She'd called them all to the ice house and everyone was now seated in their pyjamas, shivering lots and trying desperately to follow her train of thought.

'It's simple,' she said again, and the room was filled with groaning.

'If it was simple, then we'd understand you,' said Sicknote, who was wearing a plaster across the bridge of his nose which he insisted helped him breathe in the night when the weather was bad.

'It was Tusia's picture,' Brodie said again.

Tusia was obviously unsure why her picture was in any way helpful.

'The picture she painted of the front page of the Shakespeare book Granddad got me for Christmas.' She looked appreciatively in his direction.

'You like that then,' Granddad said. 'I hoped you'd like it. Books are safe, of course, but I wasn't sure if it was a bit old or if—'

'It's great, Granddad. A perfect pressie. And it reminded me,' she ploughed on, 'of all the stuff from

Riverbank Labs Fabyan brought us. And the project on Shakespeare. Remember how Mrs Wells Gallup used the cipher wheel to try and read the coded messages she thought were left in the portfolio?'

'And?' Tusia was yawning widely.

'And I remembered Mrs Wells Gallup thought there was a code at the beginning of the portfolio. Fabyan said so when he gave us the cipher wheel.'

Fabyan smiled broadly but gestured for her to explain.

'What was this code?' asked Miss Tandari.

'This one,' said Brodie. She took a large sheet of paper and wrote out the phrase written under the Shakespeare portrait.

O it was for gentler Shakespeare cut

'Cut?' said Sheldon. 'What d'they mean, cut?'

'Well, the picture wasn't painted like Tusia did it,' explained Sicknote. 'Not way back when the books were being printed. The picture was cut on to copper apparently so it could be printed lots of times.'

'But it's not the word "cut" that's important,' pressed Brodie.

Sicknote looked dejected.

'I mean, it's not the *only* word. *Gentler's* important too, and that got me thinking it was an odd phrase. Why *gentler* and not just *gentle*?'

'Maybe that's why Mrs Wells Gallup thought that sentence was suspicious,' suggested Smithies, who'd pulled a coat over his pyjamas before driving in from home when Miss Tandari rang to say Brodie had made a breakthrough.

'Suspicious?' questioned Hunter.

'She thought the sentence was a code,' Brodie explained.

'Go on,' said Tusia.

'The workers at Riverbank thought the sentence was an anagram, and what it really said was this.' Brodie scribbled out another phrase.

Seek sir for a true angle at Chepstow

'Oh, I see,' said Hunter. 'Same thirty letters,' he added. 'Makes sense.' He pulled back a little. 'Except it doesn't make sense.'

'Why not?' snapped Brodie.

'Because what's so special about Chepstow? What has any of this got to do with MS 408 and the Knights of Neustria?'

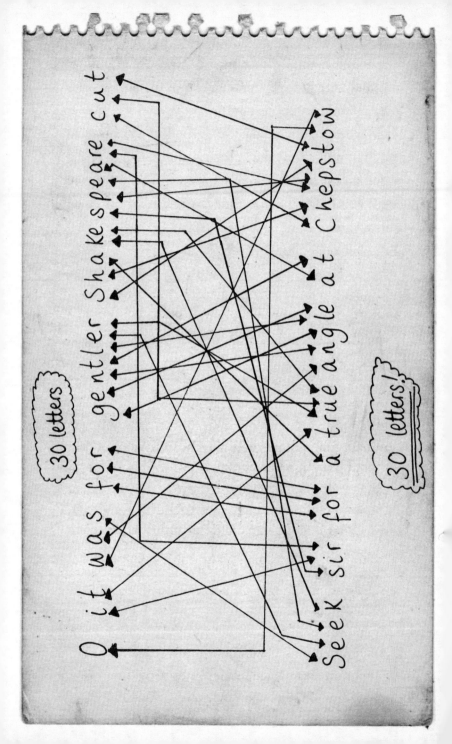

'Sir Francis Bacon,' said Brodie triumphantly.

'What the bacon baguette has it got to do with him? I thought the Riverbanks team proved he wasn't Shakespeare.'

'They did,' said Brodie. 'But it doesn't mean there aren't codes in the Shakespeare portfolio like there's codes in *Morte d'Arthur*. Sir Francis knew how codes were hidden in important works and I think he knew about this code.'

'And you think that, why?'

'Because of what happened when Sir Francis died . . . or didn't die.'

'You mean when he faked his death and escaped to Europe to keep the Knights of Nesutria's secret.'

'I mean before then.'

'Before then?' groaned Hunter. 'When he was at the Lord Arundel's house?'

'No. After then.'

The frustration in the room was palpable.

'Can you *please* explain what you're talking about?' said Sicknote, rubbing his forehead rather aggressively.

Brodie took a deep breath. 'There's three years between the date the portfolio was published and the date Bacon was supposed to have died. Bacon must have been planning his new life for years. I reckon he knew about the anagram. Perhaps he even told

Shakespeare or the printers to add it.'

'What? Why?'

'Because of what the old woman said.'

'I'm trying really hard, B. And I know you're on to something but I really can't see what.'

'The old woman who showed us round Old Hall said Sir Francis Bacon had unfinished business to deal with first and do you remember where that business was?'

The room felt suddenly warm again.

'Chepstow,' gasped Tusia.

'Exactly,' said Brodie. 'Sir Francis Bacon, our Knight of Neustria, had unfinished business in Chepstow.'

'We need all the information you can find on Chepstow and the links between Bacon and Shakespeare,' said Smithies, taking off his coat and putting it on the back of the chair.

Brodie pulled her hair across her shoulders and twisted the strands into a plait. 'I'll look through the books Fabyan brought over from the Riverbank Labs,' she said. 'Who's with me?'

Hunter, Sheldon, Tusia and Sicknote raised their hands. 'OK,' said Brodie. 'That's the past covered. What else?'

'We should think about the future,' laughed Smithies. 'Why don't Tandi and Fabyan find out what they can on the internet about Chepstow and look for anything that may be relevant?'

'I'll get us all a working breakfast,' said Granddad keenly.

'And I'll go home and change and then get the Matroyska full of chip oil and plan our route,' added Smithies.

'We're leaving the Station, then?' asked Hunter, shock reddening his face slightly.

Smithies looked a little embarrassed. 'Nothing's safe. We know that. But as you all persuaded me before, sometimes you have to break the rules to break the code.'

'Amazing,' Brodie said, rubbing her eyes, which were itchy with tiredness. 'It's a brilliant theory if it's true.'

They'd once again joined forces in Hut 11 and were sharing notes.

'It looks like,' said Hunter, 'Dr Orville Owen, the guy who made the cipher wheel, was just *slightly* obsessed with Shakespeare. He learnt all the Shakespeare plays off by heart! Can you imagine! You should try that if you call yourself a real reader, BB.' He watched her consider this. 'Anyway, knowing them off by heart made him think parts of the plays were in code. He thought sections were out of context and didn't quite make sense to the flow of the stories.'

'Like the use of the word "gentler" by Shakespeare's picture,' said Brodie, who'd been slightly distracted, and excited, by the challenge of learning the Shakespeare plays off by heart. 'That must have been added because the person who put together the portfolio needed those exact letters to leave their code.'

'The message which included the word "Chepstow"?'

'That's right.'

'So what else did you find?' asked Fabyan, who seemed quite impressed so far.

'I think you'll like this,' Brodie said. 'Look.' She pulled out a copy of a newspaper article. It was yellowed round the edges but clearly showed a picture of men digging. 'This was tucked inside the notes you brought by Elizebeth and William Friedman.'

Brodie made sure everyone could see.

'So what is it?' asked Smithies.

'A sketch of Dr Owen's men digging in the River Wye, looking for something connected to Shakespeare.'

'River Wye?' said Sheldon. 'Elgar moved to live by the River Wye just before he died.'

'Nice connection,' said Brodie. 'But you'll like this

connection more. The section of the river Dr Owen chose to dig by was in Chepstow.'

'Nice one, B!'

'Did they find anything?' asked Smithies.

'Nothing,' said Brodie. 'But Dr Owen was positive there was something there.'

'And he was sure of this just because of the anagram at the front of the Shakespeare portfolio?' Smithies asked.

'No,' explained Hunter. 'Look, we found more.' This time he took another printout from the computer and laid it next to the article Brodie had found. 'The story was reported both in London and America. Look. The *New York Times* ran an article too.'

HOAXED DR ORVILLE OWEN

CHIMNEY SWEEP SAID HE HAD PAPERS ABOUT SHAKESPEARE AND BACON

CHEPSTOW, Oct 1 – Dr Orville Owen of Detroit, who in 1911 made an extensive search of the bed of the River Wye for Shakespearean manuscripts or documents without success, is here, seeking documentary proof that Bacon wrote the Shakespeare works.

A Chepstow chimney sweep sent word to Dr Owen in the United States that when the doctor was excavating the river bed he himself discovered documents elsewhere relating to the controversy. Dr Owen crossed the Atlantic and offered money to the sweep for his alleged secret. They came to no satisfactory arrangement, and Dr Owen has now withdrawn his offer, saying that he has discovered that the sweep has no information to give.

'But Dr Owen must have believed there was something hidden in Chepstow that it was vital to find,' Hunter continued to explain. 'Maybe something Sir Francis Bacon hid just after he'd faked his own death and before he escaped to Europe.'

'But why in the river, though?' said Sheldon. 'That's a bit nutty, isn't it? Hiding something in a river?'

'Maybe,' said Brodie. 'But you've just said yourself about the River Wye being important to Elgar. Maybe the river's important to the Knights of Neustria.'

'Still seems a crazy place to hide something, if you ask me.'

'Yeah, well, maybe the treasure wasn't hidden in the river anyway. Dr Owen certainly looked for long enough. And he never found anything.'

'Well, what was the "anything" he was looking for? I mean, what sort of treasure are we after?'

'Something which will give us more information about the Knights of Neustria, I guess,' suggested Sheldon.

'And what about the sweep?' Tusia urged, looking back at the newspaper article. 'How's he important?'

'Well, he claimed to have got information about what was hidden.' Brodie checked the article. 'Maybe he never gave that information to Dr Owen. Doesn't mean it was all a hoax, though. The information could still have been good but the sweep just backed out of telling Owen.'

'So who was this sweep?' asked Tandi. 'We need to find out.'

'Where in Chepstow did he live?' asked Sicknote.

'We couldn't find anything about that,' Brodie said despondently.

'We could start with family connections,' mused Smithies. 'See if we can find the sweep's family. Maybe one of them can tell us more.'

'It's worth a go,' said Miss Tandari. 'We've said if a secret's worth having, then there's a chance it'll pass through the family.'

'So that's where we start, then,' agreed Smithies.

Tusia stood up suddenly. 'I've got it,' she said.

'Hope it's not contagious, then,' laughed Hunter, at which point Sicknote took out his handkerchief and covered his mouth.

'I mean, I bet I know what the sweep's name was.'

'Any chance of you telling us before the jelly sets?' sniffed Hunter.

'I bet the sweep's name was Mr Salem,' Tusia said confidently. 'I bet he was a descendant of Mr Ben Salem.'

A Light in the Darkness

'I don't believe it,' huffed Smithies, red blotches appearing on his cheekbones as they always did when he was annoyed. 'What date is it?'

'Thirtieth of December.'

'Priceless,' snapped Smithies. 'They're running Christmas opening times and the place isn't open again until the New Year.'

They'd pulled up outside the Chepstow Record Office to be greeted with a sign which said 'Closed for Christmas. Happy Holidays'.

Brodie stared out of the Matroyska window at the Record Office. 'There's a light on upstairs,' she gasped.

'There's a what?' asked Sicknote, who, since Fabyan and Granddad had stayed back at Station X again, had the back seat to himself.

'A light on,' said Brodie. 'In the Record Office, look.'

Hunter jumped down from the Matroyska and hurried to the door.

'What you doing?' yelped Tusia.

'If there's a light on, there must be someone inside,' he argued.

'But they won't let us in,' said Tusia.

'Want to bet a cheese sandwich on that?' he laughed as he began to hammer on the door. 'I'll throw in the pickle if it takes longer than ten minutes.'

After precisely seven minutes the door swung open.

A tall teenage girl, with her hair swept back in a high ponytail, stood in the porch. She had an apron on, was wearing bright-pink rubber gloves and had a mop in her hand. 'We're closed,' she bellowed over the tinny accompaniment of music playing from her iPod. 'Can't you read the sign?'

Miss Tandari pushed to the front of the group huddled in the doorway and began to apologise. 'Look, I'm really sorry,' she said. 'We don't mean to be any bother.'

'You can't come in,' the girl said far too loudly, then blew a bubble with her chewing-gum. 'I'm here to clean, not let people in.'

She pushed the door hard but it didn't close.

Sheldon's foot was jammed in the opening. 'Nice track,' he said, pointing up at the girl's earphone.

'What?' She blew another bubble.

'I said, nice track.'

The girl blushed and the door swung open a little further. 'You into this?'

Sheldon took his own iPod out of his pocket and flicked to a playlist. The girl looked impressed. 'Like this one better, though.' He scrolled through the list and she beamed when the playlist stopped. 'Want to listen?' he said, stretching his own earphone out and offering it to her.

'I should really get back to work,' she said guiltily, but the sentiment didn't reach her eyes.

'Oh, come on,' insisted Sheldon. 'It's the holidays. Who else is working with you, keeping you company?'

Her shoulders tightened a little.

'Just you here, then. Working when everyone else is at home relaxing. Hardly seems fair to me.'

This time her shoulders lowered.

'Look, why don't you and I have a coffee break together? Just a little rest while my friends come in and take a look around.'

'I really shouldn't . . .'

'. . . be working so hard in the holidays,' he finished

for her. 'Now, come on. Just ten minutes. You, me and the magic of music.'

'He's a total genius,' said Hunter.

They'd made their way, undisturbed, to the top floor of the Record Office and were busy searching through news reports from 1911 and 1912.

Tusia suddenly pushed the filing cabinet drawer shut.

'Guess she's got something,' whispered Hunter, hurrying across the room to join her.

Tusia *had* found something. A file packed with cuttings and articles detailing Dr Owen's search of the river-bed. 'Says here he got permission from the Duke of Beaufort for the digging,' read Tusia, turning the pages carefully. 'He believed the treasure was buried near Chepstow Castle. Makes sense,' she added. 'Treasure and castles. They tend to go together.'

'And Ben Salem, the ancestor of the chimney sweep. Anything about him there?' asked Smithies, pushing his glasses up on to his forehead.

Tusia flicked the pages, then froze. 'Hold on. There is.'

'Well, tell us then,' urged Miss Tandari.

'It talks about the sweep who contacted Dr Owen and it says he worked at Piercefield House.'

'What's that?'

'A large country house. The sweep used to live there all year round. In the summer he did the gardens.' Tusia pushed a rather yellowed drawing across the table.

'Looks quite a place,' Hunter said, unclipping a series of notes fastened to the top of the picture.

'What do the notes say?' urged Tusia.

Hunter scanned the pages. 'It's just a history of the house. About how it was probably built in Tudor times and then added to. The Clay family owned it when Dr Owen came on his digging expedition.'

'So the Clay family employed the sweep, then?'

'Guess so.' Hunter returned to the notes. 'Seems lots of people have stayed at Piercefield.'

'Like who?' asked Brodie.

'Oh, you'll like this one,' he said, jabbing his finger at the notes. 'What with your story obsession.'

'Who?' pressed Brodie, leaning in further.

'Coleridge. Samuel Taylor Coleridge. Wasn't he an author?'

Brodie sniffed. 'A poet. He was a poet.'

'Same thing, just fewer words used,' said Hunter. 'I told you everything comes down to numbers.'

Brodie groaned. 'Well, actually, Coleridge used loads of words when he wrote. He liked writing epic poems.'

Hunter was clearly not in the mood for details.

'That means long poems,' she added, barely concealing the annoyance from her voice. 'You must have heard of the *Ancient Mariner*.'

'Was he one of Coleridge's mates?' Hunter asked.

Brodie felt her cheeks colour. 'It's one of Coleridge's most famous poems. Surely everyone's heard of it.'

Tusia lowered her head and began to scrabble in her pocket in the obvious pretence of searching for a tissue.

'It's one of the most famous poems in the English language,' went on Brodie. 'One of the longest Coleridge wrote. It's in seven sections, you know.' The look Hunter gave her suggested he didn't know, but was in fact vaguely interested. 'I learnt it off by heart once,' Brodie continued, 'when we had to learn a poem for homework.'

'Bet that made you popular,' whispered Hunter.

'It didn't actually,' said Brodie sadly. 'No one in my class learnt anything longer than three lines and they all said I was showing off.'

'They might have had a point,' Hunter whispered again.

Brodie flicked her hair behind her shoulders, lost now in memories of the poem.

'Beyond the shadow of the ship,
I watched the water snakes:
They moved in tracks of shining white,
And when they reared, the elfish light
Fell off in hoary flakes.'

'Very nice,' said Smithies, tapping her on the arm and breaking her flow. 'Very nice dear.'

Brodie felt self-conscious. 'I always loved the bit about the elfish light,' she said, and then something weird happened to her breathing.

'You OK, BB?' said Hunter, putting the notes down on the table. 'I didn't mean anything about you learning the poem. Kids at my school never liked me knowing the seventeen times table up to sixty-five places either. It's a good job that—'

He never got to finish his sentence.

'Elfish light,' blurted Brodie. 'Like Elfish Urim and the Firebird Code. Part of the clues of the Firebird Code,' she went on, trying to keep calm even though her mind was racing. 'The code which started this whole adventure. Remember?' The code had led them to Brighton and the Royal Pavilion where a special musical box was hidden. 'We found Elgar's song after following the code about the Elfish Urim,' added Brodie. 'Maybe Coleridge's poem's got clues in it

216

about the treasure at Chepstow.'

'You think Coleridge was a Knight of Neustria and knew about the "true angle at Chepstow"?' Hunter said. 'That's a bit of a leap, isn't it?'

'Maybe,' said Brodie. 'But Coleridge was considered mad, you know. People didn't believe what he said half the time and he used to worry loads and be very secretive. He could have been involved with the Knights of Neustria.'

'Lots of people worry, B.'

'I know. But if he'd lived now, people would have taken time to try and understand him.' She wasn't sure why the room suddenly felt cold around her. 'I'm talking about someone who was misunderstood,' she snapped defensively, suddenly working out whom the others were probably thinking about. 'I'm *not* talking about Friedman.'

'No one said you were,' Tusia said softly.

'And anyway,' her mind was twisting and turning and her head thumping, 'remember how we saw a sign saying Coleridge lived in a house right next to Lord Arundel's house when we were in London? And we went in to the Institution and there was a Coleridge room?'

'I remember you spent ages in there and we went and got ourselves pasties,' laughed Hunter.

'I reckon,' said Brodie, 'if you put all those things together, then there's at least a chance Coleridge was a Knight of Neustria. I mean, Elgar was. And Malory. Why not him?'

'We have to have more proof than him staying in places connected to the code, B. At this rate, any artist or writer could be in on the act.'

Brodie huffed and leant forward and grabbed the pile of notes about Piercefield House and pretended to examine them closely. 'I was just saying,' she mumbled.

There was an awkward silence until Smithies spoke. 'So this sweep,' he said in a voice which sounded far too jovial for the occasion. 'Are there any details about him? He, after all, is why we're here.'

Brodie couldn't focus on the paper and thrust the pages towards Tusia who took them and began to scan them studiously. 'Great news,' she said at last.

'Go on,' urged Hunter, obviously grateful for a change in direction. 'Does it say about him being descended from Ben Salem?'

'Afraid not.' There was a pause.

'What's great about that, Toots?'

'It gives the sweep a name. So I reckon tomorrow, we go to Piercefield House and ask the present owners if they know what happened to the descendants of someone called Mr Willer. According to this, that was the sweep's actual name. Now, let's go and get Sheldon and get out of here!'

'She's my granddaughter,' said Mr Bray quietly. 'You knew that, of course.'

The guard in the mansion gate-office folded his arms. The dragon tattoo puckered. 'I kind of knew that.'

'Brought her up myself after her mother died,' Mr Bray went on, his gaze never shifting for a second. 'Can you imagine how hard that was? I mean, I'd lost her mother and then I was left with this scrap of life and . . .' He took a slurp from his tea. 'What could I do? I was all she had.' He put the mug down. 'She *is* all I have.'

The guard nodded.

'I'd do anything to protect her, you know. Anything at all. And when you get to my stage in life, well . . .'

'I'm not sure I follow.'

'No. I think you do. You see, when people get to my age, they sort of become invisible. Greying old man. Can't have a clue about much, can he? But I do have a clue. About a lot. And perhaps the being old thing and the being invisible's sort of like a super-skill. I mean, I'm just a funny old man. What could I possibly do if I found out anything that could hurt those I love?'

The tattoo on the man's arm flexed. The teeth

elongated in the dragon's jaw. 'I'm not sure I understand you.'

Mr Bray took a final sip of his tea. He pushed the mug away. 'Nice chatting to you,' he said. 'We must do this again sometime, if you're still working here, I mean. Of course, you might have a change of heart. Might see things differently if you looked really carefully.' He slid a tatty old newspaper cutting across the desk. It was of Brodie on the day of her mother's funeral. 'I think history's important, don't you?'

The guard looked down at the newspaper cutting.

'Sometimes it's important to see the big picture.'

The guard unfolded his arms. 'And do you always think that? Is seeing everything always important?'

'Like I said,' went on Mr Bray, 'I'll do everything I can to protect my family.'

18

Discovering Ben Salem

After several hours of desperate searching for a place to stay, they found a bed and breakfast in nearby Sedbury which was willing to accommodate all of them. Smithies paid with a wad of cash Fabyan had given him before they left, then pulled the Matroyska into the driveway.

Brodie led the way up to the attic room she was sharing with Tusia and collapsed on to the bed. The room smelt of cabbage and there was a dusting of cobwebs hanging from the lampshade. A stack of flyers sprawled on the top of a chest of drawers advertised a rather dodgy-looking New Year's Eve party in the town hall.

'So Ben Salem wasn't the sweep,' sighed Brodie, unpacking her toothbrush and putting it in a grubby glass by the sink.

Tusia shrugged and dragged the bedside cabinet towards the centre of the room. 'What?' she said in response to Brodie's questioning face. 'You know I won't be able to sleep until I balance the shui.'

Brodie shrugged and pushed her hands into her pockets. Tired as she was, she knew she wouldn't be able to get to sleep without reading first. She felt a pang of regret she hadn't had enough space to bring the Shakespeare portfolio with her as she wanted to make a start on learning as much as she could off by heart after Hunter's challenge. Instead, she reached into her bag and pulled out a copy of *The Intermediate Guide to Concertos*. 'Oh, what? How did this get in here?'

Tusia held out her hand in a gesture which Brodie supposed meant 'do you want me to go and give that to Sheldon?'

She returned some moments later with a book Brodie recognised from the pile of Christmas gifts her granddad had given her. 'Great. What's Sheldon like?' she huffed. 'Taking my presents.'

'I thought you'd read all the things Bacon had written,' said Tusia, glancing at the book cover as she pulled on her pyjamas and yanked the duvet up to her chin.

'All his academic stuff,' yawned Brodie, slipping into her now rather tatty nightie with the rabbit on the front. 'This is some fiction he wrote. Granddad bought it for me.' She climbed into bed herself and stared at the cover which showed a ship sailing towards an island. *New Atlantis* by Sir Francis Bacon. She wouldn't read for long. Her eyes were growing heavy.

'I'm telling you I know who Ben Salem is,' hissed Brodie across the breakfast table as the landlady carried in plates of greasy breakfast and dropped them on to the table.

'I thought we hoped he was someone connected to the sweep who offered information to Dr Owen,' said Smithies, taking his glasses off to wipe them on his sleeve.

'We did,' she said. 'We were wrong.'

'Oh. OK,' said Smithies, putting his glasses back on and then frowning at the plate of food in front of him. 'So who is he, then? This Ben Salem, if he's not an ancestor of the sweep?'

'Not a person at all,' said Brodie brightly.

'But I thought you said you knew who he was.'

'I did. I should have said I know *what* Ben Salem is.'

'Well, what is it?' said Hunter through a mouthful of food.

'A place.'

'Where?'

'I don't know where. But it's a special place. There's amazing things there. Places where you can find things out and learn stuff. And there's strange flowers and castles.'

'Castles?'

Brodie traced her finger across her locket. She could hardly contain her excitement.

'And where exactly did you find out about this place?' said Smithies, watching to ensure the landlady was safely back in the kitchen.

'In a book I read called *New Atlantis*.'

'No surprise there, then, BB,' laughed Hunter. 'Where d'you get this book?'

'From my granddad for Christmas,' she said proudly. 'And here's the best bit. Who d'you think wrote the book about Ben Salem?'

Tusia put her fork down gingerly on her plate. 'Who?'

'Sir Francis Bacon.'

Kerrith was trying desperately to avoid the crowds racing past her for the sales. Why anyone would want to fight their way through hordes of people and rummage through clothing racks as if they were at a jumble sale was totally beyond her. The idea of chain-store shopping repulsed her.

She looked at her Rolex. The old woman from the Highgate Institution had better turn up. The Director seemed particularly anxious she was dealt with swiftly.

Kerrith glanced down at her instructions. She was now used to meeting the Director at places which didn't exist. 'Down Street' underground station this time. Like 'British Museum' station, this one had been removed from all new maps although it was marked on the oldest versions.

The station next door had simply changed its name from Dover Street to Green Park, but Down Street had disappeared. Officially vanished.

Kerrith stood outside the red-tiled newsagent's shop and waited.

She spotted the old woman at once, in the ill-fitting duffle coat and garish suede boots, looking like a child about to visit a pantomime. Kerrith detested everything about her, but she forced a smile. The Director had warned it was important not to unnerve her. He'd been particular about that.

'Miss Longman.' Kerrith forced the name through her teeth. 'How wonderful to see you again.'

The old woman looked like she'd been offered ice cream in the interval of the pantomime.

'I see you've brought your overnight things as suggested.'

More inane grinning.

Kerrith turned and strode past the door to the newsagent's and to a brown door beside it, unpainted and unmarked. There was a blast of cold air, and a scattering of snow swirled at her feet.

Miss Longman mumbled something behind her, but there was no need to answer or reassure her now. She'd got her inside. The door was firmly closed behind them.

The Director had explained to Kerrith how 'Down Street' station served a different purpose to 'British Museum'. The overall aim was the same, though. Suppression. But Down Street dealt with people and not the printed word.

Kerrith took a sheet of paper from her bag. The light was a little dim but she could just make out the plan. Apparently, the abandoned station had been used in the war as a safe meeting place for people making important decisions. It was perfectly designed to take guests. For however long they needed to be 'looked after'. It made Kerrith feel strangely excited to think the Black Chamber could also make use of places utilised in World War Two. Station X wasn't the only location with secrets. And she had a sneaking suspicion the secrets contained in Down Street were just a little more exciting than those at Bletchley Park Mansion.

'As I was saying, I'm not altogether sure about this.' The old woman was twittering behind her.

Kerrith shook the plan open. It showed the layout of the disused station. She opened the door to the Gas Lock Area and led the way towards Office 8.

'My boss is very keen to meet you,' she said. 'As we've explained, we feel it's necessary to hear your theories in detail.'

The high-pitched, grating whine of a voice continued behind her.

Kerrith paid no attention to the words said.

'So Bensalem's not a person but a place,' said Tusia, wrestling with the seat belt of the Matroyska and narrowly avoiding being hit on the head by the white fluffy pompoms hanging from the reattached curtain.

'Well, an imagined place, right?' said Hunter, moving slightly to the left to give Tusia more room.

'I suppose,' said Brodie. 'But if it was imagined, it was beautiful.'

Smithies pulled the Matroyska out of the drive. 'So tell us about it, then. What's Bensalem like?'

Brodie mentally shuffled what she was going to say into order. 'Well, Sir Francis wrote the story imagining he'd actually been there. He talks about finding a great wilderness in the waters of the world.'

'So Bensalem was an island?' asked Sheldon.

'Yep. Sir Francis imagines in his story that a boat of European sailors is blown off course somewhere in the Pacific Ocean.'

'Nice,' quipped Hunter.

'At first no one wants the sailors on the island. The people who live there know lots about the outside world but the outside world knows nothing about them.'

'Literally a "secret society", then,' said Sicknote, who, Brodie noticed, had failed to remove the breathing strip plaster from the bridge of his nose and was wearing a rather vibrant pink pair of earmuffs.

Brodie returned to her explanation. 'Anyway, eventually the sailors are allowed on to the island. They see amazing things there.'

'Like what?'

'Well, there's loads of strange flowers used for medicines. There's pools where people bathe and then get better from terrible diseases. And there's these things called "houses of learning" where all sorts of experiments are carried out.'

'And the sailors stay here?' asked Miss Tandari.

'Yep. On the island.'

'So what happens to them? Do they ever return to their own world?'

228

Brodie felt her cheeks colour a little. 'The novel's unfinished.'

'What?' blurted Hunter.

'There's no ending.'

'But then how did the thing get published?' asked Hunter.

Brodie scratched her head. 'The notes inside the cover of *New Atlantis* say the story was printed after Sir Francis died.'

'Or pretended to die,' cut in Tusia.

'So Sir Francis may not have wanted the work to be published and have people read it,' suggested Sheldon.

'Maybe not. But he certainly hadn't rounded up the end of the story.'

'If it was a story,' said Tusia.

Everyone in the Matroyska turned to look at her.

'Sir Francis may have written *New Atlantis* and pretended the place was imagined. But maybe it was real.'

Hunter narrowed his eyes. 'And perhaps the Knights of Neustria knew about Bensalem and that was the secret they were trying to protect.'

'Because, *"the Knights of Neustria serve Bensalem"*,' said Brodie, 'just like the code in Sir Francis's death-bed letter says.'

'And perhaps,' said Smithies, 'if Bensalem's a real

place, then MS 408 is the book which tells us all about it.'

'Written in code,' added Brodie, 'because no one's supposed to know about it really existing.'

'And,' said Hunter, his eyes wide with excitement, 'maybe Sir Francis was scared people were on to his secret. So he planned his escape and hid the final pieces of evidence about where Bensalem was in the river in Chepstow.'

'It makes total sense,' said Miss Tandari.

'Sir Francis left a clue behind in Chepstow knowing anyone who read the clues carefully would know if they searched at "the true angle at Chepstow" they'd find it,' summed up Smithies.

'It's all coming together,' encouraged Brodie. 'We're this close,' she said, making a tiny gap between her hands.

'All we need to do now,' said Hunter, 'is track down the Willer family who are related to this sweep. We need to know exactly where Sir Francis hid the final clues. Then we should be able to get hold of the thing we need to be able to read MS 408 properly and find out where Bensalem really is.'

Brodie could hardly keep herself seated in the van. She felt her chest would explode.

Smithies laughed as he drove. 'Once we reach

"New Atlantis"

not Ben Salem then!

Ship lost in the Pacific Ocean → Discovered the island of (Bensalem)

Free from pollution

House of strangers

House of healing

House of science and learning

Singing of songs

Amazing plants and flowers

Island of secrets

The sailors were told not to tell anyone what they had seen.

Piercefield House,' he said, 'we're home and dry.' He blew out a deep and satisfied breath. 'And if I'm not very much mistaken, as soon as we round this bend we should be able to see the house coming into view.'

'Brilliant,' chorused Tusia and Brodie together.

'Triple chocolate with nuts on perfect,' laughed Hunter.

And amid the celebrations, the Matroyska turned the corner and pulled up the hill towards its destination.

19

Piercefield House

The guard ran his finger along the rim of his mug. This was ridiculous. The guy was just an old man. Probably nutty. Nothing the old geezer said the other day was important.

He scanned the article the old guy had left. It didn't make happy reading. There was no proof of course. About Level Five. And it was years ago and what he was doing now, here at the mansion, was different. He was following orders. Someone had to.

He took a final swig of the tea. It was cold and he shivered.

Maybe that someone didn't have to be him.

'No!' It was the only word Brodie could find.

'This can't be right,' moaned Hunter. 'What the

chicken drumstick's happened to the place?'

Smithies stopped the Matroyska and they clambered out. No one said any more. There was nothing to say.

Piercefield House was in front of them. The roof was caved in. There were gaping holes for windows and the crumbling walls were choked with ivy and weeds. It was a derelict, empty shell.

'It doesn't make sense,' groaned Tusia. 'The records said the Willer family lived on the estate in 1912.'

'Exactly a century ago,' Hunter said. 'A lot can happen in a hundred years.'

'It looks tragic,' Brodie said quietly. 'Like all the life's gone.'

'The life *and* the answers,' moaned Smithies. 'What chance have we got of tracking down the sweep's family now?'

Hunter folded his arms across his chest and his eyes seemed to be focused on something far away.

'You OK, Hunter?' Brodie asked.

'I was just thinking a hundred years is a long time.'

Brodie knew Hunter's skills with maths usually stretched to something a little more taxing than the blatantly obvious.

'And I was also thinking it's a hundred years since MS 408 was found. 1912. An important year. The sweep with clues about secrets in the river won't hand over information at more or less the same time Voynich found our book.' He paced up and down. 'If the secret from the river and the coded manuscript had been put together a century ago, the world would have known the answers. But now we're at another dead-end.' He stopped pacing and kicked at the ground.

Brodie didn't know what to say. 'But this can't be it,' she mumbled. She was aware her words were a plea and not a statement. 'We don't have to go back to Station X yet.'

No one said anything.

'We're not giving up, are we?'

Miss Tandari stepped forward and slipped an arm around her shoulder. 'We just need to regroup and think again. It's not over. It's just ended here.'

'But . . .'

'Brodie. Look at the place. We're not going to find anyone who knows the family of a man who knew a secret a century ago in a house that's only a shell.' She patted Brodie's arm comfortingly. 'You have to see that.'

Brodie shook her arm free. She didn't have to do anything. 'But there may be answers here.'

'Come on,' said Smithies, jangling the keys to the Matroyska. 'There's no answers. Not any more.'

She shook her head. The building may be broken and damaged, but she wasn't ready to leave. Maybe there was something in what Tusia had said about Old Hall. About buildings having souls. She knew somehow Piercefield House had something to share. Still had a story.

'Brodie?' Miss Tandari's voice was gentle and somehow this made Brodie feel more cross.

'I want to go inside.'

'It's derelict! It's not safe.' Miss Tandari was looking scared now. 'We really should go back.'

The Director sat at the end of the table. He ran his finger along the line of his collar, then he leant forward and rested his hands in front of his face. 'We need answers. I'm tired of watching.'

There was a general shuffling around the table. The Director could practically feel them all squirming.

'We have to know what they're closing in on. Where this is all leading them. I need to know how close they're getting. And to what.'

Those seated around him looked down. The shine on the table acted like a mirror. He could still see their faces.

'Why Sir Francis Bacon?' the Director blurted. 'How does he connect to MS 408?'

Kerrith put the computer printout of the death-bed letter on the table. The Director glanced over.

'I wondered, sir,' said Kerrith, 'if it's the Shakespeare link. You know, the idea that Bacon was Shakespeare.'

'I'd like to leave Shakespeare out of this if we can.' The Director did not have happy memories from his English lessons at school.

'Yes. But there's the possibility, sir, that MS 408 was written by Bacon.'

The Director raised his eyebrow. 'It's not enough, though, is it? The manuscript a long-lost play by someone who was really Shakespeare. MS 408 just a story. What's the point?' He took a deep breath and banged the table with his palms 'We have to watch more closely. We have to see the links they're making and we have to make them too. They've been at it too long now. We've given them enough rope and I'm getting edgy.' It was the closest he'd got to being honest. 'It's a good plan. Let them dig and let them discover, but we have to be on top of things. We have to know how close they're getting. We have to really watch!'

'We are watching, sir.'

The Director looked to his left. Howard was getting cocky. He should know to keep a low profile after the disasters at the Royal Albert Hall and Cambridge. The man was taking a chance speaking at all.

'And what are you learning from your watching? How close are they getting?'

'I don't know, sir.'

Kerrith raised her hand slightly as if attempting to wave. 'Sir, there's the old woman. The one from the Institution. We could ask again. Press her for more details.'

The Director felt as if he could smell a particularly vile odour just teasing at his nostrils. 'The woman's mad. Totally batty. Dead people who aren't dead. Empty coffins. Frozen chickens.' He shook his head. 'She stays where she is. Whatever she's rambling on about can't fit with our truth. And it doesn't help us. Doesn't make it clear what those oddballs and has-beens are really on to.' He could hear the frustration in his own voice. It had been weeks since the arrival of the scroll and he'd hoped for more by now. And there was nothing. And this watching and monitoring and waiting. That was giving them nothing either.

The Director stood up and walked to the window. The light was fading. There was a threat of snow. 'We've been charged with keeping things quiet. Suppressing truth. But I want to know, need to know, what truth they're getting close to.'

'What truth could it be, sir?' Kerrith said quietly.

The Director clasped his left hand around the four fingers of his right. 'Never mind. Let's just keep watching and looking. I want to know everything they know and I want to know when they know it. Understand?'

The reflections in the table made it clear that everybody did.

'And we need a back-up plan. More than one. To keep up the pressure. I want to know the truth they've broken. Or I want them broken. Or I want both!'

The wind blew as the first flakes of snow fell. Brodie pulled her coat tighter round her shoulders.

The sky was the only ceiling. Around her, the jagged walls of the ruin stretched up into the clouds.

Piercefield House had been beautiful once. Brodie tried to see it in her head. She imagined guests chattering in every room, fires burning in every grate.

She hesitated. The smell of the smoke was real.

Rounding the corner, she saw him.

An old man, wrapped in a shabby overcoat tied at the waist with string. A cloth cap pulled around fragile, greying hair. He was stooped, his back curved against the cold, and with a long stick he was prodding a tiny fire in a broken fireplace. A plume of thin and wispy smoke snaked upwards.

Her footsteps crunched on the frost.

He turned and raised the heated stick in the air above him.

'Hello,' she said softly. 'My name's Brodie. Can I come in?'

The old man looked at the collapsed doorways and crumbled walls. 'Of course,' he said. 'Come inside from the cold,' and he took off his cap and bowed gently, welcoming her to the grand and stately home the building must once have been.

Brodie moved forward, then in response to the old man's gesturing she sat down on an upturned crate by the fire.

'Do you live here?' she said, glancing at a line of tattered clothing strung across an opening for a window, and a pile of crockery and cooking implements arranged around the fireplace.

The old man prodded the fire once more with the poker.

'So d'you remember the place before it looked like this?' she said.

'Just,' he said quietly. 'Piercefield's been abandoned for eighty years now. She was empty when I first remember her – but I heard talk about how the place had been before.'

'And you've lived here all this time?' she asked.

'Bless me, no. I never lived in the big house at the beginning. I was born and raised in the cottage over there.' He pointed feebly down the hill and Brodie could just make out a dilapidated building through the trees. 'But I reckoned if this house and my own were crumblin' then no one would mind me taking up a place here. I think my mother would have liked that. She was mindful of position. It would've made her smile to see me living on in the mansion.' He jabbed the fire again with the poker.

'And you never thought of moving on? Finding somewhere safer? Somewhere warmer to live?'

'Not me, young lady. I'm not moving from here. I've a promise to keep.' He smiled and Brodie could see his teeth were yellow stumps.

'A promise?'

'Aye. To my father. A promise to watch over things, just as he did.'

'Your father lived at Piercefield?'

The old man stood for a moment and with the end of the stick he traced a detail carved in the brick above the fireplace. Brodie looked up and her heart tightened in her chest. There, marked in the stone, was a crest of a branch. Brodie's pulse quickened. Eneuvac's symbol? A link with the Knights of Neustria?

The old man lowered the stick. He turned and looked at Brodie as if he was seeing her for the very first time. 'I've been waiting here for a worthy alchemist of words to come,' he said.

Brodie's heart did something strange. Van der Essen had used that phrase! When he'd written the Firebird Code he'd said it was for a worthy alchemist of words.

'I think it's time I asked what brings you here,' the old man said gently, 'if we're going to get to sharing secrets.'

Brodie swallowed. Her heart was pounding. Something about the way the man was looking at her, the way his eyes darted now and then towards the crest, confirmed everything she felt. This man had answers. She knew it.

But Smithies had warned them to be careful.

Her mind was spinning. She looked at the crest. She looked at the fire. She looked at the old man. And she remembered her granddad and the letter to Zimansky.

She swallowed hard and her voice burnt in her throat as she whispered the words. But she knew without doubt it was right to say them.

'I'm looking for the true angle at Chepstow,' she said.

'It's OK, BB,' yelled Hunter, bursting into the room, his body poised defensively, just about to launch into a flying karate kick. 'We saw the smoke! Then the shadow of someone there! Then the weapon and . . .'

His voice tailed away as he saw the old man standing by the fire, the stick lowered into the crackling embers of the fire.

'Oh,' was all Hunter could manage. 'You're not being attacked, then,' he added, glancing once more in the old man's direction.

Brodie knew the horror of the suggestion was clear on her face. 'No!'

'But from back there, it really looked like . . .' Again his voice tailed away.

'I'm sorry,' said Brodie, turning to the man, who was by now looking bemused. 'These are my friends. They're quite protective of me.'

Hunter seemed pleased by this comment.

'I was just chatting to this man about how he was staying here to finish something important,' Brodie explained. 'To keep a promise to his dad.'

'And the young lady was just explaining to me why it was she was in Chepstow.'

Brodie felt her cheeks colouring.

'How could you tell him anything?' hissed Sicknote. 'Have you forgotten how careful we need to be about Level Five?'

Brodie's cheeks felt decidedly warm. 'But he said he was waiting for a worthy alchemist of words.'

Only Sheldon didn't seem to follow this argument. 'Firebird Code,' said Tusia. 'That's what Van der Essen said.'

'So is he,' Sheldon pointed at the old man as he raked the embers in the fire, 'is he a you know what?'

'A Knight of Neustria?' whispered Tusia. 'I suppose we'd better find out.'

'I wouldn't be too hard on your friend,' the old man said as he turned from the grate. 'Seems as luck would have it, your business in the area and mine might in fact be linked.'

Smithies was obviously searching for something sensible to say.

'I've stayed in this ruin years after I should have left,' went on the old man, 'because my father believed one day someone new would come looking for answers. If I just kept trusting.' He rubbed his hands together and Brodie could see they were gnarled with the cold. 'If what this young lady has said is true, then I think perhaps you lot could be the ones I've been waiting for all these years. The ones who'll allow me to keep my promise.'

Brodie stood up from the crate. 'And what was that promise?' she said.

'To share something very special.'

'So will you show us then, Mr . . .'

'Willer,' said the old man. 'The name's Mr Willer.'

Keeping a Promise

Smithies and Miss Tandari carried in extra logs for the fire and Hunter and Sheldon dragged crates as seating beside it. Then they sat, the flames dancing in the hearth and snow falling silently all around.

'I knew someone would come,' said the old man. 'But my father warned me trust was important.'

'Was it difficult to know who to trust then?' asked Miss Tandari.

The old man looked very sad. 'My grandfather, long ago, trusted someone from America. Dr Owen, his name was.'

Brodie tried to hide her recognition of the name.

'The doctor didn't believe him. Laughed at all my grandfather had to say. Called him a hoaxer and a liar.

My grandfather never recovered from the slur on his character.' He turned to look into the flames. 'It rots you away inside knowing those you trusted with the truth don't believe a word you say. Not being believed cost my grandfather his life.'

Brodie's mind was racing. She knew the old man was telling his grandfather's story, but she couldn't shake the thought of Friedman from her head. Her heart ached. When she looked up, Smithies was speaking.

'And how d'you know you can trust us?'

'I don't. But time's running out. I stayed here to try and ensure the chain of knowledge is never broken. If I'm wrong to trust you then the chain will break. If I don't trust you the chain breaks anyway. I've waited too long. It's time to pass on my part of the story.'

Brodie rubbed her chest with the heel of her hand. 'We came here to find the "true angle at Chepstow",' she said. 'And you have something to show us. Is it some sort of map? A drawing? Or a chart?'

'No maps or drawings or charts. But three things. Parts of a promise I've protected and watched over but never really understood.' He smiled his toothless grin. 'My father said they would make sense to the right person.'

The group was so quiet Brodie could almost hear the snow falling around her.

'Would you like me to show you?' the old man said.

'They won't come.'

The old lady in the brown suede boots turned from the closed door and lowered her fist. She'd been knocking for over an hour. 'But they must,' she said. 'They said once they'd thought about all I'd told them, they'd come back for me. They said I'd been very helpful.' Her eyes looked haunted. 'They said they'd come back.'

Robbie Friedman rocked forward, lowered his pen and put it on the sheet of paper balanced on his lap. 'I'm telling you, they won't come.'

'But they said . . .'

'I know,' whispered Friedman. 'I know.' He gestured to an empty plastic seat. 'Here. Why don't you sit down for a while?'

The old lady shrugged. She lifted her duffle coat from the floor and walked towards the chair. Her eyes were wide as if shocked by sudden brightness. 'What is this place?' she said.

'It'll be OK,' he said, lowering his gaze.

'But how long have you been here? How long have any of you been here?'

Friedman looked up. People were seated around the room in white plastic chairs. They looked as if they were waiting for a bus. Some rocked backwards and forwards. Others mumbled quietly to themselves. Most stared forward at the whitewashed walls. Friedman decided once again it was best not to give an answer.

'What's your name?' he said gently.

'Molly,' she whispered. 'Molly Longman. I volunteer at the Highgate Institution and I'm a cleaner. I didn't always do that, though,' she said. 'I was a researcher once. That's why I came.' Her eyes darted to his face. 'I thought they wanted to hear what I knew.'

Friedman rolled the pen across the paper.

'You see, before the lady came there was a man and some children and they seemed genuinely interested in—'

The pen slipped from Friedman's grasp. It clattered across the stone floor. Ink leaked from the nib. 'There was a man and some children, you say?'

'Four children and an oldish man and a beautiful black lady. And another man, but he seemed a bit nervy.'

'And they spoke to you about what you knew?'

'Not all of them,' she said. 'One of the boys was hungry, I think, so some waited outside. But the two girls stayed. And the man. And I showed them what I knew.'

'And what you told these children? Is that what you told the people who brought you here?'

'I guess.'

Friedman closed his eyes and tried to breathe slowly. 'And what you told them. You think it's important?'

'Very.' Her mouth twitched into a nervous smile. 'The lady in the coat with the sharp red nails and the designer bag said it was important too.'

'Molly.' He tried to say the name gently. 'Molly, is there any way, the things you told these children; the information you shared with them; is there any way it could lead them into danger? Any way at all?'

Mr Willer was stoking the fire.

Brodie shuffled forward on the upturned crate. 'You said you had three things to show us, Mr Willer. Are you ready to show us the first?'

The old man's nose wrinkled as he concentrated. 'The first is the tree,' he said purposefully. 'Most likely you'll find it a little odd.'

The tree was incredibly odd.

It was an oak, still growing and already tall and

wide. Beautiful in fact. But sliced completely in two by a metal fence.

The old man leant on the fencing. His knuckles whitened like the snow.

'Wow,' said Tusia, trying to balance what she saw with her need for order and feng shui. 'That's got to hurt the tree. Why on earth weren't the railings moved?'

The old man seemed glad to see the tree was provoking a reaction. 'There were orders.'

'Orders?'

'Yes. Instructions. The tree was never to be felled and the railings never moved.'

Tusia ran her palms across the bark.

'Who were the orders from? The Clay family?' asked Brodie, remembering the name of the owners of the house.

'Not the Clays,' Mr Willer said, and plunged his hands deep into his pockets. 'So the story goes, the tree was planted in this exact location by a very famous visitor to Piercefield.' He let them look a little while longer. 'Shall I show you the second thing?' he said eventually.

'Absolutely,' said Brodie. 'Show the way.'

'Not quite as odd as that one, though,' Mr Willer said, as he strode forward. 'But part of the promise all the same.'

They followed him across the park, their feet lifting newly fallen snow in tiny clouds.

'Here,' he said at last. 'What d'you think?'

This time the old man had led them to a large undamaged tree standing in the centre of a field.

Railings circled the tree rather than slicing it in two but at the base of the trunk was a stone slab. Brodie knelt down and cleared away the dusting of snow from the writing. Her fingers tingled.

'Well?' asked Smithies, stepping closer. 'What does it say?'

Brodie read the text aloud. '*This Tree planted to commemorate the birth of RICHARD, son of Captain Clay, Oak Grove, St Arvans. By S. Waugh in 1898.*' She shrugged her shoulders.

'Does it mean anything to you?' Mr Willer asked hopefully.

'Nothing,' Brodie said. 'Do you know anything about this son of Captain Clay? Or S. Waugh? Or even St Arvan? Who or what was he?'

'St Arvan's is a church in Chepstow. Named after the local saint.'

'And do you know anything about this St Arvan?' asked Tusia.

'He was a hermit. Bit like me, I guess,' he added with a laugh.

'There's a hermit in the *Ancient Mariner* poem by Coleridge,' cut in Brodie.

'I don't think now is really the time for one of your poems,' grinned Hunter. 'We're supposed to be looking for clues.'

'I was just saying.'

Sicknote coughed and cleared his throat, obviously desperate to move the conversation on. 'You said there were three things you swore to protect, Mr Willer. Do you think you could show us the third?'

'I think you'll find this one the most intriguing,' Mr Willer said. 'It's inside the house.'

'In the house? You sure?' said Hunter, peering back towards the ruined mansion.

The old man's eyes sparkled. 'I thought you'd learnt today not to judge by appearances, young man. There's more to a house than what you see above ground.'

Mr Willer strode purposefully towards the mansion. The seven of them followed behind, with Sicknote lagging at the end muttering about how cold he felt.

'We're making for down there,' Mr Willer said, waving towards a circular hole in the ground.

'OK. He's totally lost it now,' hissed Hunter, struggling to keep up.

'Shh. He'll hear you,' begged Tusia, wrapping her tassle-edged shawl more tightly round her shoulders.

'Good if he does, Toots. What sane man plans to take us down a rabbit-hole?'

Tusia struggled to find an appropriate answer but didn't need one as Mr Willer turned to the left then bent down to clear the light dusting of new snow from a trapdoor buried in the ground. 'Now, mind you take care,' he called authoritatively over his shoulder. 'We don't want any mishaps on the icy steps.'

'Mr Willer,' called Sicknote, from the end of the procession. He appeared to be clasping his chest and his face had whitened to match the snow. 'Mr Willer, where exactly are you taking us?'

The old man winked, and then, without a word, he disappeared.

21

The Third Piece of the Puzzle

It took Brodie's eyes a while to get used to the change in light but it soon became clear she was in some sort of wine cellar. The walls were whitewashed and rounded, the roof domed with a hole in the middle which was obviously the other end of the circular hole Mr Willer had pointed out to them in the ground. Built into the whitewashed walls were a series of brick wine racks.

'This would be my main residence,' Mr Willer called as he led them onwards. 'This part of the mansion survived whereas the cottage and main house have decayed.' He sniffed and wiped his nose on the sleeve of his jacket. 'No matter. I always liked it down here. Even as a child. My father would bring me and I'd play for hours in the tunnels.'

It looked like there were several tunnels leading off to various chambers and storerooms. The old man had filled spaces with rickety furniture and belongings and on the walls were candle fixings which he lit with a lighter as he walked. 'Now,' he said, slowing the pace a little, allowing Sicknote to catch up. 'The third part of the promise. This I have kept most safely.'

He began to scour the numbered shelves of the brick wine rack, discarding tins of beans and a squashed loaf of bread, before settling on a squat ceramic jar. It looked to Brodie like the sort of container you'd keep coffee in. 'Aha,' he said with an air of celebration. 'This would be it.' He unscrewed the lid and pulled out a handful of straw. 'The house was cleared of all the Clays' possessions when the building was sold, but I kept this safely here.'

Hunter was obviously wrestling with the idea of keeping straw safe, but Brodie shot him a withering look to make sure he said nothing.

Mr Willer pulled out more straw and then a small leather book. 'Here,' he said. 'The third part of the promise.'

Brodie took the book from him. A strand of straw scratched her hand. She turned the book gently and read the name from the spine. 'Samuel Taylor Coleridge. I knew it,' she yelped. 'I told you Coleridge was important. He just had to be.'

'Coleridge,' mused Mr Willer thoughtfully. 'It was him.'

Miss Tandari narrowed her eyes in concentration. 'What do you mean, *it was him*, Mr Willer?'

'The tree. It was Coleridge's tree. He planted the tree which has grown through the railings. He was the special visitor here.'

'You're absolutely sure?' pressed Hunter.

'Yep. Said it should never be moved. The tree, the memorial and the book. Three parts of the promise, all connected.'

Smithies had a look of deep satisfaction about him.

'So I've helped you, then,' the old man said quietly. 'And I've kept my promise.'

Smithies nodded. 'We can use what you've told us to help solve our puzzle,' he said. 'You'll want to come with us?' His question really more of a statement. 'To see if we can use what you've found to help us reach the "true angle".'

The old man shook his head. His milky blue eyes flickered in the light of the burning torches. 'I don't think I do,' he said gently.

'But don't you want to know?' urged Sheldon incredulously. 'Don't you want to see what the things you've protected lead to?'

Again Mr Willer shook his head. 'I've done what I wanted to. I've passed on what I know and that's all I ever really needed.'

Brodie held the Coleridge book tightly. She didn't understand.

'All I hoped for,' went on the old man, 'was to one day have someone believe what this family knew. I just wanted to be listened to. That's the treasure for me.'

They sat in the Matroyska. The pompom-edged curtains tapped against the windows as an icy breeze whistled through joins in the window frame.

'So?' said Tusia keenly. 'Where do we start?'

Hunter's voice was unusually soft. 'I hate to admit it, but I think we should start with the Coleridge book. If we don't, we'll never hear the end of it.' He grinned at Brodie as she blew the cobwebs from the leather volume and opened it.

On the first page there was a handwritten dedication.

Richard Clay
On the occasion of your baptism
Be never steered from the family line.

'No pressure there then,' joked Sheldon.

Brodie turned the page. The contents listed a collection of poems. She ran her finger down the list and stopped at the last title. 'See,' she said with conviction. '*The Rime of the Ancient Mariner.*'

'We're back to her elfish lights, then, are we?' said Sheldon jokily.

'But I was right, wasn't I? I had a gut feeling if Coleridge stayed at Piercefield then his most famous poem might be important, but you wouldn't listen.'

Hunter raised his head to argue then obviously thought better of it. 'OK, B. So it looks like you're right. The poem might be important. But how? Like you say, it's a pretty long poem.'

Brodie winced. 'I reckon we need to think about everything Mr Willer showed us and see how they connect.'

'So the tree and the fence line cutting it in half,' said Tusia, this memory causing her some discomfort.

'And the plaque by the memorial tree?' added Miss Tandari.

'All of it,' said Brodie. 'What was the most striking thing about what we saw?'

'What, apart from an aged hermit who lived underground in a wine cellar?' laughed Hunter.

'That's it!' said Brodie.

'The wine cellar?' said Sicknote nervously. 'Because I think if health and safety knew about the risks involved in using naked flames in that confined space there'd be an outcry.'

'No,' groaned Brodie. 'The *hermit* bit.'

The others looked at her expectantly. She tried to organise her thoughts to make her explanation clear. 'OK. So from the very beginning of this challenge, we've been taught to make connections, right?'

Smithies beamed with pride. 'Yes. The key's in the connections.'

'OK. So we have to try and find a connection between the tree and the plaque and this book. And so what about *this* connection? There's a mention of St Arvan on the memorial tree and then, given as a present to the boy they planted the tree for, there's a poem which ends with talking about a hermit. And what did Bedivere do after Arthur made him the Duke of Neustria? He became a hermit, right? What do you think?'

Hunter was looking dubious. 'OK. I get what you're trying to link, B. But aren't you stretching it with the poem? It's a long poem, right? Epic, you said. It talks about loads of things, not just a hermit.'

'It's hugely long,' agreed Brodie. 'But it ends with the hermit. *Ends*, you see. We're trying to make these connections because we're looking for the place where Bacon hid something important when he told the world his life was at an *end*. I think the hermit's important.'

'OK,' said Tusia. 'We can go with that idea to start. We can see the hermit as the link between the three things and a connection with Bedivere. So what does the poem say about this hermit?'

Brodie didn't need the book. She cleared her throat and began to recite.

> '*He kneels at morn, and noon, and eve –*
> *He hath a cushion plump:*
> *It is the moss that wholly hides*
> *The rotted old oak stump.*'

Even Hunter looked impressed. 'Nice one, B.'

'Yep,' said Tusia. 'A bit weird but nice. How's it help us? How d'we find out where this hermit left the treasure we need?'

Brodie felt a little despondent. 'I'm not sure.'

'Well, we have to find out where this hermit lived,' said Miss Tandari.

Hunter led the clamber down from the Matroyska and followed a single set of footsteps in the snow towards the door of St Arvan's Church, ducking to avoid a prickly holly wreath hanging from the overhead lintel.

3 parts to Mr Willer's promise...

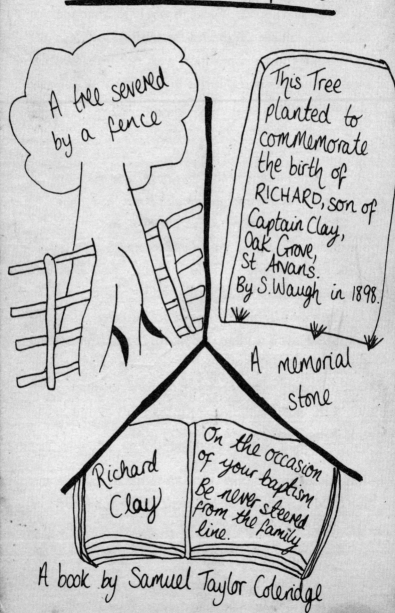

A tree severed by a fence

This Tree planted to commemorate the birth of RICHARD, son of Captain Clay, Oak Grove, St Arvans. By S. Waugh in 1898.

A memorial stone

Richard Clay

On the occasion of your baptism Be never steered from the family line.

A book by Samuel Taylor Coleridge

'Will be nice to warm up a little,' said Sicknote, hurrying to the front of the procession. 'This cold weather's playing havoc with my arthritis.'

Brodie followed him inside and pulled the door of the church shut.

'Nice,' said Tusia, looking up at the intricately patterned ceiling painted in scarlets and golds.

Brodie moved to look more closely at a broken stone cross laid on a windowsill.

'Weird,' laughed Hunter. 'If the thing's broken, why don't they throw it away?'

Somehow Brodie knew why. 'It's still beautiful,' she said.

'Interesting observation.' A voice Brodie didn't recognise came from behind. 'I think your friend's idea about the beauty of the broken cross is lovely. We keep it here to promote discussion. There's often more than one way to see things. The story of the cross made it clear that only when things are broken can we really see the truth inside.'

Hunter raised an eyebrow.

'Father Jacob,' the speaker said, grinning broadly as he strode down the aisle towards them.

'D'you *get* all that, B?' Hunter whispered. 'What he said about things being broken?'

'I did,' snapped Tusia, but Brodie didn't have time

to answer. The vicar was speaking again in a voice that would have reached a church full of congregation. 'Fantastic to see so many of you joining us for our New Year procession and tableaux.' He glanced down at his watch. 'You're a little early but I'm sure I could rustle up some mince pies and coffee while we wait for the Angel Gabriel to arrive.' He leant in and tapped his index finger sharply against his nose. 'Truth is, Angel Gabriel's in charge. This is my first festive season in the parish and I'm new to all this.'

Smithies stepped forward. 'Father Jacob, you say?'

The vicar patted his dog-collar, checking it was still firmly in place.

'And you're waiting for the Angel Gabriel?'

'Not the *actual* Gabriel, you understand, although everything's possible. No. I was referring to Beryl, the leader of the village council. You know Beryl, of course.'

Smithies' face showed he didn't. The vicar's eyes seemed to dull a little. 'Then you're not here for the festive walk around the village and re-enactment of the Christmas story in tableau form,' he said despondently.

Smithies did his best to let the vicar down gently.

'No matter,' the vicar said stoically. 'Always good to have visitors. Whatever reason's brought you to St Arvan's, I'm grateful.'

Brodie seized the opportunity while she could. 'We

wondered if we could ask some questions,' she said.

The vicar's beaming smile returned. 'Of course. Of course. The quest for answers is my thing,' he said. 'Meaning of life; good and evil; free will versus destiny. Questions are my business.'

'We really wanted to know about St Arvan,' Hunter said.

The vicar puffed his chest out rather like a bird trying to keep warm. 'Ah well, St Arvan. Where do I begin? The story is, he was a hermit round here and he helped the poor and sick and lonely.'

'Bit of a saint, then,' quipped Sheldon.

'Yes, yes.' The vicar beamed appreciatively. 'He gave his life to helping others. Met a tragic end, I'm afraid. Apparently, he drowned.'

'Drowned?' Brodie said again, as if she wasn't entirely sure what the word meant.

'Well, yes. In a boating accident. Died in the River Wye.'

'River Wye?'

The vicar looked puzzled. 'You seem to be repeating everything I say, dear. Is there anything wrong?'

'No, no. I know. It's just. It's sad. Very sad that he drowned,' said Brodie, trying to make her voice sound sympathetic. 'Have you any idea where that was? Or where he lived?'

'I do indeed,' he said. 'Lived and died right near the church. He caught salmon, you see, and he'd sail in his little boat in the calm part of the river which flowed near the side of the wood. The townspeople planted a tree in his memory just by the shore. I've never seen the tree myself but I know it's there.'

Brodie felt her stomach twist. Another tree. They had to be getting closer. She could almost taste it.

'Wood, you say?' pressed Sicknote.

Father Jacob nodded. 'Where the land slopes down to the river. The best salmon are found there.' He allowed his words to sink in. 'Now, how about those mince pies I offered? Never one to go back on a promise, me. What would that teach about the Church, eh? I ask you.' He tapped his finger once more against his dog-collar. 'Just give me a moment to heat them up in the vestry,' and with that he strode towards the back of the church.

The Director paced in a circle around his office. His hands were plunged tight inside his pockets. This time he was determined not to rush himself.

The second scroll was on the centre of the desk. The thin black ribbon shone in the glare of the overhead lighting. The ends of the ribbon were cut to sharp points, almost like blades.

He was unsure of the system. How could he be? It was an ancient practice stretching back centuries. No recorded documentation for him to check. Only whispers. His own breath was whispering on the air. The office was totally silent apart from that. Until he lifted the scroll and untied the ribbon. Then he could hear the thud of his own heartbeat.

This time the message between the four emblems was short.

The committee are in discussion.

He twisted the end of the ribbon around his index finger and it was a while before his hand began to throb and he realised he'd cut off the blood supply. When the untwisted ribbon fell to the table, the tip of his finger was the same crisp white colour as the scroll.

'It's the tree!' Sheldon could barely contain himself. 'You heard him. Father Jacob said the hermit had a tree. And your poem, Brodie, went on about a rotting tree-stump. And there were those two trees at Piercefield. I reckon we need to find St Arvan's tree down by the river. That's all! Dr Owen was digging in the wrong place.'

'Dr Owen thought Bacon's treasure was hidden in the river by the castle,' said Brodie. 'He dug near the castle because castles and treasure fit together.'

'Well, they do,' said Tusia.

'Yes, but not all types of treasure. Mr Willer said being believed felt like finding treasure. So a church is a better link than a castle. It's to do with what people *believe* not what people *have*. It's a different sort of treasure.' Brodie could barely contain her excitement. 'Sheldon's right. The tree's important. St Arvan's tree. We don't need to dig in the river at all. We find St Arvan's tree in the woods near this church, and we've found the treasure!'

Sheldon was nodding enthusiastically.

'So when do we go?' asked Tusia. 'If we're going to go digging we need to be sure we're not seen.'

'We may have taken enough risks today,' suggested Smithies, 'talking to so many people. If we are as close to an answer as I feel we are, then we need to be really sure we don't draw attention to ourselves. We have to be extra careful. You do all understand that, don't you? We can't afford to mess things up now.'

Just then Father Jacob returned from the vestry laden down with a tray of steaming mince pies and the door of the church burst open to reveal a plump lady dressed from head to foot in white, garlands of golden tinsel draped around her head and waist, and a pair of cardboard wings attached lopsidedly to her back.

The Angel Gabriel had appeared.

22

Searching for St Arvan

'I thought we'd never get away,' groaned Brodie. She glanced across the room to where Hunter was munching his way through a plate of Jammie Dodger biscuits Smithies had passed round. 'And how can you still be eating? I've never seen anyone eat as many mince pies as you managed.'

'What?' said Hunter, sounding highly aggrieved. 'It'd have been rude not to take them.'

'*Really?*'

Hunter didn't bother to reply. Instead he slurped his hot chocolate.

'So we go once it gets dark tonight?' asked Sheldon.

'I've decided New Year's Eve's actually the perfect cover,' Smithies said. 'We have to allow time for the church procession to make it through town. That "innkeeper" looked like he wasn't to be tangled with. But if Father Jacob's right, the whole town moves on to celebrate in the town hall, leaving the riverside clear. The police will be busy monitoring that, so our little adventures should go unnoticed.'

Brodie took a gulp of her own hot chocolate. She had to admit the thought of being noticed by anyone connected with Level Five, when everything was coming together, churned her stomach. 'How easy do you think it will be to dig?' she asked, appreciating time was against them.

'Whatever's hidden there,' said Miss Tandari, 'has been hidden for hundreds of years. I think it'll take a lot of finding.' She moved towards the window and lifted the curtain. Her bracelets jingled together on her wrist. 'But the snow's beginning to melt and the sky's clearing. Hopefully the ground won't be too hard for spades.'

Hunter put his mug down and grabbed another biscuit from the half-empty plate. 'So have we got a map? We need to find this wood between the church and river the vicar talked about.'

'We've got the map I used for our journey here,' said Smithies, reaching into his jacket pocket and pulling out a rather crumpled sheet of paper. 'It shows the town centre and the area along the Wye.'

He spread the map across the table.

'So where's the church?'

Smithies pointed.

Brodie traced her finger across the map. 'OK, well, this area looks like there's a few trees. But do you think that counts as a wood? Do you think it's here? Or it could be this way?' She dragged her finger in the other direction from the church.

Hunter stared closer. 'Places change over time, don't they? And this is a modern map. And St Arvan lived centuries ago. How d'we know where exactly his tree is if things might have changed?'

'Words,' said Sicknote. 'We look at the words used. Places on maps usually take on names of things that were there in the past. We just have to see if any of the names of places near the church suggest an area that was once much more wooded.' He put his bottle of tablets down on the table. 'Like this one,' he said confidently. 'Can't get a better name than that.' He jabbed the map purposefully with his index finger. 'Elmdale. Perfect.'

'It is?'

'Of course. Elms are trees and dales are sloping areas. I reckon in the past, right here on the map in the place marked "Elmdale", there was a really big wood sloping down to the river. I reckon that's where we start digging.'

'Well, that's right opposite the castle,' said Hunter. 'Dr Owen was so close!'

'Shame for him, but lucky for us,' grinned Sheldon.

'OK,' said Smithies, rubbing his hands together like a football manager about to give the half-time pep talk. 'Miss Tandari and I will go into town and collect all the equipment we think we'll need. Then, as soon as it begins to get dark, we head off.'

Brodie couldn't help being worried. 'I wish Mr Willer had come back with us. I feel bad about him staying in that ruined house. '

'But it's what he wanted,' said Sicknote. 'He wanted to be there.'

'But d'you think it's safe?'

'He's lived there for years, Brodie. Whatever we may think of the arrangements, the Piercefield cellar's his home. And he's happy. Especially now he's kept his promise.' Miss Tandari lifted her coat from the end of the bed and slipped it on. 'He trusted us with his secret and we have to trust he's where he wants to be.'

'I suppose,' Brodie said quietly. 'I just feel bad about leaving him.'

Smithies folded the map on the table. 'Is that the only reason you feel bad?' he said gently.

* * *

They sat on the back steps of the bed and breakfast as behind them a neon sign flickered and flashed the words 'Merry Christmas' in the window.

'The old man made me think, that's all,' Brodie said, hugging her knees to herself to keep out the cold.

'It's never a bad idea to think, Brodie.'

She sniffed in answer. 'Yeah, well, this particular thing I'd been trying not to think about.'

'Particular *thing* . . . or particular *person*?' Smithies asked.

Brodie shrugged. His question didn't need an answer. 'Friedman left my mother when she needed him,' she said at last. 'What possible excuse can there be for that?'

'There might not be an excuse. But there might be a reason.'

Brodie looked up at the sky. Stars pricked the darkness. Fragments of light on black. Just enough to be beautiful.

'Then why hasn't he come back? Why can't he face us and tell us what he did?'

Smithies shook his head. 'Perhaps for the same reason you can't ring him. Because he's scared.'

'I'm not scared. I'm angry!'

'Perhaps while Miss Tandari and I pop into town you should just ring the number he keeps sending,' offered Smithies.

She pulled a crumpled postcard from her coat pocket and stared at the telephone number printed along the back. 'And then what?'

Smithies didn't offer an answer.

It was a long time before the phone was answered. A woman's voice asked what she wanted.

Brodie couldn't bring herself to say 'want'. She wasn't sure it was the right word.

'I need to speak to Robbie Friedman,' she said.

There was a silence on the end of the line. 'I'm afraid that isn't possible at the moment. He's asked not to be disturbed.'

'Oh.'

'Can I ask who's calling?'

'Brodie. Brodie Bray.'

Another pause on the end of the line and the noise of scratched writing on paper. 'Can I take a number on which you can be contacted?' asked the voice.

Brodie rubbed her forehead as she thought about what to say. 'Erm, he knows how to reach me. My granddad can take a message.'

'Very well, Miss Bray. Will that be all?'

Brodie wasn't really sure. But the line was already dead.

The screen on the mobile flashed green. The guard put down his mug. The tea didn't taste good today anyway.

He looked at the incoming number. Strange. It was the first time the facility had rung him at Bletchley, but it was part of the protocol. Part of the system to make sure that all the links in the chain were connected. But recently he was less and less comfortable about being part of the chain.

He held the mobile in his hand and the light from the screen made his dragon tattoo look alive and ready for attack.

But he wasn't ready. He watched the screen flash but he made no attempt to answer it.

The phone rang four more times and then the light went dark.

Kerrith cradled the receiver by her ear. 'You're telling me the call was patched through to you?'

'Yes, ma'am. It was the young girl. She must have dialled the number from the postcard and the call was transferred here just as you instructed it to be.'

Kerrith couldn't help but smile. 'But she has no idea where her call was really directed to?'

'Oh no, ma'am. I made it all sound very caring.'

'Well, that's great news.' Kerrith thought for a

moment. 'And you've informed the link at Bletchley? The operative handing on the postcards.'

'I tried, ma'am, but I couldn't get through.'

Kerrith was only slightly troubled by this information. The important thing was that the child was trying to make contact at last. This was a positive thing. A very positive thing indeed. And finally they could move on to the next stage in the plan. 'I'd like you to listen very carefully,' she said clearly into the receiver. 'There are some changes we need you to make now.'

It was night. The year was dying. December breathing her last and January waiting to be born. The sky was heavy with the threat of rain.

Smithies led the way down to the riverbank.

To a casual observer, they may have looked perhaps like New Year partygoers clad in fancy dress. Seven of them, armed with spades and ropes and blankets.

'Are you sure we need all this clobber?' moaned Hunter.

'Best to be prepared,' smiled back Miss Tandari, recoiling one of the ropes.

Beside the river, Smithies drew them around him. 'OK. This is Elmdale,' he said. 'There was probably a big wood here once. If we've followed all the clues correctly then we should be somewhere near St Arvan's tree and if we are, then we're near to Bacon's treasure.' He allowed time for the weight of his words to sink in. 'We've about eight hours of darkness and a huge area of ground to cover. Let's get searching!'

It was true Elmdale was no longer a huge wood but there were more than a few trees growing along the line of the river.

'So we're looking for a plaque like the one at Piercefield?' asked Tusia, wrapping her shawl more tightly around her and shivering as the first specks of rain began to fall.

'Perhaps,' said Sicknote.

'People mark the passing of special ones in all sorts of ways,' added Smithies, and Brodie wondered how he and his wife had marked the passing of their little girl. 'It might not be as obvious as a plaque.'

'No. That would make it too easy,' huffed Hunter. 'Why have jacket spuds when you can have potato waffles?'

They spread out, leaving the spades and equipment stacked together by the shore, but in the gloom of the torches it was difficult to see.

'This weather isn't good,' groaned Sicknote. 'We'd be better coming back when that storm's blown over.'

'We're here now, so we do this,' said Smithies, and

his voice made it clear he wanted no arguing.

Suddenly Hunter gave a yelp, lurched forward and performed an Eskimo roll across the ground. 'What in the name of coffee mochaccino was that?' he said, reaching up and running his hand along the back of his neck.

In the beam of her torchlight Brodie could see Tusia was looking a little guilty.

'Did she throw something at me?' Hunter yelped, rubbing his neck with more vigour. 'I swear that girl's dangerous. An absolute liability.'

Brodie tugged him towards her. 'Well, she's obviously found something and wanted to let us know.'

'Oh yeah. The fact she chose to let *us* know by pelting *me* in the neck with rocks the size of turnips makes me feel so much better.'

'It was a pine cone,' hissed Tusia. 'Hardly a weapon of mass destruction. And I was just trying to get your attention.'

Hunter was still moaning and rubbing his neck as the group gathered round the tree Tusia had singled out. The rain was falling more heavily now and the ground had begun to squelch underfoot.

Brodie stepped through the group. 'What have you found?'

Tusia took Brodie's hand and pressed it against the

trunk of the tree and moved her palm smoothly across the wet bark. 'Feel that?' she said.

'Oh, not more of her tree-hugging,' groaned Hunter, clutching his neck.

Brodie ignored him. 'Oh, well done, Tusia!' she said. 'That's really very clever.'

Even in the swooping light of the torches it was clear the others didn't understand.

'There's an icthys,' explained Brodie.

Sicknote recoiled as if she'd mentioned some highly contagious disease.

'The sign of the fish,' went on Brodie. 'I've read about them.'

'Makes a change,' snorted Sheldon as Hunter, still rubbing his neck, winked in agreement.

Brodie turned and shone the torch directly on to the trunk of the tree. Through the line of drizzle they could just about see a cut in the wood, reddened by the tree sap. It looked like a fish swimming on its side.

'It's a sign. For a fisherman,' said Brodie confidently. 'St Arvan was a fisherman.'

'And it means more than that,' pressed on Brodie. 'Early Christians used it as a sign to show themselves to each other. A sort of secret code.'

'That I'm liking,' Hunter cut in.

'The fish meant Jesus was "a fisher of men", and so early Christians wore the fish sign like a badge really, to say they belonged.'

'Bit like a crest then?' asked Tusia.

'Exactly. A crest, which could mean two things. Fisherman or Christian.'

'Or, in St Arvan's case, both things at once,' added Sheldon.

Brodie ran her finger once more over the pattern in the bark. 'This is it, then,' she said. 'We've found St Arvan's tree.'

'So let's get digging!' exclaimed Sheldon. 'Before this storm really hits. What are we waiting for?' He raised the spade behind him and swung the blade down hard towards the ground.

'Hold on!' Tusia reached out and grabbed Sheldon's arm.

'What you doing?' yelped Hunter. 'It's Arvan's tree. This is where we dig!'

'It's not enough!' said Tusia.

'What you on about, Toots?'

'I don't think it's enough. Just digging by his tree.'

Sheldon gritted his teeth. 'But we worked it out. We all agreed—'

'I know! I know! But it doesn't seem right.' She

281

looked pleadingly at Hunter. 'You're the numbers man. You've got to see it too. This is just too easy. We haven't used all the clues Mr Willer gave us.'

Sheldon's spade thudded against the trunk of the tree.

Hunter looked up and rain dripped down his face. 'OK. There's three clues. But one was a tree . . . this is a tree . . . one was a memorial . . . this is a memorial . . . and one was a poem about a hermit . . . and this is the hermit's memorial tree. *Surely* we've used all three clues. I say this is where we dig.'

'Tusia's right!' said Miss Tandari. 'We're rushing. The clues have to be cleverer than that. If we really only had to dig here, then the memorial tree at Piercefield would have been enough of a clue. We have to think about the other things we were shown. What about the tree which was split by the fence? And the poem? There must be more details we need. Measurements maybe. Distances.' She was screwing her face up in concentration. 'Are there any distances in the poem we should use to work out how far away from the tree we should dig?'

Brodie was suddenly aware everyone was staring at her. 'Well, I don't know,' she pleaded. 'It's a long poem.'

'But one which you learnt *off by heart*,' said Smithies. 'Can you remember any measurements? Any at all?'

Brodie closed her eyes to concentrate. The phrases she'd learnt danced in her mind. It wasn't the cheeriest of poems and for a while her mind swam with words like the leaves floating on the river behind her. Suddenly it came to her.

'Nine fathoms,' she blurted. 'That's it. Nine fathoms.'

> *'And some in dreams assured were*
> *Of the Spirit that plagued us so;*
> *Nine fathom deep he followed us*
> *From the land of mist and snow.'*

'You're good,' grinned Hunter. 'Really good.'

Brodie felt herself blushing.

'And that's wonderful,' Sheldon added. 'But what an earth do you mean by a fathom?'

'I think most people mean about six feet,' said Hunter.

'Oh OK.'

'Nine fathoms would be about fifty-four feet.'

Tusia nodded eagerly but then her face fell. 'Fifty-four feet. But in what direction? It could be fifty-four feet at any angle from the tree.'

Brodie's heart was racing. 'Angle,' she blurted.

'What?'

'It's an odd word.'

'It's not that odd,' mumbled Hunter.

'No. But it's something else which could mean two things.' She began to pace now. 'It could mean to fish. *To angle.*'

Tusia pulled a suitably disgusted face.

'And it could mean a measurement of distance arcing out from a place.'

'So we have to work out at which angle from the tree we should measure fifty-four feet,' urged Smithies.

'We have to use the "*true*" angle,' cried Brodie.

'Wait a minute,' said Tusia, clearly getting agitated. 'We've used the clue from the poem and we've used the memorial tree to help us. The only clue we haven't used is the one where the tree was sliced by the fence. What were the words which were part of Coleridge's order about the tree?'

'That the line should never be broken. The fence never removed.'

'So it's a marker, then. A sign.'

'It is!' yelped Brodie. 'And wasn't there a message about a line in the front of the poem book?'

'Yes,' said Miss Tandari. 'The family line. Don't stray from the family line.'

Brodie gulped in breath. 'Where's Piercefield House compared to where we are now?'

Smithies looked down at the map and tried to shake it dry. 'Here,' he said.

'So,' continued Tusia. 'If we draw a line on the map from where the sliced tree at Piercefield is and we connect it to this tree here, then we'll have our "true angle". A connection to the family line, d'you see?' She wiped the rain from her face. 'We must dig on that line nine fathoms away from the tree.'

Sheldon didn't need telling twice. He grabbed the map and gestured to Brodie to hold the torch carefully above it. Then he took a pencil from Tusia's topknot and began as best he could to score a line on the wet paper. 'Our tree's here,' he said proudly, 'Piercefield's tree is here.' He connected the two positions on the map with a line. 'And if I continue the line along, then we should be digging fifty-four feet away in that direction.' He turned and pointed. 'Just there.'

Even in the driving rain it took only a few seconds for them to recognise the problem before Sheldon lowered his hand.

'Ahh,' he said. 'Could be a little awkward. Maybe Dr Owen wasn't so wrong after all.'

Brodie frowned. The position the clues had led to seemed to be the point where the borders of England and Wales touched, slap-bang in the middle of the River Wye.

A Gathering Storm

Mr Bray followed Fabyan up the stairs to the Listening Post. The American took the newspaper article and smoothed it flat against the pinboard, tacking each corner with a silver pin. It was a short piece. Untrained eyes would have missed it. An elderly guide missing from her voluntary work. Hardly worth noting. Unless noting these things was what you'd been asked to do.

'Should we let Smithies know? It proves Level Five is circling close.'

Mr Bray took a moment to consider. 'No. We record. We keep track. We do the worrying. We let them get on with the task in hand. Sometimes knowing the whole truth doesn't help anybody.'

The American angled his head to the side. 'You

really think that, my friend?'

The older man didn't answer.

'The river must have moved,' said Tusia desperately.

'Yeah. They tend to do that, rivers. Move. Sort of part of being a river,' Hunter said dismissively.

'No, what I mean is, the location of the river must have moved.'

'Really,' said Hunter, his eyes wide. 'That makes *so* much more sense.'

'Not moved far! Just changed a little over time, as the edge of the river wore away.'

'Sounds like my Year Five teacher back at school. She was always going on about erosion. She eroded my brain with all her rambling.'

'That would explain everything,' said Brodie, grinning at Hunter sympathetically.

'What I'm trying to say,' said Tusia through gritted teeth, 'is that Dr Owen was right *and* wrong to dig in the river! Years ago, when Bacon hid whatever he did for us to find, nine fathoms in this direction from the tree maybe wasn't in the middle of the River Wye. There may have been an outcrop of land which has worn away since.'

'Or an island,' said Brodie, peering through the light cast by her torch, glancing at a shape in the river she hadn't noticed before.

'Well, probably not an island,' said Tusia.

'Oh, that's a shame, because there's an island there,' said Brodie, pointing. True enough, marked out by the weak beam of light was a small clump of earth jutting from the river, which appeared to support a few small bushes and rocks. 'Measure out nine fathoms,' she said confidently. 'I bet if we do, it'll finish at that island.'

Hunter shrugged and stepped back so his heels were against the root of St Arvan's memorial tree. 'Fifty-four feet from here, then,' he said, beginning to pace.

He stopped when he reached the number thirty, his feet precariously close to the edge of the river.

'How much further do you think to the island, then?' pressed Brodie.

'Twenty-four feet, I reckon.'

'So the island's right, then?'

'Looks like it, B.'

'Perfect. So how do we get across?'

Even in the feeble light cast by the torches it was possible to see Sicknote had turned a little green. 'We don't, *obviously*,' he said. 'We can't possibly get across to the island tonight. This rain's getting worse. We'll have to come back another time.'

'But we can't come back in daylight,' pleaded Miss

Tandari. 'We don't want to be seen.'

'I thought New Year was the perfect cover. The ultimate distraction,' added Tusia. 'We can't let this chance slip by. We managed to do all this without any interference from Level Five. We can't give up now. We're so close.'

'Yes. Twenty-four feet close,' said Hunter.

Sicknote was visibly wobbling and began to dab at his forehead with a rather large handkerchief.

'I vote for wading across,' said Hunter.

'But the river!'

'Is the reason I used the word "*wade*",' he said deliberately. 'Come on. This I *can* do. Mice, spiders, cockroaches, confined spaces, clowns and wasps are all off limits.'

'But you're really all right with water?' Brodie checked nervously as a rumble of thunder rolled above them.

'Of course. Humans are about eighty per cent water, after all. What's there to be scared of?'

Brodie glanced at the foaming water of the River Wye as it buffeted against the shoreline, lashed now by the rain. In the distance the castle was lit up for a second as forks of lightning clawed at the sky.

Brodie decided there was quite a lot to be scared of. But the thought of returning to the Matroyska and driving away, the treasure uncovered and MS 408 still silent, seemed unbearable. 'I should come too,' she said.

'Don't be ridiculous. I can manage.'

'But you'll need someone to shine a torch where you're digging. It makes more sense for two of us to go.'

At this point Sicknote looked like any air in his lungs was escaping through his ears and Brodie knew she had to press on with her suggestion before he passed out entirely. 'You should tie us both to the tree,' she blurted to Smithies.

Lightning tore at the sky again. 'We're going to try and wade over to the island,' said Hunter. 'What you talking about tying us to a tree for?'

'A safety rope. My teacher went on about them when we did river surveys. If we tie a rope around our waist, then if we slip we'll be secure.'

Hunter didn't seem daunted by this idea. 'OK.' He shook the rain from his shoulders.

'We can feed out the lines to you as you move across,' said Sheldon. 'That way everyone's safe.'

'This isn't my definition of safety,' groaned Sicknote, wincing as more thunder boomed.

It was difficult to see in the rain and the semi-light. Tusia worked as quickly as she could with the wet ropes, fastening them first round the nearest tree-trunk and then one each round Brodie and Hunter's waists. 'Secure?' she said, tugging on the lines to check.

Brodie tried to ignore the straining noise the tree-trunk made in response.

She hitched a spare torch to her rope belt and tied the string handle of her own torch safely next to it. Hunter, meanwhile, swung the spade up behind him and pushed the handle down through the rope at his waist so the metal blade of the spade framed his face like a halo. Sheldon and Miss Tandari took charge of the rope secured round Hunter while Smithies and Tusia worked on Brodie's rope. Not being involved didn't stop Sicknote shouting instructions. 'Take it slowly and steadily! Walk sideways against the current, then you're less likely to slip. And if it's too much, come back,' he added rather desperately.

'It's twenty-four feet.' Hunter's face radiated in the torch light. 'Twenty-four feet and hundreds of years between us and the answer.'

Brodie tried to swallow but she seemed to have forgotten how to.

'Are you ready, B?' said Hunter, holding out his hand.

She hoped her steps towards the riverbank were enough of an answer.

There were no words to explain how cold the water was. Brodie's boots and jeans were no protection. It felt like tiny rotary blades were moving through the water, cutting into her skin. Air seemed unwilling to enter her lungs in case it was turned to ice and so she could barely breathe. Her legs felt so heavy it seemed impossible to lift them, and she couldn't feel her feet at all. It was as if they'd separated from her body and floated off down the river.

'You OK, B?' Hunter's voice trembled and she wasn't sure if it was from fear or from the cold. 'Sure you want to do this?'

Everything in her wanted to tell him no. Of course she didn't want to do this. To be wading through an icy river towards a darkened island in the pouring rain. But did she want to find whatever Bacon had hidden? Did she want to find the next piece of the puzzle? She wanted that more than anything in the world.

'B? You OK?'

'Just keep going,' she called out to him as the sky lit up again with scars of light.

Hunter looked up at the storm. 'Do you want to turn back?'

'Just keep going!'

It seemed unbelievable. That a distance which could

have been covered in moments on dry land could be so difficult to travel. She'd lost all clear memory of how to move her body and every action and every step required maximum concentration. She could hear Hunter trying to encourage her, but his words made no sense. The only thing which made any sense to her was the need to get to the island. To feel firm ground under her feet.

The water surged around her legs, lifting in waves around her. The rope, wet and heavy, cut into her waist, dragging like a chain behind her. Her breath, so cold now, formed clouds on the air. And the light from the torch bubbled on the swirling water. Her muscles burnt with the effort to keep upright and her hand clung tightly to Hunter's as the rain drove into her back like needles.

'Nearly there,' he said, his voice shaking obviously now as he abandoned the urge to ask her if she was OK. 'Just a few steps more.'

And then her foot struck the edge of the island. Her toes scrabbled against land.

Hunter clambered beside her, the spade swaying on his back like a giant antenna. 'Take my other hand,' he gulped. 'Let me help you.'

The earth was slippery, like butter. It pressed through her fingers and folded under her knees. Brodie squirmed like a long-distance swimmer who'd just reached a foreign shore. She pulled tightly on Hunter's hands and, for a moment, he tottered above her. The spade slid from the fastening and landed dagger-like in the earth. Brodie lowered her head and the light from the spare torch flickered and died. And so in the light of a single torch beam and as the rain fell, she and Hunter surveyed their landing place.

'OK,' he said, helping her to stand then shaking water from his arms. 'Mission accomplished. Sort of.' It was obvious he was shivering. 'The island looks bigger than it did from over there.'

He took the edge of his coat and wrung it out, pooling water on his feet. But it was useless. The rain was relentless now. Brodie was sure they'd never be dry again.

'Where should we start?'

Brodie wrapped her arms around herself. The torch light cut a line in the dark sky. She was too cold to answer.

'Here, you think? By this bush?'

Brodie shook her head. Now she was here, she knew exactly where to dig. 'There,' she said and there wasn't even a tremor to her voice. 'We dig there.' She pointed to a gnarled tree-trunk, half hidden by moss and rotting leaves.

'Because you think that's exactly nine fathoms from

St Arvan's tree?' Hunter asked.

'That and another reason.' Brodie clapped her hands again against her arms. 'Seems today's all about double meanings.'

Hunter lifted the spade but his eyes narrowed in question.

'It's nine fathoms from St Arvan's tree but it also fits another bit of the poem, remember?'

'Go on,' he said.

'The hermit,' she said. 'It's where he prayed.'

'He kneels at morn, and noon, and eve –
He hath a cushion plump,
It is the moss that wholly hides,
The rotted old oak stump.'

'Nice one, B,' gasped Hunter as the rain pummelled his shoulders. And in the pool of light from her torch and at the base of the old oak stump, he began to dig.

Far behind them, in the shadow of the castle, the sky was suddenly ripped apart by lightning. The air rumbled with thunder. And as the river surged around the island, Hunter dug for answers.

Brodie's shoulders ached from hunching over. Her clothes hung wet to her body. Her fingers burnt with cold. But her heart beat steadily and loud.

They'd find it, she knew. All their trials and false turns had led them to this. The dirt and the mud beside the river under a sky torn apart by fire.

Hunter pressed his foot down on the top of the spade face. He swept his fringe back from his eyes to see more clearly and he trod down again.

And then, about half a metre below the base of the rotting tree-stump, he struck something solid.

'Here,' he yelled. 'It's here!'

Brodie knelt beside him. The river roared. Rain lashed down. They churned the earth with their hands.

Then stopped.

Below the soil, revealed after centuries of hiding, was a small metal box.

Brodie lifted it carefully from its muddy grave and wiped the rusty lid. Raised and pronounced under her fingers was an intricate pattern proud against the metal. A single crest with three images linked in one design.

A phoenix. A griffin. And a branch.

The marks of the Knights of Neustria.

Then, without any warning, the ground below their knees fell away.

24

When the World Fell Away

Brodie hit the river like a fist breaking polished glass. Water closed over her like the lid of a coffin. She could see the sky on fire above her, glowing and sparking out of reach, but as she stretched her empty hand towards it, she carried on falling. The rope round her waist was tugging tight, snaking down her leg, and even in the closing darkness she could feel the pull of something heavy on the end of the rope. She understood then – the tree the rope had been tied to had fallen. The thing supposed to keep her safe and alive was dragging her down. Under the dirty, churning water. To a watery grave.

She could see the whole event as if it was happening in a film. As if the falling, twisting, struggling body in the water belonged to someone else. And in her head she screamed to the person to fight, to swim, to push for the surface. But the water was too cold, the current too strong and the rope too twisted around the fallen sprawling body for anyone to hear.

Brodie knew she was going to die.

Was this how her mother had felt in her last breathing moments? Had she been alone, knowing the end would come? Knowing her friend had abandoned her? Had her mother known she was dying? Did she struggle? Did she remember Brodie? Did she think of the daughter she'd leave behind?

Brodie felt the metal box against her chest like a weight pushing her deeper into the water. If she freed the box she clung to, would she rise in the water like a phoenix from a fire? If she let go of the box, would she live?

Her chest was burning. Blazing like the sky she could no longer see. It was so dark her eyes were useless.

Her limbs felt disconnected. The only thing she could feel was the box.

And the dark.

'You have to let me out!'

Friedman's hands were raw, his nails torn, his knuckles bruised.

'Mr Friedman, please. You're disturbing the other guests.'

Friedman struggled to form words to contain his anger. 'We're not your guests!' he spat. 'We're your prisoners. And you have to let me out. I have to be with them! I have to speak to her. I have to . . .'

'Mr Friedman, please.'

'I have to explain to Brodie. I have to tell her.'

The woman moved her face closer to the grille. 'Mr Friedman. You really must calm down.'

'But I need to speak to Brodie. I just have to.'

The woman took a clipboard from the wall on her side of the door and flicked through the pages clasped to the board. 'Brodie, you say?'

'Please. If I could just speak to her. If I could—'

The woman held up a hand to stop him continuing. 'It seems from your notes, Mr Friedman, a young lady called Brodie has in fact been in touch with the facility.'

'She has? But when . . . what . . . ?'

'It seems to me, from the notes written here, she asked to speak to you.'

'When? When did she do that? Why wasn't I told? Why—'

'Mr Friedman. I can only tell you, it was made clear to her you were unavailable. And I have to say if she calls again, she'll be given the same answer.'

'But, please. I just need—'

'Mr Friedman. I think it's about time you began to accept your situation. You're in Down Street to stay. There's no opportunity for escape. There's no chance of parole. You'll remain as our guest. All this striving for the outside world is just causing you distress.' She tapped the clipboard with her finger. 'I think our improved plan for you will help with that. Let me explain.'

Brodie burst through the water.

Her lungs fought for air.

Her head pounded. Her eyelids burnt red. Rain sliced at her face like a knife.

She was turning and twisting and the water was still raging against her. But it was losing. She hadn't given in. She wouldn't go quietly.

The river roared around her but there was another sound churning in her mind.

The sound of her name. 'Brodie, Brodie, stay with me.'

Was it her mother calling for her? Her mother reaching out when she needed her most, to help her?

The current tugged again at her legs and dragged her back under. Water, clogged with earth and soil, seeped into her lungs. Her stomach heaved. She spluttered for air. Fibres tore at the back of her throat.

'Brodie, please! Hang on,' the voice came again.

Once more she was thrown under the water, but this time she felt a hand searching for hers. Someone pulling her upwards not down.

There was shouting. The roar of the river again. Twigs and branches from the shoreline scratching her skin. The roots of the fallen tree scraping her body.

But in the darkness and the noise and the terror, someone held her hand.

'It's OK, Brodie,' the voice said again. 'It's OK. I've got you and I'm not going to lose you.'

And when darkness came this time, Brodie wasn't scared. This time she wasn't alone.

The nurse moved her face closer to the grille. 'We've decided to take away your writing privileges, Mr Friedman.'

The words pressed the air from his stomach. 'You can't stop me sending letters,' he blurted. 'You can't—'

'We can and we will.' The nurse slid the shutter across the grille and blocked out the light.

He could still hear her final words as they died on the air.

'We can do anything, Mr Friedman.'

* * *

Brodie wasn't sure how they pulled her from the water on to the shore.

When she opened her eyes, a single beam of torchlight scorched her tears.

Her lungs screamed for breath.

Then she turned on her side and vomited.

'Nice,' said Sheldon, kneeling beside her.

Brodie wiped her mouth with the back of her hand and tried to sit.

'Not yet. Not yet,' said Miss Tandari softly. 'You're a little woozy. You need to take it easy.'

Beside her, Sicknote was blowing rapidly into a brown paper bag. 'This was the very thing I was scared of,' he blurted between rasping breaths. 'I knew it would end in tragedy. I knew it!' he yelped.

'I admit that was a close thing,' said Smithies, his words suggesting a calmness his face didn't display. 'If it hadn't been for Hunter, we'd have lost you.'

Brodie tried to process what had happened. The fallen tree, the raging current of the water, and Hunter. Hunter who'd saved her.

'It was nothing,' said a croaky voice from beside her.

Brodie moved her head slowly to see Hunter wrapped in a blanket, huddled against the easing rain. 'I can think of better ways to celebrate a New Year, though,' he added.

Brodie tried to force her mouth into a smile. She wasn't entirely sure she succeeded.

Tusia knelt and wrapped a blanket round Brodie's shoulders. 'Certainly kicked the year off with a bang,' she said, her voice trembling as she spoke. 'But you did it, Brodie.'

Brodie struggled to understand.

'You found the treasure,' explained Smithies quietly.

Brodie looked down to her side and in the light of a sudden vein of lightning, fragmenting in the falling rain, she saw it.

The box from the island, still gripped tightly in her hand.

'You open it,' said Hunter, his voice hoarse and strained from the rescue.

Brodie pulled the blanket tight around her shoulders. The room in the bed and breakfast smelt of the river and, despite the pumping of the wall heater, it was still cold.

Miss Tandari had put the box on the table. It looked strangely ordinary sitting on the intricate lace tablecloth, a rusty pool of rain and river-water leaking from its lid.

'Hunter's right. You should do it,' said Miss Tandari, gesturing to Brodie. 'After the efforts you made to keep it safe, you should be the one who lifts the lid.'

On the table in front of her was an answer. Something Sir Francis Bacon had risked his life and faked his death to leave behind. Something so important it had remained undisturbed for centuries. Waiting until now.

Brodie thought of the pages of MS 408 and the Knights of Neustria, who'd promised to keep their secret safe. She ran her fingers along the edge of the lid. It was caked in mud. She rubbed the mud away. Silt ran through her fingers, grit caught under her nails. 'I can't open it,' she said.

Hunter scrabbled in his wallet. He took out the phoenix medallion. 'Try this.'

Brodie pressed the edge of the disc under the lip of the lid. Like a walnut prised open, the lid strained a little with the pressure.

Brodie steadied the box, then she hooked the medallion more firmly under the lip of the lid and lifted.

Rain fell against the window and the last cracks of thunder rumbled.

Brodie lowered her hand inside the box.

'Well, what is it? Let's see.'

Brodie lifted her arm and opened her hand.

There, on her palm, was a ring.

The Broken Cross

Smithies filled a glass with water. They lowered the ring inside and washed away the silt and mud.

'I've seen that ring before,' gasped Sicknote. 'It's Nicholas Bacon's ring! Nicholas was wearing it in the portrait back at Gray's Inn. Bessie showed us. Maybe he wore it to show he was Lord Keeper of the Great Seal. You remember Bessie said the title came with signs of office.'

'I've seen it too. Coleridge wore it in his portrait at the Institution in London,' added Tusia. 'But this can't be the same ring as the one Bacon wore if it's been buried in the river for hundreds of years.'

'So there must be two,' said Hunter. 'Two rings the same. Well, two at least.'

'Symbols for those who were Knights of Neustria

perhaps,' said Sheldon. 'Like the ichthys marking out Christians.'

Brodie picked the ring from the glass and let it lie still in her palm.

It was beautiful.

A flat face secured to a thick golden band. Across the face of the ring sparkled row after row of tiny coloured gems. Some red. Some green.

In the flickering light of the overhead bulb, the gems dazzled and shone.

'Put it on,' said Brodie, slipping the ring on to Hunter's finger. 'Imagine the stories it could tell if it could speak. A ring which might have been worn by Sir Nicholas Bacon or Sir Francis Bacon and has been hidden in the river for centuries.'

Hunter lifted his hand and the ring's gems swam in colour.

'It can't speak, though, can it.' said Sheldon at last. 'It's a ring. Beautiful and all that. But it can't tell us anything.'

The windows rattled from the beating of the rain. There was no sound inside the room.

'This can't be all there is,' said Miss Tandari at last.

Brodie struggled to find her voice. 'This *is* all there is.'

'But it's not enough without words,' said Sicknote.

'What can a beautiful ring tell us? How can we make sense of the coded manuscript and the stories of Bensalem with just a ring?'

'It's useless,' said Sheldon quietly.

Hunter rested his hand in his lap and above them the overhead bulb buzzed and faltered. The ring's sparkle faded.

And Tusia watched. Then she took a piece of paper from the table, a pencil from her topknot and began to draw.

It was a simple sketch. The outline of an ornate cross.

Then she took the picture she'd drawn and held it up.

And she tore it. Top to bottom, she ripped the paper in half.

'You wanted a plan, sir. A back-up plan. Two maybe.'

The Director lifted his head. 'Go on, Miss Vernan.'

'Well, I've taken the liberty of organising a change in the care regime. For Friedman. I think it may prove effective.'

'Very good, Miss Vernan.'

'And I just wondered if perhaps we need to intensify our level of watching.' She paused a little, a flicker of hesitation betraying her resolve. 'I was just wondering if perhaps we need to get right inside Station X, not just its gatehouse.'

'Go on.'

Kerrith put a photograph on the table. It was of a teenage girl. She was wearing an apron.

The Director picked it up.

'She's needy, sir. At a bit of a dead-end.'

The Director flicked the photograph between his fingers. 'You think they would be accepting?'

'Isn't that their biggest downfall, sir?'

The Director frowned. There was a memory of a similar conversation involving a photograph. Something about that recollection jarred but he batted the thought away. 'I like your style, Miss Vernan.' He passed the image back to her. 'Have it arranged. And the change with Friedman. See to it that's arranged as well.'

'I already have, sir.'

'What are you doing, Toots?' Hunter lurched forward and grabbed her outstretched hands as the severed sections of paper flapped in the air.

'It's the cross,' she said. 'The cross we saw at St Arvan's church.'

'The one on the windowsill? The broken one?' pressed Brodie.

Tusia nodded but no one else seemed to be clear where she was going with her argument.

'Go on,' said Sicknote, who'd finally put his paper bag down on the table and was concentrating intently.

'Don't you remember what Father Jacob said?' asked Tusia.

'What, apart from help yourself to mince pies?' winced Hunter, the colour at last returned to his cheeks.

Tusia batted his answer away dismissively. 'No. About the cross being broken?'

Dawning realisation suddenly flashed across Sheldon's face. 'About how they kept it. To keep people talking.'

'And how the story of the cross,' cut in Brodie, 'was all about how when things were broken they had important truths to tell.'

'Yeah. I didn't really *get* that,' said Hunter.

'It doesn't matter,' said Brodie. 'What's important is that the broken cross could still teach people things.'

'It could?'

'Absolutely,' Tusia said.

'No. I'm sorry. You've lost me, Toots. No idea what you're talking about.'

'I think if we want to get the full story of the Knights of Neustria we have to "break" something.'

Hunter looked rather scared, as if he thought he might be in line.

But Brodie knew she wasn't talking about Hunter. The realisation of what Tusia was suggesting seemed too incredible to be real. 'You've got to be kidding me.'

'It has to be broken to tell us what we need to know,' Tusia said softly. 'Piercefield House was broken, just like the cross. It still gave answers.'

'It can't be that,' said Brodie. Her stomach was clenching. She was pretty sure she'd be sick again.

'Will someone please tell me what's going on?' begged Sicknote, reaching once more for his paper bag.

'Tusia thinks we've got to break the ring in order to understand its message,' said Brodie. 'She thinks it's the only way to work out what it means.'

Six people speaking all at once made quite a noise. It was Miss Tandari who raised her hands to stop them. 'This can't possibly be the way,' she said. 'This ring's been kept safe for centuries and you're suggesting we break it apart only hours after we've found it?'

'I can't let you do it,' gulped Sicknote, the paper bag now torn and flapping round his face like a disfigured beak.

'There has to be another way,' begged Smithies.

'But this is the way it must be,' said Tusia. 'Secret

breaking. That's what we do, isn't it? Remember how we had to break the wax seal to read the scroll Sir Nicholas left behind?'

Smithies' eyes clouded. 'I'm not sure about this.'

But somehow Brodie knew now Tusia was right. 'The Firebird Code,' she said, trying to process all the thoughts colliding in her head. 'Van der Essen said it was for "worthy alchemists of words". And Mr Willer used that phrase too.'

'And?' Smithies' brows were drawn tight together.

'Phoenixes rise from the fire,' she said. 'After being broken, they fly again.' She was pleading now, not only with him but with her mind, for the words she said to be true.

'But it's such a risk. Suppose you're wrong. Suppose we destroy everything we worked for?' begged Smithies.

'But suppose we're right?' Brodie begged. 'The ring's beautiful and intricate, but to mean anything, we have to look further than what's on the surface.'

'Look for a second meaning?' said Hunter. 'Like you're always teaching us to do.'

'So. Are you all with me?' Tusia said in barely a whisper.

Brodie waited in the silence.

Then, slowly, Smithies nodded his head.

The nurse opened the door and stepped inside.

She took the pages of paper then crumpled the letters he'd written into a ball.

'Please, I need you to understand!' Friedman pleaded.

'You should save all that for her.'

'I'm sorry?'

'The girl. The one you kept writing to.'

'But—'

'Oh, now we're stopping our little game, Robbie. You can no longer try and explain. But the truth is, we haven't let you explain anything from the very beginning.'

'But the other letters?'

'Not a single word of it's been read by those you wanted to reach. Funny, don't you think? Makes your writing a bit like MS 408. Unbreakable.'

'But they know I'm being kept here? They understand that?'

The nurse shook her head. 'It's our secret, Robbie.'

She didn't look at him as she closed the door but she knew he had slid down to his knees on the cold concrete floor behind her.

Looking carefully, it was just possible to see that in places the gems on the face of the ring were a little loose. Tusia took a silver hoop earring from her ear. Then, with the sharp metal point, she levered against one of the gems.

Brodie felt the room hold its breath with them.

The green gem resisted for a moment and then lifted. It slipped from its bed and rattled on to the table.

Tusia paused. 'Do I go on?'

Brodie wasn't alone in nodding.

Tusia pressed the metal point against the casing. This time a red gem slithered from its fastening. Tusia swallowed and held the ring up higher in the air and peered at the broken face. Then her own face broke into a smile. 'I knew it,' she said. 'Look.'

In the spaces left by the fallen gems, pressed into the golden setting of the ring, were shapes. And the shapes were letters.

'I reckon it's got something to say after all,' said Sheldon.

The rain had stopped and the first light of morning was leaking into a frosty sky by the time Tusia removed the final red gem from the ring and put it down on the table.

Hunter lowered his pencil and rested it on the piece of paper where they'd recorded the removal of the stones.

Brodie took a deep breath.

Under the red gems, there'd been eleven letters pressed into the gold.

Under the green gems, there'd been ten letters, and a symbol.

Tusia took the paper and ordered the letters according to the placement of the stones they'd been under.

'It's the answer,' she said, and pushed the paper into the middle of the table.

It was the secret Bacon had risked his life to hide. It was what they'd searched for and it had nearly cost Brodie her life. It was the truth the Knights had guarded.

The Director stepped inside the lift. He held his security clearance against the touch pad and then tapped in his six-digit code. The lights flickered slightly as the lift descended.

'Sir, we had no idea you would be—'

The Director raised his hand. 'Not now, Wheeler.'

'But, sir. If we'd known you were going to make a visit we would—'

'I said, not now!' He lowered his hand. 'Show me what you have.'

'But, sir, we're still working and trying to make links. We have the computers working through various

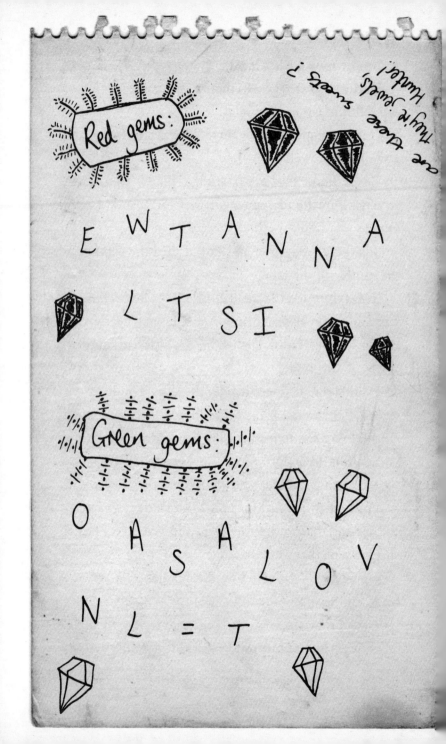

algorithms. And Miss Vernan suggested that—'

'I'm not interested in methods, Wheeler. I want to know what you've found.' He passed a whiteboard with photographs attached. He paused a moment.

Wheeler lowered his head. 'Operatives, sir. Out in the field. Those we have watching.'

The Director recognised many of the faces. He jabbed at a photo peeling free from one corner. 'Nice shoes,' he said.

'Sir?'

'Never mind.' His hand slid along the line of photos. One of the images had been scored through. A thick red cross obliterating the face. The Director removed the photo from the board. The tattoo on the arm of the photographed man rippled as the picture moved, as if the dragon was waking and stretching ready to pounce. 'Would you like to explain this?'

'Missing in action, sir. No contact for the last few days. We think perhaps the team were on to him.'

'And what else are they *on to*, Wheeler? What are they seeing that we are missing? What connections are they making that we can't?' The next board was covered with notes and writings about Sir Francis Bacon. Pages of MS 408 copied beside the notes. 'What are they looking for?'

Wheeler shook his head. 'We're trying our best, sir.

I just think if you give the computers time, we really are . . .'

The Director turned his head. He took a scroll from his pocket. A small white sheet of paper that was coloured slightly now, from fingerprints and constant rerolling. The Director flicked the page open. The movement was practised and well rehearsed. Slowly he pointed to each of the four corners: the earth; the wind; the water; and the fire. Then he rested his finger on the monogrammed letter 'T'. 'What have the team at Bletchley worked out, Wheeler?' he hissed between his teeth. 'We need to know.'

26

The Treasure in the Water

Brodie took the piece of paper and read the message aloud.

New Atlantis = Lost Avalon

'Avalon?' said Brodie quietly. The word slid around her mouth like honey.

Smithies pressed down on the table. 'That's what it says. New Atlantis is the Lost Avalon.'

'So the story Sir Francis wrote,' said Brodie, 'wasn't imagined, then? It was real.'

Tusia's face was wrinkled with confusion. 'Is that what you think? Avalon really exists?'

'It's taken us ages to connect everything, but that

must be what it means. It must be the answer.'

'So the Knights of Neustria were set up to protect information about a *real* place,' said Sheldon.

'Somewhere Bacon wrote about, as if it was pretend,' added Brodie.

Smithies let out a sigh. 'You know, in the past, when people came up with theories about MS 408 being about an incredible land that existed alongside our own, people said they were mad. All their theories were discredited.'

'So that's why the Knights of Neustria went to all the trouble of hiding their secret, then,' said Miss Tandari. 'If people knew the world of Avalon talked about in the myths of King Arthur was real, then the whole belief system about the world as we know it would be shaken.'

'Why?' said Sheldon. 'What's so incredible about Avalon?'

'I've read lots about it,' Brodie said.

'That figures,' cut in Hunter. 'What haven't you read lots about?'

His comment didn't stop her explaining. 'Stories say Avalon is magical. It's where the ladies of the lake made a weapon for King Arthur to make him invincible. Can't get more magical than that. It's where Sir Lancelot grew up and trained and it's where King Arthur went when he was injured in the battle of Camlann.'

'I remember that bit,' said Hunter, joining in. 'He was taken away by seven ladies to be restored.'

'Restored?' said Sheldon quizzically.

'Made well again.'

'But it's just a story, right? A myth?'

'I don't think so,' Brodie said. 'Look, the ring tells us that the story of the Bensalem which Bacon wrote about in *New Atlantis* is really about the Lost Avalon. The Firebird Code Van der Essen hid for us was based around King Arthur and the sword Excalibur. We even found the story about the Knights of Neustria hidden in *Morte d'Arthur.*'

'Does that mean Avalon exists, though?' said Hunter sceptically. 'We've been told enough about the danger of making leaps.' He glanced across at Smithies.

'No, it doesn't,' conceded Brodie. 'But what about all the effort taken to hide and guard the secret? Would the Knights of Neustria have done all that just to protect a story?'

'And you're forgetting MS 408,' said Tusia.

'I am?'

'A book entirely in code,' said Tusia. 'Containing weird drawings of people and flowers and places we've never seen.'

'You think the pictures show Avalon?' said Hunter. 'The real Avalon?'

Brodie felt her heart thumping in her chest. That's what she thought. It was almost too incredible to believe, but all the evidence they'd found was fitting together like pieces of a puzzle to show that.

'Well, if MS 408 is the story of the real Avalon, d'you think that means some of the Knights in the past managed to get there?'

No one spoke for a moment.

'I mean,' pressed on Hunter, 'do you think the Knights recorded what they saw in the manuscript, protecting what they wrote by putting it in code?'

'No wonder the authorities wanted no one to have anything to do with it,' said Tusia.

Everyone turned to face her.

'Imagine what would happen if people knew there really was a place where there were flowers growing which could heal you and weapons which could make you invincible. How could anyone control who went there?'

Brodie felt the colour rising to her cheeks. 'So you think the Knights were protecting a bad secret?'

'Not a bad one,' said Sicknote. 'But a complex and dangerous one.' He paused. 'Finding Avalon could be wonderful and amazing and life-changing. But you've got to remember the stories about how Avalon was magical could be how writers explained what happened there. The stories contain ideas we think the Knights of Neustria wanted to protect at all costs. Not being careful with those ideas could be harmful.'

Brodie felt a bead of sweat prick on her forehead despite the cold. 'But we're supposed to be the good guys. Looking for answers. Trying to find the truth.'

'But sometimes the truth's hard to handle,' said Miss Tandari. 'Life doesn't fall neatly into goodies and baddies. Good decisions and bad. The truth can be dangerous. Hard to control.'

'If we manage to read MS 408 and find the location of Avalon, should we keep that secret, then?' she said almost desperately.

Smithies put his hand on hers. 'Brodie, life's full of difficult questions. Sometimes there's no right or wrong answers. Sometimes you just have to go with what you believe is the right thing to do.'

'But what if you don't know what's right?' She wiped her forehead, stood up from the table and walked towards the window. The New Year sun was climbing weakly into the sky, while across the road, fairy lights on a dying Christmas tree flickered in the window. One year dying, one beginning, standing side by side in the half-light of morning. 'I've thought all along, the Knights must be protecting a secret but maybe they were just too scared to share what they knew.'

'Scared?'

'Worried about what would happen if people knew there was an Avalon to find.'

'But it's still out of our reach. Still beyond the cave.'

'Now you're really confusing me.'

Smithies looked wistful. 'Do you remember once, I told you the story of Plato's cave?'

Brodie scrambled through her memory.

'People had been raised forever, deep inside a dark and gloomy cave. The only reality they knew was shown to them by shadows moving across the cave walls. One day, someone brave broke free of the chains and walked out of the cave. But when the young explorer returned and told what he'd seen, no one in the cave believed him. They said he was mad. People have always wondered what's outside the cave, Brodie. It doesn't mean they'll necessarily believe what they hear.'

'So we should tell people about Avalon, then, and have them call us mad?'

Smithies considered what she'd said. 'I think we should keep searching and reading and try to make sense of the book of Avalon which came to us as MS 408, not because of what other people may say, but because we've got a chance to.'

'And if people don't believe us?'

'We worry about that when it happens.'

'But what if they *do* believe us? What if everyone wants to find Avalon? There would be chaos, right?'

Smithies waited. 'Maybe it isn't up to anyone else to decide who can and can't find Avalon?'

'So maybe that's the real reason the Knights protected their secret.'

'Maybe it is.'

Brodie's hand slid down the windowpane, leaving a print in the mist. Outside the window, the lights from the Christmas tree flickered and spluttered in the rain, then went out.

'Like I said,' whispered Smithies. 'There's no right answers to what we're doing here. We've chosen to put together pieces of a puzzle and we must deal carefully with the picture formed.'

'Or,' said Sicknote tentatively, 'we could walk away.'

Those around the table looked up at him.

'Smithies tells us the chains keeping us in the cave are loosened,' Sicknote said, tugging gently on the chain he used, even here, to attach his mug to the radiator. 'That doesn't always make you free.' His eyes were dark, his lips thin as he struggled to form the words he needed to explain. 'It'd be so much easier if we could turn off the need to know. If we could walk away from the hope of Avalon. If we could turn back now and say that even if Avalon is really out there, and even if reading MS 408 will show us where it is, then we don't want to go. If we could say putting together the pieces of the puzzle didn't matter. But we can't say that, can we? Any of us?'

Brodie walked back to the table and sat down. 'None of us will walk away,' she said quietly. 'Not now we've come this far.' She looked around the table and realised her statement was really a question.

'I'm not leaving,' said Hunter in answer.

'Me neither,' said Tusia.

'You're stuck with me,' said Sheldon.

Miss Tandari watched as Smithies folded his arms in an act suggesting resolve. 'So none of us are walking away, then,' she said.

'If Avalon's out there and MS 408 will tell us where it is,' said Brodie, 'then we keep looking.'

'I suppose you could say this isn't really an ending then,' said Smithies gently. 'I think we could say it's really just another beginning.'

'It's started.' Kerrith's voice was husky through the speakerphone.

The Director unbuttoned his suit jacket and swilled

the last dregs of New Year's champagne from the glass. 'Good. Good.'

'So do we let Station X know the situation?' Kerrith said.

The Director moved away from the office window and sat down in the leather-backed chair behind the desk. 'Not yet,' he said deliberately. He traced his finger round the edge of the empty champagne flute. It hummed.

'Will that be all, sir?'

'That'll be all, Miss Vernan. You've done well.'

There was a pause and then a whispered thank you before the line went dead.

The Director leant back in his chair. From his office window he could see revellers returning from their parties. It was, after all, an extremely good time to celebrate.

He reached forward across his desk and traced his finger over the copper statue positioned on the corner. Then, in a smooth and fluid movement, he drew the sword from the stone and let it glint a moment in the breaking dawn of a brand-new year. He did this not because he was strong or because the ornament had weakened. He did it because it had always been possible. People had just never tried.

* * *

Smithies waited in the Matroyska with the others while Hunter and Brodie made the delivery. 'We don't want to overwhelm him,' said Sicknote, as they turned back to the van to look for reassurance.

'We've brought you these,' said Brodie, handing over a rather battered box of sugared almonds they'd managed to pick up from the local newsagent on the way back to Piercefield House.

Mr Willer took the sweets gratefully and put them down on the upturned crate in front of him.

Brodie glanced through the ruined archway to where the tree severed by the fencing stood. She could just make out the memorial tree to the left of it. She held the Coleridge book. 'And we brought you this,' she said quietly and held the book towards him. 'It's right that it comes home.'

The old man smiled his toothless grin. 'Did you find what you searched for?' he said, his eyes widening with his smile.

'We did. We found the true angle at Chepstow. It was—'

The old man cut Hunter off. 'I don't want to know what it was.'

'But after all these years, don't you wonder? Don't you want to know?'

'All I want to know is that I passed the secret on to

someone who believed. That's all I ever wanted. Passed it on and kept it safe.'

'Well, you've done that,' Brodie said, and the old man closed his eyes. 'You could move on now. From this place,' she added. 'Find yourself somewhere warm and cosy. Now the Coleridge book's given us the answers, you could sell it perhaps. First edition. I bet that'd be worth a bit.'

The old man opened his eyes. 'I didn't stay here because I didn't have the money to move,' he said quietly. 'I stayed here because there was a job to be done.'

'Well, if you ever wanted to,' she whispered, 'the job's done now.'

They sat for a while, talking and watching the flames in the fire. They shared the sugared almonds. But they didn't mention the treasure again.

'I didn't ever say a proper thank you,' said Brodie.

Hunter slowed his step. 'What for?'

'Erm, for rescuing me and basically saving my life,' laughed Brodie.

'Oh that. It was nothing, B. I was in the area, nothing better to do. Glad I could help.'

She prodded him in the arm. 'Seriously, if you hadn't helped me, I'd have drowned.'

Hunter shrugged. 'Yeah. Well. Some things are worth hanging on to,' he said, and then turned and led the way back to the Matroyska.

Epilogue

'Let's listen to some Elgar,' said Sheldon. He passed the CD to Smithies at the front of the Matroyska and then flicked open the case notes and began to read.

Smithies switched on the sound system and music filled the van as it pulled along the motorway.

'Do you think Elgar knew some of the Knights had found Avalon?' Tusia asked, pulling her shawl tight around her as rain pummelled against the windows.

'Who can tell?' said Hunter, rummaging in the back seat pocket and searching for something to eat. He smiled eagerly and pulled out a rather sticky mint imperial, blew the fluff from it and popped it in his mouth.

'You're truly disgusting,' said Tusia. 'Absolutely truly disgusting and if I had my way—'

She never got to tell him what would happen if she had her way.

'Skip the track!' shouted Sheldon from near the back of the Matroyska.

'What?' Smithies was trying desperately to keep his eyes on the road as the windscreen wipers beat frantically across the glass.

'Skip to the last track!' Sheldon yelled.

'What? Why?'

Miss Tandari was fiddling with the controls on the sound system as the CD jumped and skittered forward.

'*Because Elgar knew*,' said Sheldon forcefully. 'Listen.'

They sat in silence as the music played. It was soft. It was calm. It was unremarkable.

'Well?' said Sheldon, as the final strains melted in the air.

'Well, what?'

'What d'you think?'

Brodie frowned. 'I think it's OK,' she said. 'Why?'

Sheldon beamed in answer. 'It's one of the last things Elgar wrote. We heard it at the Albert Hall. Remember?'

'And?' said Tusia.

'And it's called "Arthur's music",' said Sheldon proudly, flapping the notes from the inside of the CD case wildly in the air. 'It's about the death of Arthur.

Like the "Enigma Variations", it's got friends in it. Not Elgar's this time. But King Arthur's.'

Brodie watched the rain lash against the windows.

'I think it proves Elgar knew about Avalon,' said Sheldon quietly.

'Which means,' said Tusia, 'it's likely there's more clues out there. More signs left behind by Knights of Neustria.'

'All we've got to do,' said Hunter, crunching on his mint imperial, 'is be brave enough to find them.'

Brodie leant her head against the window. The rain fell like tears, washing away the final traces of snow from the ground. Everything looked clean. A brand-new world perched on the edge of a brand-new year.

She felt an excitement coursing through her like a charge of electricity. This was the new beginning Smithies had talked about.

The air pulsed again with the strains of Elgar's late work. The music of Arthur. The song of his friends. Brodie thought of Sir Bedivere, who stood by the King as he lay dying. His most trusted friend. The one Arthur passed his secret to. The knowledge of Avalon.

And Sir Bedivere and the Knights who followed him who'd tried to find the truth of the secret. Just like she and her friends tried to find answers too.

Modern-day Knights of Neustria on a quest which might lead them to Avalon.

In the distance, Brodie could just make out Bletchley Mansion appearing on the horizon. She could imagine the zebras running in the field, Fabyan preparing them a 'welcome home' feast. And her granddad waiting for her.

Brodie closed her eyes. In her excitement she thought of Friedman and she determined now she'd give him a chance. She'd ring again and she'd try to listen. Her stomach knotted inside her at the thought, but this time she didn't weaken. If the journey of the last few days had taught her nothing else, it had taught her the importance of seeking the truth.

The truth, after all, was what Operation Veritas was all about.

AUTHOR'S NOTE

Once again, lots of the best ideas for this *Secret Breakers* adventure
came from real life, real people and real places!

COLONEL GEORGE FABYAN

When I planned the Secret Breakers series, I read about the amazing
Colonel George Fabyan. I think it was the fact that he drove around in
a carriage pulled by zebras that made me determined to use him in my
story. Everything I've written about him is true. Fortune magazine once
listed him as one of America's top ten millionaire eccentrics. His father
ran the Bliss Fabyan Corporation which was the biggest cotton goods
organization in the world. But, at the age of 17, George ran away from
home and was disinherited by his father. Using a fake name and a secret
identity, George got a job at his father's firm without his father
knowing. He worked hard and rose up the ranks of the employees, selling
more stock than anyone else. Eventually, his father sent for the person
who'd made the most money for the company and was staggered to see
his estranged son George arrive in his office! George was welcomed back
into the family and inherited millions of dollars when his father died.

It was this determination to succeed and his ability to keep a secret that
made Fabyan so interested in codes. He brought together many of the
American code-crackers who would be so vital to the code-breaking
work done in World War Two, including William Friedman and his wife
Elizebeth. They all lived and worked together at George's Riverbanks
Estate. Then, when the American army formed an official Cipher Bureau,
its first 88 officers were people who'd been trained at Riverbank Labs by
Fabyan and Friedman. (I hope keen *Secret Breakers* readers will smile
when they see that number 88!)

George Fabyan was a fanatical collector of artifacts and mysteries. He really did keep bears (called Tom and Jerry!) and a troupe of monkeys who used to live in his loft. The windmill on his estate helped the Secret Breakers make important connections and who knows, maybe other interesting objects he had might eventually prove useful to the team! Fabyan once said 'you never get sick of too much knowledge'. I think this is a great motto for Secret Breakers looking to unlock the truth!

THE SHAKEPSEARE ENIGMA

Fabyan was sure that Sir Francis Bacon was the real writer of the Shakespeare plays. The Shakespeare Mangle or Cipher Wheel, described in the story, was used to try and find out the truth about the great playwright. It was an incredible machine and Dr Owen, who invented it, really did dig in the River Wye looking for hidden treasure that might connect to the puzzle. The story about the sweep reported in the *New York Times* is all true too, yet more proof that fact is often stranger than anything you can make up! It is incredible to think that at about the same time as Wilfred Voynich was discovering the encoded manuscript MS 408 in the dungeon of Mondragone Villa, Americans were digging in the bed of a British river looking for coded clues and stories!

PIERCEFIELD HOUSE

Secret Breakers readers will know that I love to write about fascinating real locations – like Piercefield House. At the time of writing *The Knights of Neustria*, Piercefield House was abandoned and derelict. A quick online search showed how amazing it looked. The broken building was covered with ivy and creepers. It was a real house of mystery. But it was the photograph of the tree growing through a fence that most caught my attention. I knew I had to use that image in my story. Maybe one day soon Piercefield House will be restored to its former glory or turned into a housing complex, but I think it looks particularly beautiful in its derelict form and full of endless story possibilities.

THE MAN WHO DIDN'T DIE

There are hundreds of stories written about Sir Francis Bacon. He was a very clever man and his life was full of secrets. His Bilateral Cipher is a great way of hiding a message in plain sight. This is, as Smithies would say, the very best type of 'secret keeping'. Whether or not he died in the house in Highgate has been debated by scholars, but the Old Hall really did have secret tunnels built into it for hiding works of art and precious things that needed to be kept out of sight. I like to think Sir Francis used these tunnels to make his escape to Chepstow.

Don't forget to find out more about all these links and connections at *The Knights of Neustria* section on **www.hldennis.com**

HOW TO MAKE A
SECRET BREAKERS CIPHER WHEEL

The Cipher Wheel, or Shakespeare Mangle, is vital for helping Team Veritas find out about the Knights of Neustria. Follow these simple instructions to make your own Secret Breakers Cipher Wheel that will make it quick and easy to send secret messages to your friends!

1. Trace or scan the two letter wheels below.

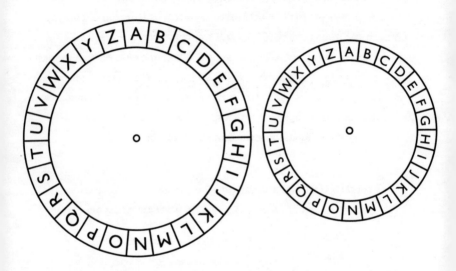

2. Cut them out and fix the smaller one inside the larger one, securing it with a paper fastener. You should be able to spin the smaller wheel inside the larger one. Notice how each letter finds a 'partner' in the larger wheel.

3. Decide on the message you want to send in code.

4. This coding device uses something called the CAESAR SHIFT method to work. Match the letter A on the outer wheel with the letter F on the inner wheel. This is a CAESAR SHIFT 5!

5. Find the letters for your message on the inner wheel. Use its 'partner' on the outer wheel to write it in code. (The pairings will change each time you move the inner wheel.)

6. To decode the message your friends must find each letter in the outer wheel and write down its 'partner' in the inner wheel.

This Secret Breakers Cipher Wheel is easy to use and a tiny turn forwards or backwards will give you a totally new way of encoding a message.

Brodie has encoded the following message for you:

Avwpgjpn nzxmzo wmzvfdib!

Decode it by aligning the outer A with the inner F.

Discover the world of the Secret Breakers.

For more information about H. L. Dennis
and the Secret Breakers visit

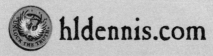

hldennis.com

You'll find competitions, code cracking lessons
and discover lots more secrets!

SECRET BREAKERS

Imagine the chance to solve the secret code of the Voynich Manuscript - a puzzle that has defeated adults for centuries.

Together with her new friends, Brodie Bray must break the rules to break the code, at every turn facing terrible danger. For someone is watching them - and will even kill to stop them.

The Secret Breakers series is Dan Brown for kids. As real codes are being cracked a thrilling adventure unfolds taking the characters across the globe.

www.hldennis.com
www.hodderchildrens.co.uk

Hodder Children's Books